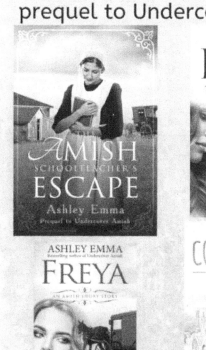

Other books by Ashley Emma

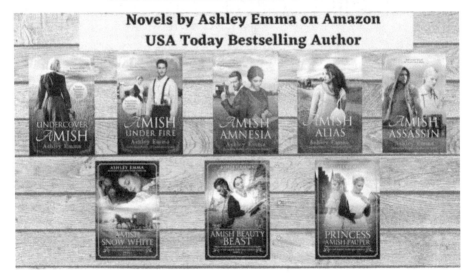

Novels by Ashley Emma on Amazon
USA Today Bestselling Author

Special thanks to:

Julie

Ryan

Tammi

Kit

Gail

Vickie

Janet

Kimberly

Sara

Swati

Sharon

Dianne

Bonnie

There were so many readers from my email list who gave me helpful feedback on this book, so I couldn't list you all here. Thank you so much!

Check out my author Facebook page to see rare photos from when I lived with the Amish in Unity, Maine. Just Search for 'Ashley Emma, author and publisher' on Facebook.

Join my free Facebook group 'The Amish Book Club' where I share free Amish books weekly!

The characters and events in this book are the creation of the author, and any resemblance to actual persons or events are purely coincidental.

PRINCESS AND THE AMISH PAUPER

Copyright © 2021 by Ashley Emma

Princess and the Amish Pauper

Ashley Emma

"The Amish have many denominations. Just like Christians, there are many different styles, if you will. Baptist, Catholic, Pentecostal, etc. Only theirs are named Old Order, New Order, Swartzentruber, and Beachy. Then under those titles are many different churches with different rules, depending on the community or state."

-Hannah S., formerly Amish

Table of Contents

Chapter One

No matter how many times she'd seen it, the sunrise through the kitchen window always took Damaris Kauffman's breath away. She placed her flour-covered hands on the kitchen counter and admired the view above a sink of dirty dishes.

The fields stretched for miles, and at this time of the year, it was easy to see the land's beauty: the fiery colors of the leaves on the trees, the crisp scent of fall in the air.

Damaris stretched as the feeling of fatigue swept her entire being. The day had barely begun, and she was already tired.

"You stayed up too late reading last night, didn't you?" *Maam* said, rolling out dough beside her for pies. "I saw your battery-operated lamp on late last night in your room."

How could Damaris deny it? "*Ja*, I did. Now I'm regretting it."

"You knew we have to wake up at five-thirty to start baking. You're twenty-three years old. You know better. Why do you keep staying up so late?" *Maam* asked, placing the homemade pie crust in a dish. "You're a grown woman. It's up to you how late you stay up, but really, Damaris. You're going to get run down if you keep doing this."

"I know. But I was at such a good part of the book last night. I just couldn't stop reading. It was a Tony Graham book, of course." Damaris sighed, playing over the scenes in her mind. The story took place in Germany. Oh, how she wished she could travel there, or anywhere in Europe.

But that was out of the question. As Old Order Amish in Unity, Maine, they were forbidden from flying on airplanes. She didn't know any Amish who had traveled that far. How could she ever get there? Besides, she knew it would be outrageously expensive.

1

Sure, she could travel by boat, but it would result in her being away from her family for far too long. Her family needed her help around the house, and they also needed the money she earned. Even one week away from them without her help would cause her family to struggle.

No, Damaris couldn't see herself going to Germany any time soon—maybe not ever.

What Damaris couldn't tell *Maam* was that reading was her escape. There had been so many changes in her life over the last few years. A few years ago, Damaris' father had passed away, and her older brother Dominic had left the Amish for a few years.

After Dominic returned to the community, he married Adriana. Yes, he had only moved to a house down the lane from them, but Damaris was still sad to see him move out after he'd finally come home.

It shamed her now to think how mean she had been to Adriana when they'd first met, how Damaris had spread rumors about her, trying to get her to leave. In the end, Adriana had still married her brother, and after Damaris had confessed the truth to her, she and Damaris became close friends.

"You better get those cinnamon rolls out of the oven so we can bring them to the Millers," *Maam* said, snapping Damaris out of her thoughts. "Mae, Laura, and Lydia will be waiting to take some of those to the market, and you need to deliver the rest to the Community Store."

Ever since Dominic had taken over the furniture business of their deceased father, Damaris and *Maam* now made a living baking for the Millers' Bakery. The pay wasn't much, but they got by. On top of baking early in the morning with her mother, Damaris also worked at the Unity Community Store during the day.

But it wasn't enough. Yes, Damaris enjoyed baking with her mother, even though it was long, hard work. They'd grown closer than ever and managed to keep their heads above water by baking for the Millers.

Yet Damaris knew she was made for so much more. She longed to open a business of her own and to travel to places she couldn't even imagine. She didn't want a Plan B. She dreamed of owning her own bakery, and in her dreams, that bakery wasn't in Unity, Maine.

She was beginning to understand why Dominic had left the Amish a few years ago. The thought stabbed her with another pang of guilt at having been so angry with him for so long. Had she really been angry that he left, or had she been angry that he left her behind?

As if reading Damaris' thoughts, her mother said, "I know you want to do more than bake for the Millers and work at the store, Damaris. One day, when you are a mother, your focus will be raising your children, which may come sooner than you think. For now, this is good for us. You won't be worried about a career once you get married and have children."

She's right, Damaris thought. Something shifted inside of her, and she lifted her head to look out the window.

No. Maybe she's not completely right.

Yes, if she met the right man, she would love to have a husband and children one day, but it was the last thing on her mind.

She would also be content with being single forever, if it came to that.

Damaris blinked, bringing herself out of her thoughts as she put on oven mitts.

"So, how is Gilbert?" *Maam* asked, her eyes twinkling. "He is such a nice young man. Do you think he will ask to court you soon? I sure would love to see you get married to a man like him."

"*Maam!*" Damaris blurted, her face heating, and it wasn't from the heat of the woodstove as she pulled out the cinnamon rolls. "We've only seen each other a few times. We aren't even courting yet."

"I know you've been in love with him for a long time. It was rather obvious."

3

"Well… I thought I was, but now that we've gotten to know each other better…" Damaris let her voice trail off as she set the cinnamon rolls on top of the woodstove. "I think I was just infatuated with him. I'm not the only one. So many of the other young ladies are after him. He's kind and handsome—"

"What's the problem?" *Maam* asked, hands on her hips. "Do you have your eyes on someone else?"

"No, it's not like that," Damaris said. "I guess I thought I was in love with him, but I don't think I am. I mean, I've never been in love, so how would I know? How did you know when you fell in love with *Daed*?"

"Well, you don't always fall in love head over heels like in your romance novels," *Maam* said. "Sometimes love just gradually sneaks up on you. You get to know the person, and before you know it, every time you think of them you feel like you're floating on air. Even after years of marriage, your father's smile still made my heart flip. You realize you can't live without that person…until of course, they're gone." *Maam's* eyes teared up, and she wiped at them with the corner of her apron. "I still miss him every day."

"Me too." Damaris hugged her mother.

"When you love someone, you'll know, my dear," *Maam* said. "But I was hoping you'd say you were expecting a proposal from him one day. I was hoping you'd get married. With your father gone and Dominic married off and moved out, we could use some financial support. I know Gilbert's carpentry business does well, so I was hoping…" *Maam* shook her head. "I'm not going to put that burden on you. I want you to marry someone you truly love. That's worth waiting for. I want you to have with your husband what I had with your father. A love so strong it can't even be broken by death."

Damaris smiled, warmth filling her heart with memories of how much her parents loved each other. She knew it was rare.

"Thanks, *Maam*. I hope one day I can have that."

"The Lord has someone for you. Don't you worry. Well, you better get going before the Millers have to leave and bring only their baked goods to the market."

After loading up the pies, cinnamon rolls, and pastries into the buggy, Damaris clicked her tongue to get their horse, Apple, moving. She sighed over the beautiful colors of the trees. Every year, it seemed to become even more majestic.

It was a picturesque community, and an ideal place to live, but something inside Damaris wanted more.

She wanted to use her creativity to run a bigger business than a local bakery. Her mother would tell her that was pish posh, to be content, and to bloom where she was planted.

And, of course, she wanted to fall in love and get married, but she had the feeling her soul mate did not live here in Unity, Maine. She'd known all the young men here her entire life, and she couldn't imagine marrying any of them.

What if the one for her wasn't here in this town, or this state, or even this country?

God, I'm sorry I'm so ungrateful, she prayed silently. *I do love it here, and I'm thankful I was raised here, but I want to see the world. I know I should be content, but I confess I want more.*

Was it wrong that even though she lived in a wonderful place, she yearned to travel across the ocean?

***

Twenty-three-year-old Arabella Blackwood happily baked alongside Blackwood Bakery employees. The many bakers bustled around the kitchen. Though so many of them were working here together, it was not chaotic, but calm and peaceful.

This was what Arabella loved to do—to bake with her hands, to come up with new recipes. When her parents tried to teach her how the business worked and went over spreadsheets and finances, it just made her head hurt.

Arabella wiped her flour-covered hands off on her apron and gazed out the window. In the distance, she could see the mansion where she lived. The entire estate and lush green lands would be hers once her parents died. She was expected to take over the Blackwood Bakery empire when they retired, which would be in the upcoming year.

"Arabella!" Ms. Libby's screechy voice shattered Arabella's thoughts, rising an octave at the end of her name. Several of the bakers turned to the woman. As the manager of the estate and Arabella's parents' personal assistant, Ms. Libby held a position of power.

"Dinner is about to be served. Your parents have told you before that you should be learning the business, not baking the inventory. That is for the *employees* to handle, not a Blackwood," Ms. Libby said, making the word *employees* sound like something distasteful. She sniffed, raising her thin eyebrows, eyeing the flour all over Arabella's apron. "You should go make yourself more…presentable…before dinner."

Oh. Her stomach sank to the floor. She'd completely forgotten about dinner with her parents tonight.

She reached up and felt her long brown hair in a bun, which was matted with flour from the hours she'd spent baking. Sometimes she dreamed about moving to a quiet corner in the world, where she could spend her time inventing new recipes or baking for a small, local bakery, and not having to deal with business dealings and opening new locations nationwide.

"Now. I have the car outside. Let's go," Ms. Libby snapped, and Arabella reluctantly followed her.

Once they returned to the Blackwood estate and Arabella was in her room, she scrambled to get ready. She took off her flour-covered clothing and put on a pencil skirt and blouse. In her hurry, she stumbled while grabbing a hairbrush, then quickly brushed through most of the tangles and wrapped it up in a semi-presentable bun. She'd have to finish brushing it later.

Arabella pulled on some heels and walked down the stairs.

Dinner would be served any minute, and she could not keep her parents waiting. It was quite rare to have a family dinner since her parents were so busy.

They were never interested in her new recipes. Most of what they knew about her life was from the folder prepared by the security team.

As an only child, she was the heiress to one of the most successful, profitable companies in Germany—the Blackwood Bakery company. They had locations all across Europe and had tried opening locations in the United States, but the business deals had been unsuccessful.

She said hello to her parents in the dining room. They answered with a nod and waved her into a seat across from them at the long table, next to her grandmother, Elizabeth.

Arabella was surprised to see that for the first time in a long time, there were no phones in her parents' hands. Instead, they watched her with rapt attention.

"Come sit, darling. We have something to tell you," her mother, Helene, said. Her blonde hair was done up in a perfect French twist, and she wore a gray knee-length pleated dress with heels.

She sat down cautiously. What was going on? She gave her grandmother a questioning look, but Elizabeth only shrugged.

"I'm as confused as you are, dear," Elizabeth whispered.

Helene rang a small bell, and the staff rolled in the trolley holding their meal. Arabella fidgeted in her seat.

"Arabella, honey, how was your morning?" her father, Henry, asked.

"Fine," Arabella whispered in answer; her throat felt dry under the scrutiny of her father's eyes.

She watched as her mother took a helping of soup before she spoke again.

Arabella could only drink the cup of water in front of her; her stomach was in knots as she watched her mother's robotic actions. Why had they wanted to have dinner with her tonight, and why were they paying so much attention to her? What did they have to tell her?

Helene said, "You do know that our business has been in a bit of financial trouble for some time now. We took out a loan several years ago that we thought we'd be able to pay back by opening more locations, but that didn't work out, and now we are unable to pay back the loan."

"Yes, Mother," Arabella answered, but her mother waved her hand, hushing Arabella, motioning for her to stay quiet and listen.

"However, we have met with some investors who would indeed help fund the new locations and pay back our loan in full," Henry explained.

"Really? Who?" Arabella asked, sitting on the edge of her seat.

"Our biggest competitor, Castle Cakes," her father said.

"Castle Cakes?" Arabella retorted. "We can't trust them. They've been trying to buy us out for years now."

Elizabeth nodded. "I agree. Why would you want to get involved with him?"

"Well, Philip Castle has been my rival since business school, yes," Henry admitted. "But now we finally agree on something."

Arabella wanted to roll her eyes. She seriously doubted that.

"It's true, Arabella. We don't want to lose our family business. This bakery has been in the family for three generations now, and it will be four once it is passed down to you. As you know, we would go to great lengths to keep it successful," Helene said.

"Of course," Arabella said. She couldn't imagine having to sell the company or losing it to the bank.

"So, Philip Castle has agreed to pay back our loan and help fund the new company locations, which would indeed save the company, but there is a small condition that must be met." Henry steepled his fingers together in front of him, avoiding her eyes.

Arabella could sense the increased tension in her parents as they looked at each other before turning their heads back to her.

What was going on? She felt the skin on her neck and scalp prickle with dread. What could be so hard for them to tell her? Elizabeth gave her a concerned glance.

After a brief pause, Helene spoke. "What your father is trying to tell you is that Castle Cakes has agreed to invest and pay off our loan, but only if we unite the two companies."

"What? A merger?" Elizabeth argued.

Oh no. This wasn't good.

"And one more thing. Philip Castle says he will only do this if you marry his son, Stefan," Henry stated.

Arabella felt the blood drain from her face. Had she heard that correctly? Her parents wouldn't ask her to do something like that, would they?

Unable to speak, Arabella stared at them.

Elizabeth scoffed. "You mean an arranged marriage? What is this, the Middle Ages?" she spat out.

Oh. She had heard them right. Arabella slowly turned her head to look at her grandmother, whose face was red with fury.

"Philip agreed to pay off the loan and to fund the new company locations in exchange for part of the profits. Paying off the debt would be his wedding gift to both of you. One day, when we retire and Philip retires, you and Stefan will run the company together," Helene explained calmly, as though talking about the weather.

"Henry, Helene, what are you two thinking?" Elizabeth demanded. "This is preposterous. You can't ask this of her. Besides, what does Mr. Castle get out of them getting married?"

"Philip Castle fears that his son will never get married. He's a bit of an awkward young man with no social life. He prefers to stay home, reading science and sci-fi books. Now that Mrs. Castle has passed, Philip is concerned that his son will be alone after Philip is gone, so he wants him to find a wife."

Elizabeth threw her hands up. "He could meet the right woman, eventually."

"He also wants to leave him a large inheritance, since Stefan is his only son. Castle Cakes would profit greatly if the merger can make our companies expand. If the merger and marriage don't happen, we will lose the company. Of course, we would never force this on you, Arabella," Henry said. "It has to be your own decision."

"Arabella knows what's at stake. This business is important to her," Helene explained to Elizabeth. "We aren't forcing her to do anything. She will do the right thing."

"No." Arabella gasped, her spoon falling out of her hand and onto the floor. She felt as though she was floating, her head spinning with dizziness. Putting a hand to her temple, she took in deep breaths.

"This is only his proposition," Henry said, as if he hadn't even heard her protest. "Please, at least consider it."

Helene nodded. "Yes. You must make this decision and choose on your own. We've invited Philip and Stefan to stay here for a few weeks so we can all get to know each other better, especially you and Stefan. He is a nice young man and the future heir of Castle Cakes. He's soon to be one of the wealthiest young men in Germany."

"No! How can you expect me to marry a man I've never met?" Arabella exclaimed, hastily pushing back her chair.

"My dear, I know you don't know him yet. But once you get to know him, you might truly like him," Helene said.

Didn't they care about what she wanted?

Elizabeth snorted, shaking her head.

"But not love him?" Arabella spat. "I want to bake in the kitchen and come up with new recipes. I'm not even sure I can run this company. You know I'm not good with the business end of it and all the numbers… I just want to bake. I don't want to marry some stranger. Yes, I love this company, but this is too much."

Arabella ran out of the room, through the door to the gardens, then sank to the ground in a blur of tears.

How had this become her life? Yes, she didn't want to see Blackwood Bakery go under, but how could they ask this of her?

Chapter Two

"Good morning!" seventeen-year-old Laura Miller called, bounding out of the Miller house to greet Damaris. Damaris slowed the horse and buggy to a stop.

"Good morning, Laura," Damaris said, chuckling at Laura's never-ending energy and smiles. "You really are a morning person."

"Not all of us stay up until midnight reading by lamplight," Laura said, wagging her finger dramatically.

"Are the dark circles under my eyes that obvious?"

Laura laughed and leaned forward, resting her hands on the buggy. She whispered, "I was kidding. Actually, I do that sometimes too. But not Lydia. She's always in bed early. She's boring like that."

"I am not boring!" Lydia called, coming out of the house. "I'm responsible."

Laura rolled her eyes. "Same thing."

Damaris smiled at the playful banter between the two sisters as they helped her unload the baked goods from the back of the buggy, leaving a few boxes behind for Damaris to bring to the Community Store.

Truly, she loved working for the Millers with her mother and at the store with Ella Ruth. They weren't her ideal jobs, but they were indeed jobs, and they supported her family. Maybe if she saved up enough money, she could get out of here and do some traveling before being baptized into the Amish church.

Realistically, she knew that would never happen. Her family needed her now more than ever.

"Thank you, Damaris!" Mae Miller called out as they brought the boxes into the kitchen. Laura and Lydia's mother smiled at Damaris, her graying hair peeking out from under her prayer *kapp*.

The spacious kitchen had two ovens, a large table where the women prepared the baked goods, and there was also a dishwasher, since they'd bought this house from an *Englisher* family. But because the Amish in Unity didn't have electricity, they didn't use it for its intended purpose. Instead, the Millers used the dishwasher to store dishes, like an extra cabinet.

"Irvin said the customers at the Community Store were raving about your cinnamon rolls, and they sold out before noon," Mae told Damaris.

"That's good to hear," Damaris said with a smile. "They're Ella Ruth's favorite too."

"Well, here." Mae took one cinnamon roll and wrapped it up, handing it to her. "Why don't you give this one to her at work? It would make her day. After all she's been through, I'm sure she'd appreciate it."

"Are you sure? Don't we need every last one if they sell out by noon?"

"Anything for your best friend," Mae said with a smile. "Now go on. We will see you tomorrow morning."

***

Arabella took a sip of her coffee as she checked the café's entrance for the umpteenth time in search of a certain redhead. Wearing jeans, a hat, and sunglasses, Arabella tried to blend in with the other people around her.

Emily, her best friend, was running late. Again. As usual.

Although she was used to her friend's habit of arriving late for everything due to constantly losing track of time, she wished that Emily would at least have made an effort for her today.

Arabella ducked her head, her cheeks flaming as the Blackwood Bakery commercial played on the television on the wall. Arabella spoke on camera about the bakery's newest products, and her face was also on the packaging. She was often recognized on the street.

As she began to squirm in her seat, hoping no one would recognize her here, she heard the door of the café open, and Emily bounced in with rosy cheeks and a sunny smile.

At five and a half feet tall, with deep green eyes and a stunning mass of long red curls, Emily could light any gloomy room, even at a funeral. Arabella had not seen that happen yet, but she was sure of it.

Arabella glanced at her bodyguard, who was seated at a nearby booth to give them a bit more space.

"Sorry. Hope you didn't wait too long," Emily said as she hurried over to her seat.

"Let me guess. You lost track of time." Arabella eyed her friend over her coffee mug.

"You know me too well. Did you order my favorite already?" Emily took a sip of the mug in front of her. "You know how I like my coffee. Tall, dark, and handsome," Emily said with a glint of mischief in her eyes, conspicuously batting her eyelashes at Arabella's bodyguard in the other booth.

Unamused, he lifted one eyebrow and continued pretending to read the newspaper he held.

Arabella rolled her eyes. "He's off-limits too, Emily. They all are."

"Still nice to look at," Emily said with a chuckle, then her smile faded when she fully took in Arabella's appearance. She was probably noticing the dark circles beneath Arabella's makeup and the way her hands trembled as she moved the mug of coffee to her lips.

"Ari, are you okay? What happened?" Emily asked.

14

Before Arabella could answer, the waiter walked to their table and took their lunch order. Emily tapped her foot impatiently as the waiter finished and walked away, waiting for Arabella to grace her question with an answer.

Arabella sighed heavily, taking a sip of her coffee yet again as she sought the best way to come up with an answer without tearing up.

She looked out of the window and said, "I am getting married."

"What?!" Emily's green eyes widened. "I don't understand. Have you been secretly seeing someone? To be honest, you don't seem happy about it. What's going on?"

"No, I haven't been seeing anyone. I am getting married to Stefan Castle," Arabella explained. "My parents aren't forcing me, but they made it pretty clear that if I don't, I'll be letting them down. Big time. I don't want to lose the bakery chain. Emily, I've never even met him. What am I going to do?"

"Are you kidding me? You're considering marrying a man you don't even know? What is this, the fourteenth century?" Emily exclaimed, earning a few stares from other customers in the café, but she clearly didn't care.

"My grandmother said something like that," Arabella said humorlessly.

"Your grandmother is right. Your parents should not be asking this of you."

A tear fell from Arabella's cheek. Emily reached across the table to take her friend's hand. "You're not truly considering this, are you?"

Arabella sighed. "The bakery has been in the family for generations, and I'm supposed to inherit it. I can't let it go under. We tried opening up locations in America, but the deal fell through. We're deep in debt, and we can't afford the loan payments." She sighed. "I can't believe this is going to happen. So this is my life now."

Then Emily laughed a little unsteadily as she tried to lighten the atmosphere. "Come on. You're from one of the wealthiest families in the country. You've been in commercials and had your face on Blackwood Bakery products your whole life. You're practically a celebrity. Do you know how many women would die to switch places with you?"

Arabella sighed, staring into her coffee. Her life was not as it seemed. Her family used to be one of the wealthiest in Germany. Arabella had confided in Emily about this before. Her parents gave her little freedom to do what she wanted, even though she was past the age of twenty-one. "I wish we could just get away and go to Paris, or anywhere but here."

"You know I'd travel with you any time. I love our trips together. I'm going to New York with my family to visit relatives in two days. I know it's short notice, but do you want to come?"

"I wish I could, but I'm sure my parents would never let me with everything going on right now."

"That's a bummer. Hey, have you ever heard of the Amish? There are some in New York, actually," Emily said, her eyes wide with intrigue. "I wonder if I will see some when I'm there. I think they're fascinating."

"Well, I have heard of them, but I don't know anything about them," Arabella said.

"They don't use electricity and the women wear long dresses and bonnets, and the men wear top hats. They drive horse-drawn carriages around, and I heard," Emily said, leaning forward, "I hear that the women don't even shave their legs."

Arabella scrunched up her nose in disbelief. "What? Come on. That sounds really far-fetched."

Emily shrugged. "Look it up online. I saw videos online about this sex trafficking gang that targeted an Amish community in Maine, which isn't that far from New York. They were kidnapping Amish girls. There were several videos about it. Isn't that terrible?"

"That's horrible," Arabella said, her heart filling with sympathy for the families.

"You know the craziest part? In one of the videos, there was a woman who looked exactly like you." Emily's eyes went wide. "You've got to check it out."

"Really?"

"I'm telling you," Emily said, slapping the table with a laugh. "You could be her twin."

"Wow! I'll have to look that up later."

"You know, Ari, there is something I have to tell you. I know now is maybe not really the best timing, but I want you to know before anyone else. Maybe it'll cheer you up. My art is going to be featured at the gallery downtown, and it will be in the next art show. Isn't that amazing?"

"Oh, that's wonderful!" Arabella took her friend's hand across the table. "I can't believe you didn't tell me as soon as we sat down. You've been working so hard to get in."

"Thanks. I'm so excited. Anyway, I didn't tell you right when I sat down because I could tell you were upset about something."

"You're such a good friend, Emily. You had huge news to tell me, and you asked me about my problems first. I have no idea what I'd do without you." Arabella shook her head. "I'm so happy for you."

"Thank you. Who knows? If someone with connections sees my work and likes it, anything is possible," Emily said, her bright green eyes twinkling hopefully.

"Of course!" Arabella said with a squeal. "I'm so excited! So, tell me everything. I need a distraction, and now I can focus on this."

Arabella was about to say something when she heard Emily whisper, "Oh no."

"What's wrong, Em?" Arabella turned to see what had gotten Emily flustered. She saw the familiar flash of the camera. The paparazzi had spotted her, despite her casual clothing, hat, and glasses, and choosing a low-key café.

Her bodyguard quickly sprang into action, covering them as they scrambled to leave the café and fight their way past the persistent questions and flashes from the cameras outside.

"Arabella, is it true you're going to marry Stefan Castle, the heir of your biggest competitor, Castle Cakes?" one reporter asked.

"How did Stefan propose?"

"Have you been dating in secret?" another reporter asked. "How did the two of you meet?"

Hiding her face, Arabella followed her bodyguard closely until they reached her car and got in.

"I can't believe they found me again. How on earth did they hear about me and Stefan?" Arabella asked, exasperated. "Nothing is secret."

"Maybe one of the staff leaked the information." Emily leaned forward, raising her eyebrows. "It is one juicy bit of gossip."

"It doesn't matter. Anyway, enough about my silly problems. I want to know more about your art show," Arabella said, a twinge of sadness within her. If she was honest, there was a bit of jealousy, too.

Her best friend would be able to spend her life doing what she loved and following her dream.

Would Arabella ever know what that was like?

Arabella smiled as she listened to her friend rave about the art show excitedly. She was happy that at least one of them was getting a better life.

Although she wished her own life had taken a different turn, at least her most favorite person in the world was going to have a happy life.

Chapter Three

Damaris tried to concentrate as Ella Ruth went on and on about how to correctly shelve new merchandise. It was Ella Ruth's father's store, after all, so she knew the store inside and out.

Damaris took a sidelong glance around the store, which was filled with the bustle of activity.

The Unity Community Store sold a variety of items, ranging from tools to donuts, dry goods to groceries. Customers milled about, chatting, which made up for the lack of music playing in the store. A young Amish couple talked, smiling at each other, and a pang of guilt filled Damaris as she remembered how she would soon have to tell Gilbert that she just wanted to be friends instead of moving forward with their relationship.

"Are you okay, Damaris?" Ella Ruth looked up at her with worried eyes.

"I'm fine. It's a lot of information, remembering what goes where."

"You'll get it in time." Ella Ruth gave an encouraging smile. "Are you going to the Singing? Will Gilbert be taking you? It seems like he just adores you."

Damaris looked around, making sure no one was within earshot. "Don't tell anyone, but actually, things aren't going so great with Gilbert."

"What?" Ella Ruth dropped a homemade can of soup on the shelf with a thud. "What happened?"

"I thought I was in love with him, but now I realize it was just a crush. I actually don't want to marry him after all. I don't love him like that. Only as a friend. I have to tell him soon," Damaris explained, wringing her hands.

"You better do it really soon!" Ella Ruth whispered. "Trust me. Don't string him along, afraid to break his heart. Just get it over with."

Damaris nodded. "You're right. I know. I just hate hurting his feelings."

"Well, do you like someone else?"

Damaris sighed. "Honestly, no one here interests me. I don't think my future husband lives in this town. Maybe not even this state. But please, don't speak a word of this to anyone. I want him to hear it from me first."

Ella Ruth touched her friend's arm. "I understand. Well, we can still have fun at the Singing. Now, let's get back to stocking the shelves."

Damaris had gone to Singings before and had even been driven home by a few nice young men, as was tradition, but she'd never really been interested in anyone romantically. Her dreams had always been to travel, which consumed her thoughts.

A group of *Englisher* tourists came into the store with their flashing cameras as they ridiculously took pictures, oblivious to how it bothered those around them. They turned to Damaris and Ella Ruth with their cameras, but Damaris and Ella Ruth hid their faces and walked away in the other direction.

"How rude," Ella Ruth whispered.

"I can't believe they did that. Maybe they don't know we don't believe in having our photo taken, but it's still rude to take photos of strangers without asking," Damaris added.

The *Englishers* moved to a different part of the store to admire the local handmade Amish furniture made through a combination of hard work and nature's finest materials.

What were these *Englisher's* lives like? What interesting places did they come from?

After a few minutes, the tourists left. Damaris spotted a woman in a black dress suit and high heels walk through the door with flawless makeup, her hair pinned up perfectly. Who on earth was that? And why was she wearing high heels out here, where they could get muddy—or worse—ruined by horse manure?

Yet, she didn't look like a tourist. She looked more like a...

"Is that a news reporter?" Ella Ruth asked, ducking to get a better view through a gap in a shelf. A man with a large camera on his shoulder waited outside by a van.

"*Ja*, I think it is," Damaris answered, wide-eyed. "Why do you think they are here? Nothing has happened here except—"

"Oh no." Ella Ruth grabbed Damaris' hand, pulling her toward the door. "They're here about my sisters. About the sex trafficking. We have to warn them. They aren't ready for this. They're traumatized enough as it is, and they don't need someone trying to interview them on TV. These people have no right!"

Ella Ruth all but dragged Damaris toward the door, right toward the reporter, who was talking with Irvin.

"You have no right to come here and try to interview the survivors of the abductions. They've been through enough," Ella Ruth said, stomping her foot like an angry toddler. "You should leave."

"Ella Ruth, please," Irvin said, raising his hands. "Please be courteous."

"*Daed*, don't you agree with me?" Ella Ruth asked.

"Wait, you're Ella Ruth? Ella Ruth Holt? Actually, you're the one we are looking for," the woman said. "Would you be willing to talk with us on camera? We want to ask you about how you went undercover to help rescue your sisters from sex traffickers."

"No." Ella Ruth crossed her arms. "The Amish don't like to have their photographs taken, and we certainly don't like to be on camera."

21

Damaris watched the exchange, wide-eyed.

"Come on, Damaris. Let's get out of here." Ella Ruth pulled on Damaris' hand again and yanked her out the door.

Damaris stumbled out behind her. "Wow! I've never seen you talk to anyone like that before."

"I'm very protective of my sisters," Ella Ruth explained, marching down the lane. "Especially now more than ever, after what they've been through."

"Of course. I totally understand," Damaris said.

They walked half way down the lane before they heard voices.

"Wait! Ella Ruth!" The news reporter followed them, now holding a microphone with her cameraman following close behind. "We just have a few questions for you. Won't you take a moment to talk with us? We want to spread awareness about sex trafficking; maybe if more people know about it, we can stop it from happening to other girls like your sisters." The reporter's eyes and voice pleaded with Ella Ruth.

Ella Ruth spun around. The woman's words must have hit a nerve. "Truly?" she asked. She lowered her voice. "Well, in that case, I suppose I can do that. But it's against our ways to be on camera, so I'll only do the interview if you don't show my face, and we need to do it somewhere no one will see."

"Well, what if you turn around, then? We will only show the back of your head," the reporter said.

Ella Ruth nodded. "Sure. I can't believe I'm doing this. If anyone found out, I could get in trouble. But if it can help people become more aware of human trafficking, I'll do it. Meet me down the street. There's an old abandoned gas station. We can do it behind the gas station. No one goes there."

"Great. Thank you. We will see you there." The reporter and her cameraman walked back to their van, then drove off.

"You sure you want to do this?" Damaris asked.

"I have to do this," Ella Ruth said with a determination in her eyes Damaris had never seen before.

"Well, let me come with you then." Damaris started walking toward the gas station.

"Thanks."

About twenty minutes later, they reached the gas station, where the reporter and cameraman were waiting and already setting up.

"Thank you again, Ella Ruth," the reporter said, handing her a small device. "Here, clip this microphone to your dress. I'm going to ask you questions, but just talk to me like you normally would. You'll be great. Ready?"

Damaris took a step back to watch as Ella Ruth turned around, facing the wall. "Ready. One more thing. Don't say my name, please."

"Of course." The woman made a motion with her hands and the cameraman held up his camera. Were they recording? Damaris didn't know how to tell.

"Today I'm here in Unity, Maine, where I am speaking with a young Amish woman who prefers to remain anonymous. The Amish do not allow themselves to be photographed or be on camera, so she will be facing away from us. Her sisters were abducted by sex traffickers here in the picturesque Amish community of Unity, Maine. This proves that human trafficking is happening right in our own back yards, right under our noses. More must be done to prevent and stop this, and you know that most of all. Won't you tell us about how you went undercover to help rescue your sisters?"

Damaris watched Ella Ruth finally uncross her arms. "Well, I wanted to do something to help find them. A police officer came here and asked me for help. There was a man pretending to be Amish who was luring young women into being trafficked by taking them on 'dates.' They would flatter the young women, make them feel special, then abduct them before they realized what was happening. The police officer said if I pretended to go on dates with this man, he might lead us to where my sisters were being kept."

"What happened? Did it work?" the reporter asked.

"Well, yes…" Ella Ruth suddenly froze, staring at the wall. Her mouth remained open, but no words came out.

"Yes, it worked," Damaris said, coming to her rescue. She stepped forward, and the reporter quickly swung her microphone in front of Damaris so she could speak into it.

"She was so brave," Damaris continued. "She risked her own safety by going on these 'dates' with the imposter, and she even got hurt in the process. But she was only worried about her sisters, not for herself. Because of her, the police found the location where her sisters were being kept and also rescued several other young women who were being held there. She is a true hero." Damaris' eyes filled with tears, and Ella Ruth gave her a grateful smile.

Oh no.

The blood drained from her face as she realized what had just happened. The camera was recording her. Her face.

Would she be on TV? She hadn't meant for this to happen. It had happened so fast.

"Sounds like your friend is selfless. Because of her, her sisters are safe now." The reporter smiled at Damaris.

"Well, that's all that matters. They're safe now," Ella Ruth said slowly to the wall, finally unfreezing.

"Well, thank you both so much for your time," the woman said, then turned to the camera. She began speaking more about Unity, and though Damaris wanted to stay and listen, Ella Ruth tugged on her hand again, and they ran back toward the store.

"Stop it! Are you going to keep pulling me around all day?" Damaris said, laughing as they ran. "We were on TV! I can't believe that just happened!"

"Me neither! Let's not tell anyone about this, okay? I don't know if we'd get in trouble. Listen, thanks so much for coming to my rescue like that," Ella Ruth said, finally slowing down on the lane. "I don't know what happened. I just froze. I guess I was thinking about all the people watching me."

"Maybe it's kind of like stage fright, except you can't see the audience. Well, too bad we won't get to see it on TV. Wouldn't that be something?" Damaris asked, just imagining what it would be like to see herself on TV.

Ella Ruth laughed. "I'm glad I don't have to see myself. That was embarrassing! Well, if they're gone, we better get back to the store."

As they walked back to the Community Store, Ella Ruth asked, "I'm sorry about you and Gilbert. The whole town has been whispering about how they think you two will get married. They're in for a shock."

Damaris sighed.

Ella Ruth asked, giving Damaris a sideways glance, "So, what happened? I thought things were going well with you two. You've been in love with him forever."

"Well, yes… I mean, I thought I was in love with him all these years. Now that we've been going on dates, I've realized I think it was just an infatuation. He is handsome, and I think I just wanted him to want me. Does that make any sense?" Damaris shook her head. "What's wrong with me?"

Even when he was in love with Damaris' other best friend, Belle, Damaris still pined for him. After Belle broke it off with Gilbert, Damaris had finally told Gilbert her feelings for him, and they had started going out on dates.

"Nothing is wrong with you, Damaris. People change. Feelings change. Now that you've finally gotten to spend some one-on-one time with him, maybe you've realized he's not this perfect man you've imagined in your head. But of course, no man is perfect," Ella Ruth said as they neared the store, leaves crunching under their feet.

"That's it!" Damaris cried. "In my head, I imagined him as someone totally different. But really, we don't have that much in common. I feel so terrible because I was the one who pursued him, and now I think I have to end things before they get too serious."

"Well, you should, because I've heard he wants to court you with the intention of marriage," Ella Ruth said in a low voice.

"Ugh. I'm a despicable human being," Damaris said with a groan.

"No, you are not." Ella Ruth stopped and grabbed her friend's arm. "You just need to be honest with him. Maybe the rumors aren't true, and he feels the same way. You don't want to wait until he proposes to you, right? You've got to tell him before you lead him on any longer. Maybe at the Singing?"

Damaris heaved a sigh. "You're right. I need to just get it over with. Yes, I can do it on our way home from the Singing tonight."

"Don't worry, Damaris. You know all the young women think he's handsome. He won't be heartbroken for too long." Ella Ruth laughed and playfully poked Damaris.

"Hey! That's not very nice!" Damaris said, poking her back, smiling.

But Ella Ruth was right. Damaris had to tell Gilbert how she felt, and she had to do it soon.

Chapter Four

Singings were always so wonderful. Damaris enjoyed the wind in her hair as she rode in the buggy through the crisp evening air. At the Singing, the music filled her with happiness. They sang several hymns without instruments, as usual, and talked jovially at the end, eating popcorn and laughing.

Soon it was over, and she again watched as the young people made their way out of the host's house and to the buggies. She always felt sad for the young people who came to a Singing hoping to find a date but leaving alone. It was customary for the young men to ask a young woman if he could give her a ride home in his buggy if he was interested in her, but not every young woman got a ride home.

Damaris knew she should feel blessed, but all she could do was fidget as she sat next to Gilbert in his buggy. They rode into the night with the black starry sky over their heads.

"I've been enjoying our time together, Damaris," Gilbert began, but Damaris cut him off.

"Before you say anything else, I have to tell you something. This isn't easy, so I'm just going to say it. I know I have had feelings for you for years, and I was the one who first asked you on a date, but as we've spent more time together, I've realized I don't think we are quite right for each other. I thought I loved you, but I think I…don't." Damaris winced at how blunt her words sounded, even to herself. In her head, they'd sounded gentler.

"Uh, really?" Gilbert let go of the reins with one hand to scratch his head. "Wow, Damaris. That's kind of funny because I was going to say the same thing."

"What? Really?" Damaris stared at him, stunned.

"Well, yes. Now that we've spent more time together, I think you're right. There's no…spark. There should be a spark. Right?" He gave her a cautious glance.

"Exactly! If we were in love, we'd want to spend every second together."

Gilbert laughed. "Wow, this is a relief. I didn't want to break your heart."

"Me too. I was so nervous about telling you." Relief filled Damaris. She hadn't hurt Gilbert after all, and she'd escaped an unwanted commitment.

Gilbert blew out a breath. "The whole community expects us to get married."

"So what? They'll find something else to talk about in a few days. It's more important that we are honest with each other."

"Well, my parents have been pressuring me to settle down and get married. But I don't want to just marry anyone." His cheeks turned red, and he stumbled over his words. "I mean, I didn't mean it like that. You're an amazing person, Damaris, and one blessed man will call you his one day. I hope you find true love. I know it sounds corny, but I do believe in true love."

"So do I. It's not corny at all. You're a great guy, Gilbert. You'll make one woman very happy one day. My mother has been pressuring me a little, too. Now that my father is gone and Dominic got married and moved out, she was hoping I'd get married soon for financial stability for the family. But she doesn't want to put all that pressure on me." Damaris sighed. "It's okay. I trust that God will provide for my family."

"That's the right idea. I'm not going to marry a woman until I'm completely, totally in love with her and it hurts to be apart from her," Gilbert said as he stared at the road ahead with a dreamy look in his eyes.

"Gilbert Schwartz! I had no idea you were so poetic!" Damaris said with a laugh, playfully elbowing him.

"Love is inspiring, I guess," he said sheepishly. "At least, the thought of love is. I guess I've never really been in love before."

"My mother says that when you're in love, you'll know it."

"I hope so. You know, Damaris, I pray one day you'll find what you're looking for."

Damaris smiled at Gilbert, relief filling her. "You too, Gilbert. I'm confident you will."

Arabella stood staring at her walk-in closet, perplexed about what to wear for dinner tonight. She couldn't focus even on this simple task.

It felt like she was about to go to a funeral. Her own funeral. It was, after all, the end of her life as she knew it.

She was to meet Stefan Castle at the family dinner later tonight.

"Grandma and Emily are right. What is this, the fourteenth century?" Arabella muttered to herself, rummaging through the dresses in her closet.

The maid knocked quietly and walked into the room. "Do you need anything, miss?"

"No, that's okay, Jamie. Unless you want to take my place tonight," she joked.

The maid let out an airy laugh. "Oh, Miss Blackwood. You're too funny. I couldn't possibly."

"I know, I know. I was just kidding." Arabella eyed her hair in the mirror, trying to come up with the right way to pin it up. Nothing seemed to work. "Though, sometimes I wish I could switch places with someone."

The maid looked at her and smiled sadly. "At least let me do something with your hair."

"Thank you. You know I'm not any good with that," Arabella said with a chuckle as Jamie gently began to brush Arabella's thick hair which was highlighted blonde.

Maybe I should just wear black tonight, she thought. *It would match how my heart feels.*

"Now let's find you something to wear." The maid finished braiding her hair and went to the closet, returning with two black dresses as if she'd read Arabella's mind.

"I think either of these will do nicely," Jamie said.

Arabella sighed, not caring at all. "Sure. That one." She took it, then went into the closet to get dressed.

As she walked out of the closet, there was a smart knock on the door. Jamie opened the door and let Ms. Libby in.

"You look lovely, Arabella. Now, let's get you downstairs right away. They're waiting for you." Ms. Libby curtly nodded her head toward the door and walked out, clearly expecting Arabella to follow.

Arabella sighed. "Thanks," she said to Jamie, then briskly made her way downstairs with Ms. Libby to the drawing room, where they would gather and exchange pleasantries until they were called to the dinner table. As they approached, she could hear the easy banter and chatter in the drawing room. She got to the open doorway and hesitated a bit.

"Arabella," Ms. Libby snapped. "Are you well?"

It wasn't too late. She could still turn back.

"I'm fine."

"Ah, there she is!" Arabella's mother called out, gliding toward her. "Darling, do come in and let me introduce you to our guests."

Well, there was no turning back now. She plastered a fake smile across her face.

Arabella made her way towards her mother and tried to avoid looking at the young man who threatened her way of life. She greeted her future father-in-law and tried as much as possible to remain smiling.

Her eyes scanned the face of her potential father-in-law and soon settled on his tall, awkward son, who wore rectangular black-rimmed glasses. He looked nervous and failed at hiding it, clasping and unclasping his hands in front of him. She smiled triumphantly, delighting in his discomfort.

"It's nice to meet you, Stefan," she said coolly.

He only nodded in response, and even that gesture was clumsy.

To Arabella's relief, they were immediately called in for dinner. Ms. Libby busied herself with making sure everything was perfect.

Though expected, but still somewhat infuriating, Arabella found that she had been seated next to Stefan. She decided to ignore him and listen to their parents discuss their businesses and the dwindling economy.

Arabella tried so hard to ignore Stefan, but he kept glancing at her, and it was beginning to make her fidget.

At last, Arabella decided to take the initiative "So, Stefan, what are your interests?"

"Reading," Stefan blurted out, his nervousness seeping into his words. "Do you like to read, Arabella?"

"No. Not really. I like to bake. I know, it's not that interesting."

"Of course, it is. That's what our companies are all about," Stefan said.

"What do you like to read?"

"I really like to read sci-fi for fun, but I also love reading about science. Lately, I've been researching alternative energy solutions that would cut our costs and increase profits."

"How interesting." Arabella nodded, pretending to be listening.

He smiled, and much to her dismay, he began to babble on more about scientific studies that went straight over her head.

Arabella pretended to hear everything he was saying until he ceased the conversation, nodding and smiling now and then. But really, in her head, she was thinking over a new recipe she'd made up, wondering how she could improve it.

"Arabella is well-versed in running the business," Henry was telling Philip Castle. "We've been training her for this her entire life."

Arabella cringed. It wasn't true. Yes, she had been groomed for this since she was a child, but she was certainly not well-versed in the business at all. She was terrible at it. If Philip knew that, would he still want to move forward with the agreement?

At that moment, the kitchen staff brought out bowls of soup.

Stefan barely seemed to notice as he rambled on more about a book he'd been reading. Arabella rolled her eyes and glanced at her parents, who were still deep in conversation with Philip Castle about the agreement.

"Tony Graham is probably the most talented sci-fi author I've read this year. At the end of the novel, there was this huge twist. I had no idea that Garrett was actually the imposter. It was a huge shock!" Stefan exclaimed, waving his hands in the air. His hand knocked over his bowl of soup, which rolled, spilled, and fell off the table—right into Arabella's lap.

Arabella gasped as the hot liquid seeped through her dress and onto her legs. "Ow!" She grabbed her napkin and jumped out of her chair, trying to get most of the offending soup off.

"Oh, I am so sorry," Stefan stammered, looking as red as the roses in the middle of the table.

"Arabella, are you all right?" Arabella's mother asked.

Oh, now they are concerned about me?

"Excuse me," Arabella muttered, marching out of the room. Humiliation engulfed her entire being. She was so filled with rage that fleeing seemed like the only logical thing to do.

Chapter Five

Stefan stared at his hands, completely horrified at how much of a dolt he'd been. He'd done his best trying to seem confident and cool in front of the beautiful Arabella, even though he could tell she wasn't the least bit interested in what he had to say and had only been pretending to listen to him.

"What happened, Stefan?" his father asked.

"I'm sorry," Stefan stammered. "I knocked over my bowl of soup, and it spilled on Arabella. She probably went to change."

His father gave him that familiar disapproving look, shaking his head slowly.

"I apologize for my son's clumsiness," Mr. Castle said to Arabella's parents.

Stefan cringed.

"Don't worry. Accidents happen," said Henry.

"Yes. I am sure Arabella will rejoin us soon," Helene said, giving Stefan a kind smile.

A pang of regret and embarrassment shot through Stefan's middle. Hopefully, he hadn't ruined this entire night—and this entire arrangement.

When he had first seen her walk into the room so gracefully, he had been stunned by her exquisite beauty. She was like a princess.

Her confident walk, high cheekbones, and intense brown eyes had made him nervous and intimidated, and just being near her had made him so uncomfortable that he'd sloppily knocked over his soup.

Yes, this entire situation was uncomfortable.

He knew he could never love someone like her, even if she was quite beautiful. They clearly had nothing in common. She didn't even like reading.

Even though he was only twenty-six, he'd always chosen to do scientific research and reading over going to social events where he could meet young ladies. When he had gone out to social gatherings, he'd often embarrassed himself when trying to talk to young women.

He knew this marriage would never be based on love but rather a business agreement. Since he knew he had a slim chance of ever finding a woman who could love him, he'd agreed to his father's wishes.

He figured he wouldn't have to face the spoiled princess for the rest of the evening, and he'd prefer it that way.

***

Arabella slammed the door behind her with a loud bang. She couldn't care less if the door was pulled off of its hinges.

She removed the ruined dress hurriedly and prepared to take a bath. They would have to carry on downstairs without her.

"Arabella!" Her mother's voice came from the other side of the door. "Come downstairs this instant."

"Please, Mother. I can't. I met Stefan, so please just let me stay here the rest of the night." Arabella stood on the other side of the door.

"Open this door."

"Mother. I'm about to take a bath. I have soup all over me. I'm embarrassed, soaked in soup, and I've had enough for one night. Just tell them I'm not feeling well and go on without me," she begged, knowing if she opened the door her mother would drag her downstairs.

Helene sighed. "Oh, fine. I understand. I know this can't be easy for you. I'll let them know."

After a pause, Arabella heard her mother's footsteps echo down the hall.

A good long soak made her feel a little better, but the tears did not stop flowing from her eyes as she realized that she would most likely be spending the rest of her miserable life with the dull and clumsy Stefan.

After getting out of the bath, she decided to distract herself by watching videos on her phone online. She scrolled through the videos, distracted by the fast-moving pictures.

Then she remembered the videos Emily had told her about, the ones about the traffickers who had targeted the Amish. Maybe she could find the one with the woman who looked like her. She searched for them and found one that immediately interested her, and apparently it had just been posted.

A young woman wearing a dress with a white, old-fashioned looking bonnet-like head covering on her head appeared on the screen, but the camera only showed the back of her head. At first it looked like an old movie. Arabella sat up, perplexed by what she saw.

Who wears that kind of clothing anymore? she wondered.

Arabella turned up the volume, her interest in the program heightened. Arabella learned that Amish communities were across America.

A female news reporter came on screen, speaking to the young woman who was dressed like a pilgrim, even though she was facing away from her. The reporter said the woman wanted to remain anonymous, so that must be why she wasn't showing her face. The reporter asked the young woman about how she helped the police find and arrest the traffickers. The young woman explained, then suddenly stopped, as if afraid.

"Yes, it worked," another young woman's voice said. When the camera moved to focus on her face instead, Arabella gasped.

This was the woman Emily had told her about.

The young woman on the screen looked just like Arabella. Yes, their hair color was different from what she could see underneath the bonnet-like head covering, and their clothing was vastly different, but that could be changed. She looked like Arabella's twin.

Arabella leaned forward and listened, enraptured as the young woman spoke.

"She is a true hero." The young woman's eyes filled with tears, then a look of fear overtook her expression.

The reporter didn't seem to notice as she went on. "Sounds like your friend is selfless. Because of her, her sisters are safe now."

Arabella listened as the reporter wrapped up the interview and spoke more about this place called Unity, Maine, which sounded too good to be true, especially now that the traffickers had been arrested. She went on to say that the traffickers who had been arrested in Maine also had ties to human trafficking rings here in Germany. Appalled that this was also happening where she lived, she listened closely as the reporter gave more information on the Amish.

Arabella's interest heightened a notch further when she heard that the Amish did not use electricity or the internet but instead chose to live simply. They didn't watch TV and lived separately from the world at a slower pace.

She wished for that kind of life but could only dream about it.

An idea began to form in her head.

That young woman looks just like me, Arabella thought. *I wonder if she'd switch places with me, even for a little while.*

And if the woman refused, Arabella could at least hide out in Unity. No one would look for her there.

She tapped her foot impatiently on the floor as she dialed Emily's number.

Emily answered the phone. "Arabella, are you okay? Aren't you supposed to be at the dinner right now with the Castles?"

Her best friend knew her too well. Emily's intuition caused Arabella's eyes to sting with tears once more. Emotion cracked her voice as she said, "No, I'm not okay. I need to get out of here. I just watched that video about the Amish that you told me about."

"Incredible, right? Did you see the one with the woman who looks like you?"

"Yes, and you were right. She does look like me. Are you still going to New York?"

"Yes, I am. Why?"

"Is it too late for me to come with you?"

Emily chuckled. "Of course not, Ari, as long as you can get a seat on the flight. You're always welcome to travel with me anywhere. What changed your mind? I do hope you are not planning to do something outrageous."

"I just need some time to think. Somewhere my parents can't find me."

"Where?"

"You said Maine is only a few states away from New York, right? They don't watch TV there, so they won't know who I am. My parents would never think of looking for me in an Amish community. It's a small, quiet, peaceful place. It's perfect!" Arabella said, excitement rising in her voice.

"You want to go stay with the Amish?" Emily laughed out loud. "Oh, Ari. Out of all the ideas you've ever had, this one is the craziest. You wouldn't last one day living with the Amish. What about your cell phone and internet?"

I better not tell her about my plan to ask that woman to trade places with me; she'd really think I'm crazy, Arabella thought glumly.

38

"Who cares? I want to get away from technology. That's why I'm going there. I will be unreachable." A clever smile played on Arabella's lips.

"Well, then. I'm not going to try to change your mind. I will send you the flight information so you can book a flight with mine."

"Thanks. I'll take a bus from New York to Maine."

"Arabella, are you sure you want to do this and go to this place by yourself?" Concern lined Emily's voice.

"Yes, Emily."

"What happened?"

Arabella told Emily about the experience at dinner and how Stefan had rambled on about scientific nonsense and spilled soup on her. "I'm about to sign away the rest of my life to a bumbling, awkward nerd. I need a getaway. This is the perfect place to go."

After ending the call, Arabella set down her mobile phone and sank back into her pillow with a genuine smile and profound relief for the first time in weeks. She was finally taking control of her life, at least for the moment.

All her life, she'd made choices and done things for the sake of others, mostly her parents. She did love helping the business prosper by being the face of the company, going to social events, and doing whatever else her parents asked of her. Maybe without realizing it, her parents had played this to their advantage.

She had to do this, for her sanity. Arabella needed to live for a while, carefree, before her new mundane, miserable married life began.

***

Before the sun was up, Damaris woke up and got ready to begin a morning of baking at the Millers' house. Then they would bring their baked goods to the Community Store and the market for the day.

On days when they sold their goods at the market, Damaris baked at the Millers' house because they baked larger quantities to fill the additional demand. It was faster and easier than baking multiple oven loads at her own house and bringing everything to the Millers' house anyway before going to the market.

"Good morning," Laura chirped, bouncing to the door to greet Damaris. "We made up a new recipe for some lemon blueberry cookies. Come on; I'll show you. They were such a success last Saturday, so that's why we need your help with making more today."

While Damaris enjoyed baking and learning new recipes, she couldn't picture doing this for the rest of her life.

Rather than the actual baking, she enjoyed the business aspect so much more, like making new signs for their booth at the market, experimenting with pricing and specials, and drawing in new customers.

There had to be something more than just selling baked goods at local stores.

"Mae," Damaris said in the kitchen as Laura and Lydia began loading the products in the buggy. "I've been thinking, and I have some ideas on how we can increase our profits."

"More of your business ideas?" Mae chuckled good-naturedly. "Well, I'm happy to hear it, but I can't promise anything. Growing a business usually costs money."

"Of course. I know. I was thinking we should open our own bakery store. Then we could start selling the goods at our own bakery in addition to the market and the Community Store."

"Well, I can't sell here. This house isn't big enough, and we need the kitchen for baking."

"I know. What if we rented a space downtown for a bakery? We'd have more foot traffic and the space you need," Damaris offered.

"But the rent or lease would cut into our profits," Mae said, shaking her head. "I'm not sure if we'd be able to afford it. Besides, you and Lydia could be married within a few years, then Laura will eventually get married too. You'll have your own families and won't have time to help me bake. By then, I'll be thinking of retiring. So, it just wouldn't work, sadly." Mae shrugged.

"What if we just tried it? I did the math and I think that even with paying the rent, it would still significantly increase our profit margins," Damaris countered, setting her notebook down on the counter. She pointed to a graph she'd made. "See? These are my estimates for profit and loss."

"We have no idea what would happen if we rented a space for a bakery downtown."

"No risk, no reward, right?" Damaris smiled sheepishly.

Mae smiled and gently touched Damaris' shoulder. "I admire your ambition and your ideas, Damaris. Your ideas have already raised our profits and brought us so many more customers, but I am happy with the way the business is now. I don't want to put more time and money into it. I'm sorry. I hope you understand."

"Of course," Damaris said, nodding, but she didn't understand. Opening the new bakery could bring in so much new business for them and increase their profits. Why wouldn't Mae at least consider it?

As Damaris helped Laura finish loading the buggy with everything they'd made that morning, Damaris asked, "Do you ever think there has to be more to this life?"

"What do you mean?" Laura asked.

Damaris set a box of donuts in the back of the buggy, turned to Laura, and lowered her voice. "Don't you ever want to get out of here? Travel the world? See what's out there?"

"Oh, yes. I'd give anything to go somewhere tropical. Maybe Hawaii or Thailand. I read about these places in books, and they sound so wonderful. I guess that's why I love to read so much because I know I'll never be able to get on a plane and go somewhere like that." Laura gave a wistful sigh, staring off into the distance.

"Me too," Damaris said. "But I wish I could go to Europe most of all. Do you think it's wrong if we aren't content to stay here forever, if we want to travel?"

"No. What's wrong with wanting to see more of God's beautiful creation?" Laura asked, grinning.

"Hmm. Maybe you're right," Damaris said with a nod.

Mae and Lydia came out of the house with more boxes of pastries, so Damaris and Laura abruptly ended their conversation. Damaris said goodbye and drove to the Community Store. Once she arrived, she noticed that a few other Amish employees had arrived at the store and were beginning to put the store in order before opening.

"So, how did it go with Gilbert?" Ella Ruth asked in a soft voice as they unloaded the donuts and pastries.

"Surprisingly well." Damaris set out a box of cherry pastries. "It was not what I expected at all. He said he felt the same way. His parents have been pressuring him to get married. He says there was no spark between us, and I completely agree. He is a wonderful man, and he will make another woman very happy."

"Well, good. I'm glad you've got that sorted out. It could have become so awkward if you had let it go on," Ella Ruth said.

As the day brightened and the shop opened, customers began to stream in. At first, they came in small numbers, but soon the Community Store was bustling with shoppers.

Chapter Six

"Drop me off at that store, please," Arabella said, and the driver pulled into the parking lot of a quaint Amish store in Unity, Maine.

Arabella stepped out of the taxi and quickly paid the driver, taking her suitcase as he got it out of the trunk for her. She wore oversized sunglasses, a scarf, and a hat that covered her hair to disguise herself. She normally wore a disguise to avoid paparazzi and people recognizing her on the street, but now she didn't want people realizing how much she resembled the Amish woman she was looking for.

Arabella welcomed the fresh air filling her lungs, shouldering her oversized purse. At the same time, she took in the entire atmosphere around her.

She gazed at the open, rolling fields in different shades of yellow, green and brown which were bathed in the light of the setting sun. Some of the barns were a traditional shade of red with peeling paint while some had fresh coats of paint. Some of the barns looked more like huge, vinyl warehouses. Some of the surrounding houses were modern with power lines and cars in the driveways.

At first, she felt free, then realization set in. She hadn't realized the Amish lived side by side with Americans who were not Amish. What if she was recognized after all?

She shook her head and laughed at herself. Who was she kidding? Sure, she was a local celebrity in Germany, but here, no one would know her name. The commercials she was in wouldn't be on TV here since they didn't have any locations open in the states yet.

Enraptured by the picturesque view before her, she stared out at the long stretch of road that passed the community. A horse and buggy drove past, the horse's hooves clip-clopping on the pavement. The large, black box-like structure had a bright orange triangle on the back, signaling a slow-moving vehicle.

She was astonished by the unabashed happiness she found around her. Here, she could find peace. Arabella knew it in her heart.

An Amish family walked by, talking amongst themselves, then greeted another group of Amish people near the store, the Unity Community Store. The sign above the door creaked as it moved in the breeze.

Glancing around, she didn't see any other shops or public places in sight where she could search or ask around. Maybe someone in the Unity Community Store would know where she could find the young Amish woman who looked like her.

Walking hesitantly, she made her way down the dirt lane she was standing on to the Community Store, side-stepping a pile of horse manure as she pulled her suitcase. She'd almost ruined her high-heeled boots.

I should have worn something much more practical, she thought, shaking her head.

As she looked around, she felt as though she had traveled back in time.

Arabella pulled her suitcase into the Unity Community Store and was instantly drawn to the smell of freshly baked donuts. Her stomach rumbled loudly, and she decided to buy one. She hadn't eaten since yesterday. It was not that she could not afford to eat or buy food, but her stomach had been in knots from thinking about the upcoming wedding and leaving her home without telling her parents. After traveling on the long flight, then taking a bus and a taxi, she was exhausted and famished.

She greeted the cashier without much attention as she was more drawn to the donuts than the server. "Hi, can I have a chocolate donut, please?" Arabella asked, then looked up at the person behind the counter.

It was the young woman who had been on TV, the one who looked like her. In person, even with the bonnet-like head covering and odd clothing, this woman looked so much more like her than on TV.

44

"Of course," said the young woman without looking at Arabella, taking tongs and putting the donut in a paper bag. "You're just in time. We're about to close."

At that moment, no one else was around, so Arabella quickly removed her hat and sunglasses.

The young woman looked up at Arabella to hand her the paper bag, then froze. They both stared at each other, stunned.

"What is your name?" Arabella eventually choked out.

"I'm Damaris Kauffman," the young woman said slowly. "Who are you?" She blinked. "Wow. You know, I think we look alike."

Arabella smiled. "You're right. We do look alike. Funny, isn't it? My name is Arabella Blackwood. I came here all the way from Germany to stay here in this community."

"Germany?" Damaris' eyes went wide, and she clapped her hands together. "Oh, I'd die to go to Germany or anywhere in Europe. I've read about Germany in books. I've always wanted to go there."

"It's really beautiful there," Arabella said.

"I'd love to hear about it," Damaris said with a sigh.

"Want to go for a walk? I'd be happy to tell you about it. I also have questions about the Amish. Maybe we could answer each other's questions. We look so much alike, we could be twins. I'd like to get to know you."

"I'd love that." Damaris smiled, then glanced at the clock. "We are closing in a few minutes. Let me finish up and I'll meet you outside."

"Sure." Arabella wandered down the aisles, grabbing a few food items to make herself some dinner later on. She planned on staying at a new local inn that was only a short walk down the road from here. If her room didn't have a microwave or stovetop, she'd just have to eat the soup cold.

She returned to the counter, paid, and went outside to wait. She put her sunglasses and hat back on so that they wouldn't look so much alike.

A few minutes later, Damaris came outside. "I only have a few minutes before I have to go home and help my mother make dinner and put my brothers and sisters to bed. Do you have a place to stay?"

"I'm going to the inn that opened around the corner recently. I made some phone calls to other inns and hotels that were farther away before I arrived, and that place was recommended. It's just a short walk from here."

"Oh, I haven't heard much about it yet. I recommend the Millers' Bed and Breakfast. I work for the Millers, actually. They bake and sell their products at the store here and several other local stores," Damaris said. "Actually, you could come stay with us at my house if you'd like. I'm sure my mother would be happy to have you."

Arabella chuckled, looking at Damaris. If she stayed at the Millers or at Damaris' house, they'd notice how much she looked like Damaris right away, which would ruin her plan. "That's okay. I already have my reservation." She smiled, unable to get over how much they resembled each other. "Sorry, this is so weird. I've never met anyone who looks like me before."

"I know. It is strange, isn't it? Have you always lived in Germany? There is probably no way we are related, right?"

"My family has lived in Germany for generations, so no. So, what questions do you have about Germany?"

Arabella wanted to ask Damaris about switching places with her right away, but she didn't feel like it was the right time yet. She didn't want to scare her off, especially after everything the town had been through with the girls being kidnapped by traffickers.

"What's it like? Where do you live?" Damaris asked.

"I live on an estate in the country. It's actually near a castle," Arabella told her.

Damaris' eyes went wide. "A castle? Really? Oh, I wish I could see a castle. I've also read about castles in books."

"And we have stables," Arabella added.

"I love to ride. Do you ride?"

"Me? No. You'd love it, though."

"Is your house big?" Damaris asked.

"Well, yes, it is," Arabella said, trying not to sound like she was bragging. "The whole country is beautiful. There are mountains, lovely towns, and the best coffee shops."

Damaris sighed. "I wish I could go there someday. So, what questions do you have about the Amish?"

There were so many things Arabella wanted to ask, but she started slowly. "So, I heard all Amish communities are different."

Damaris nodded. "Yes, they have different rules."

"And you don't use electricity or cars or cell phones? And you always dress like that?"

Damaris nodded again. "Yes. It's probably very different from what you're used to."

"Actually, I find it refreshing. That's why I came here, to get away from my life for a while." Arabella leaned forward and whispered, "My friend says that Amish women don't shave their legs. Is that true?"

Damaris giggled. "Yes, that is true. At least, we don't do it here."

Arabella laughed. "Wow. Emily was right."

"Who is Emily?"

"She's my best friend. She's really funny. You'd like her."

Damaris looked around, then whispered. "Don't tell anyone, but I break the rules sometimes and shave my legs. Many of the young people here don't always follow the rules. Some of them even have cell phones."

Arabella laughed. "I'm not too surprised. So, do you think you'll ever go to Germany?"

Damaris shook her head. "We aren't allowed to ride on airplanes. I mean, if I did, I wouldn't be shunned because I haven't officially joined the church yet. Lately I've been wondering what's out there, and I want to see it for myself before I decide whether I want to join the Amish church."

"Join the Amish church? What does that mean?"

"That means once I decide to be baptized into the Amish church and officially become a member, if I ever leave the Amish, I would be shunned. My family would not be allowed to speak to me. But if I leave before I am baptized, I wouldn't be shunned. I'm already past the age most Amish youths join the church."

"So, what's the point of joining at all?"

"Well, it's expected. Also, it shows commitment." Damaris wrung her hands. "If I do join, I want to be completely committed and do it for the right reasons."

"Of course. That makes sense."

"You know," Damaris said, lowering her voice. She looked around. "No one knows this except my brother and my two best friends, Ella Ruth and Belle, but I actually was going to go to Germany on my *rumspringa*."

"What's a... What did you call it?" Arabella asked.

"*Rumspringa*. It's when the Amish youth get to leave the community temporarily to experience the ways of the world. It helps us decide if we want to join the church or not. Well, I had planned on going to Germany during that time. I got my passport and everything. That's totally against the rules, but I did it anyway. I wanted to go so badly, I didn't care."

Arabella's eyes widened. Damaris already had a passport? "Really? Why didn't you end up going?"

Damaris looked at the ground. "My father got sick and passed away. I couldn't leave my family. The timing was wrong. After that, I never went."

"Oh," Arabella said softly. "I'm so sorry."

Damaris sighed. "I guess it wasn't meant to be. Well, I need to get home. Want to meet me back here tomorrow around noon, when I have my lunch break?"

"That would be great. I'll see you then."

"See you tomorrow."

Chapter Seven

The next day, Arabella waited outside the store for Damaris to come out during her lunch break. Arabella still wore her large sunglasses and hat, trying to keep a low profile and avoiding eye contact with anyone who walked past her.

How would she even present her idea to Damaris? What if she flat out rejected her?

Damaris walked out of the store, spotting Arabella, and smiled. "Hello. Did you have a nice night at the inn?"

"Oh, yes. It's lovely there. It's nice having all this free time to myself. I'm normally so busy at home with work," Arabella said, her words coming out too fast as her heart raced with excitement. "So, do you want to go somewhere for lunch?"

"I brought lunch for both of us." She held up a large lunch bag. "I made sandwiches. We can have a picnic. My break isn't long enough for us to go anywhere."

"That sounds great!" Arabella said. They walked to the back of the store where it was quieter and spread out a colorful, intricate quilt that Damaris had sewn with her mother and sisters.

They sat down under the trees at the edge of the woods. As a breeze rustled the branches, hundreds of gold, red, and orange leaves danced their way to the ground around them.

"Do you like working at the store?" Arabella asked.

Damaris shrugged. "It's nice. I should be thankful. It's a good job. I like working with my best friend and her father."

"But?" Arabella prodded.

"I'd really like to run my own business. I want more than what this place has to offer. I want to see the world. I know I'm supposed to be content, but I want so much more," Damaris gushed, then bit into her ham sandwich.

"If you had another chance to go to Germany, would you go?"

Damaris sighed. "I don't see how it would be possible. Now that my father is gone, my mother and siblings need me. I could never afford the ticket. Besides, I could get in trouble. It'll never happen, and I need to accept that."

A slow smile spread on Arabella's face. "Well, Damaris, I think I can get you to Germany and have your family taken care of while you're gone. Also, you wouldn't have to worry about paying for the trip."

Damaris laughed out loud. "You're kidding."

"I'm serious. This might sound crazy, but I actually came here looking for you."

Damaris gave her a skeptical look, her eyebrows knitting together with suspicion. "Wait. Why would you come here to see me, and how did you even know who I am? What do you mean?"

"I saw you online in that interview about the young woman who helped rescue her sisters from sex trafficking."

Damaris' eyes went wide. "Really? Did it say my name?"

"No. I only saw your face, and I realized how much we look alike. So, I got this crazy idea. It's obvious you want to see the world. If you hear me out, I can get you to Germany for a visit." Arabella said cautiously. "Are you interested?"

Damaris asked hesitantly, "What is your idea?"

"Well, you can see we look quite alike. With some effort, we could look like identical twins."

"It is uncanny how much we look alike. It was my first thought when I saw you."

"Yes, well, what do you think about trading places with me? I could stay here, and you could go to my estate in Germany and pretend to be me. I could do your job and all your chores and help your mother with the kids. Maybe just for a week or two. I will pay for your plane ticket and everything. You won't have to pay for a thing. Plus, you said you already have your passport. Might as well use it. So, what do you say?" Arabella bit her lip, waiting for Damaris' reaction.

Damaris continued to stare at her as if Arabella had sprouted green hair. "Trade places with…you? I could never be you, and you couldn't be me. No offense."

Arabella raised her eyebrows and crossed her arms. "Yes, you could, and I could be you. I could teach you. You could teach me to be you. It would only be for a little while."

"You want to pretend to be me, pretend to be Amish?" Damaris burst into laughter. "That's even less likely."

"What?" Arabella shrugged. "It can't be that hard."

"Oh, it's harder than you think. You don't seem like the person who would want to give up her cell phone, internet, and modern conveniences for over a week." Damaris covered her mouth, stifling more laughter.

"Why does everyone think that?" Arabella rolled her eyes.

"Why do you want to stay here and pretend to be me, anyway?"

"Mainly, I want you to pretend to be me so I can get away for a while. I am supposed to marry a man I don't know soon, and before I sign my life away, I want to do what I want for a while and do something different," Arabella explained.

"Do you mean like…an arranged marriage?" Damaris asked, her eyes suddenly filled with concern.

"Sort of. Do the Amish do arranged marriages?"

Damaris shook her head. "Of course not. Not here. We marry who we want when we choose to. Why are you in an arranged marriage?"

Arabella quickly explained the situation. "I can't stand him. He's going to be staying in our home for the next few weeks so we can 'get to know each other better'." Arabella rolled her eyes again and let out an exasperated growl. "I don't want to get to know him anymore. He's a nerd, and we have nothing in common. He likes to read and I don't, and he doesn't know anything about baking. If you take my place and spend some time with him, you can also see the sights in Germany and travel like you've always wanted to."

"What do you mean by spending time with him?" Damaris asked, arching one eyebrow.

"Oh, nothing exciting. He'll probably want to play chess and talk about the boring books he's been reading or science experiments. You'll probably go sightseeing together or out to dinner. Don't worry, it will be very proper."

"Hmm." Damaris crossed her arms. "Well, if you're going to be me, you'll have to learn the Amish customs. You'll have to do all my chores and go to work for me. You'll have to wash dishes by hand, cook with a woodstove, take care of my siblings, and do everything I normally do. I work for a bakery and we start baking every morning at five-thirty. Will that be a problem?" Damaris looked her up and down. "I know you said your family owns a bakery company, so do you know how to bake?"

"Of course, I do." Arabella's face lit up. "I love baking. I come up with new recipes all the time. Actually, I'd rather do that than run the company, but it's not going to work out that way for me." Sorrow rose in Arabella's chest as she thought about how the rest of her life would be. "Anyway, before I begin my new life, I just want to pretend to be someone else for a while. Does that make any sense? Haven't you ever wanted to be someone else, to get out of here, even just for a little while?"

A look of understanding came over Damaris' face. She clasped her hands together in front of her and looked at the ground, then looked back up at Arabella. "Yes. I know exactly what you mean."

"So, what do you think? Do you want to switch places?" Arabella asked, hope rising within her as she watched Damaris' face.

"Hold on a second," Damaris said, a little too forcefully. "How do I know this isn't some scheme? We've had several girls here kidnapped by traffickers. They used young men to lure them in. How do I know you're not working for them?"

Arabella threw her hands up defensively. "Whoa! What? No, I just want some time away from my life. I love it here. I thought we could both benefit by trading places. Look, I can prove who I am." Arabella opened her wallet and handed Damaris her ID. She held up her phone. "Here are photos of me and my parents in front of one of our bakeries."

Damaris took the phone, studying the images.

"And this is one of our recent commercials." Arabella played a video on her phone of herself speaking about the bakery. "If you can get to a computer, you can do an internet search for me. I'm not sure how else I can prove it to you that I am who I say I am."

"Sorry. Don't take it personally. This town has been through a lot. I just want to make sure I'm not getting sucked into something I'll regret," Damaris said. "I can go to the library down the street and use one of their computers. In this community, we're allowed to use computers outside our home. We just can't own them. Anyway, I can do a search for you, like you said. Just to make sure."

"Of course. I understand."

"Even if you are who you say you are and you really do just want to be someone else for a while, I'm not so sure this is a good idea. My family depends on me. They'd need a lot from you while you're here. There's a lot of work to be done. Not only that, how could we do this without anyone finding out?" Damaris asked.

"I could stay here a week or so. That way we could learn how to be each other."

Damaris drew her eyebrows together, deep in thought. She gathered up her food, stuffing it into her bag. "This is *ferhuddled*. Crazy." She stood up abruptly, shaking her head. "I can't. I'm sorry. I have to go."

With that, Damaris turned and ran back into the store, leaving Arabella alone with her disappointment.

She heaved a sigh. What did she expect? Of course, Damaris would be skeptical of her, after everything that had happened here.

Why would an Amish woman trade places with her?

***

The next day, Arabella was making notes about a new recipe idea. She was so engrossed in her work that she jumped when there was a knock on her door.

She opened it to see Damaris standing in the hallway. "Damaris! I'm so happy to see you again."

"Sorry for how I acted yesterday," Damaris said, hugging herself.

Arabella motioned for her to come in. "Don't be. I totally understand. You had to be cautious."

"Well, I went to the library and looked you up. Clearly, you were telling the truth." Damaris hesitated only for a moment before nodding enthusiastically. "Yes. Yes, I want to do it. I want to trade places with you."

"Really? Are you sure?" Surprise and relief flooded Arabella. She shut the door, and they sat on the bed.

"Yes. I know I will never get the chance to go to Germany for the rest of my life, so I feel like I have to do this. There is one more thing, though," Damaris continued. "Our hair."

"What do you mean? We both have about the same hair color, from what I can tell. Mine has highlights, but I can get it colored back to brown."

"My hair is down to my knees. I'll have to cut it."

"What?" Arabella cried. "Down to your knees? Really?"

"Yes. We believe our hair is our crowning glory, so we don't cut it. I'm guessing if I'm going to pretend to be you, I will have to cut it like yours." Damaris motioned to Arabella's highlighted blonde hair which flowed to her elbows. "It's still long, but mine is much longer."

"Yes. That would be a problem if you don't. It would be a dead giveaway. If it's against your customs, are you okay with doing that?"

"As I said, I've been dying to go to Europe. A paid trip to Germany is a dream come true for me. My hair will grow back, eventually. I think I'm getting the better end of the deal."

"No, I think I am," Arabella said with a smile.

"Oh, I just remembered. We speak Pennsylvania Dutch quite often. It's a form of German. Do you speak German?"

"Well, yes, of course. I *am* German. Is it similar to German?"

"I think the way we speak it here is probably similar enough to the German you know so you can understand it, but there are probably differences. Maybe you should spend some time around people talking and listen to them. Even if you can't speak Pennsylvania Dutch well, at least hopefully you can understand well enough and respond to people in English."

"Sure, sounds good."

"May I ask why you don't have a German accent?" Damaris asked. "We once had a customer from Germany in the store and she had quite the German accent."

"Well, I spent my summers in New Hampshire when I was younger. My friends used to think it was amazing how I could flip back and forth between a German accent and a New Hampshire accent. After a few summers there, I picked up on the New Hampshire accent so much that it stuck with me. So I guess I have a New England accent like you, but I can easily switch back to a German accent." Arabella demonstrated her German accent with the last few words she spoke.

Damaris laughed out loud. "Wow. That's incredible! You're so blessed that you were able to travel so much, even at a young age."

"I loved going there during the summer. You know, I've been told I'm pretty good at faking accents and doing impressions. When I was a kid, I was cast as the narrator in a play and I had to do a British accent. People were shocked when they realized I don't actually have a British accent." Arabella smiled at the memory.

"That's too funny." Damaris said. "Well, I better get back to work soon. I'm on my break. I just got this job, and I don't want to lose it for being late. As I said before, you're also going to have to do what I do at the store. I am still new and don't know how to do the job well myself yet. It's mostly helping customers and restocking shelves. Ella Ruth will help you." Damaris bit her lip and looked away, deep in thought. "I wonder if I should tell her about this."

"Who's Ella Ruth?"

"She's my best friend. She works at the store and her father, Irvin, who is the owner. She's been teaching me how to do the job." Damaris started walking toward the door. "I really have to go. Do you remember where we had our picnic yesterday? Can you meet me there around noon tomorrow? It's my day off. I can tell my mother I have errands to run in town. Maybe I can get my hair done then and we can talk about all the details."

"Sure. That sounds great. We can have lunch in town. My treat. I'll see you then." Arabella grinned at Damaris, who then turned and hurried out the door.

Arabella took in a deep breath, which also filled her with hope and revival. Could this really work? Would Damaris suddenly change her mind and back out?

Well, she'd find out more tomorrow.

***

As Damaris returned to work, questions swirled through her mind. What on earth had she just agreed to?

Yes, she wanted to go to Europe more than anything, but was this the way to do it?

It seemed horrifying and yet appealing, and it may be her only chance to travel abroad. What if she got caught and got in trouble with the church elders for flying on an airplane?

It would be only for a little while, she thought. *If we do this right, no one would even know I ever left. God, I know it will be a lie, but I want to go to Germany more than anything. This is my only chance.*

Guilt niggled at her at the mere thought of lying to everyone. Maybe this was a terrible idea.

What would her mother say if they were caught? Also, eventually, she'd realize Damaris cut her hair. Damaris was a terrible liar, so she'd probably end up telling her mother about the trip, eventually. Her mother would be so disappointed. Yes, Damaris wouldn't be shunned, but she might get in trouble with the church in some capacity. Would it be worth it to get to travel to Germany?

The idea filled her with a mixture of excitement and dread, making it hard for her to fall asleep that night. It was almost morning before her weary body succumbed to sleep.

58

Chapter Eight

As soon as Arabella awoke, her eyes frantically scanned the unfamiliar room of the local inn. She remembered where she was and settled back into bed. It was quite strange to wake up on her own without a maid to help her get dressed and do her hair while telling her the schedule for the day of places she had to be, like filming a commercial or attending a fundraiser.

She slowly made her way into the bathroom to get ready. As she brushed her teeth, she was grateful to have a full day to herself doing only what she wanted to do—meeting with Damaris to talk through the details of their plan. She stretched out on her bed, enjoying the solitude. She had a whole room to herself without anyone coming in to give her details of a social event or a business meeting she was supposed to attend. It felt absolutely wonderful.

Yet, time seemed to pass slowly as she slipped into boredom. She grabbed her sketchbook and drawing pencils from her bag. Arabella loved to sketch, but hadn't had the time lately, and she'd missed it. She began several sketches, inspired by the new breathtaking scenery in Unity. For some reason, she couldn't get any of the sketches right, and grew frustrated. Unable to focus, she finally gave up and threw the sketchbook onto the bed.

What if the switch was a bad idea? What if they got caught? If they did, she would be hurried back home, and this time, she would be locked away until her wedding to Stefan. She stifled a shudder as she remembered the shy, awkward young man who had poured soup on her at their first meeting.

What would her parents say? They were adept at giving her the illusion of a choice, yet they made her feel like her only choice was to please them. What would they have done if she had told them no?

She braided her hair and smiled at the fact that this was the second day in years without fully applied makeup or having to change her outfits to keep up appearances. In addition, she had even eaten donuts as a meal. She burst out laughing at herself, basking in this newfound freedom.

But what about Damaris? What could be so wrong in her life that she wanted to get away so badly and pretend to be someone else? Though Arabella barely knew Damaris, she felt a deep connection to her. They had more in common than she had first thought.

What if Damaris backed out of the plan? Arabella feared what could happen, but at the same time, she desperately needed to have a vacation without guilt weighing her down.

***

Arabella arrived at the spot where they'd shared their brief picnic, down the lane from the Unity Community Store where she and Damaris had agreed to meet.

Would Damaris even show up? Arabella tapped her foot in the leaves anxiously. What if Damaris had changed her mind after thinking it over?

Just then, a buggy pulled up and Damaris hopped down.

"Hi," Damaris said, walking over to Arabella.

Relief filled Arabella at the sight of her. "You still want to go into town to talk about everything?" Arabella asked, worried Damaris had changed her mind.

"Yes. Let's do it. Shall we take my buggy?" Damaris gestured to the black box-shaped buggy hitched to a horse.

"Are you serious?" Arabella asked, scrunching up her nose at the unpleasant scent of the horse.

"You want to learn how to be Amish, right? Come on. Let's go." Damaris sauntered over to the buggy. "Also, you need to learn how to drive."

Arabella didn't bother hiding her shock as her eyebrows shot up. "Me? Drive that thing?"

Damaris laughed. "You're going to need to get around. I drive it all the time to make my deliveries and run errands, and people will get suspicious if you don't drive it for a while. It's not that hard." Damaris waved Arabella over. She approached her horse. "This is Apple. He's very gentle."

Arabella took a step back. "Whoa! I'm not so good with horses. To be honest, they scare me."

"Really? You didn't take riding lessons when you were younger?" Damaris knew Arabella was wealthy and was only joking, but Arabella frowned.

"My parents tried to get me to when I was a kid but gave up after I cried at each lesson."

"Oh. Sorry. I was only kidding."

"We have horses in the stables at home, but I haven't gone near them in years."

"It's okay. Come pet him and let him smell you."

Arabella took a few slow footsteps forward. She slowly extended her hand to the horse's nose.

Damaris took Arabella's hand and guided it along Apple's nose. "See? Isn't he sweet?"

Arabella smiled as the horse sniffed her hand. "Yes." She giggled when his scratchy tongue licked her hand. "Do you think you can put up with me for a little while, Apple?"

The horse snorted, and both women laughed.

Just then, a buggy rumbled down the lane and was about to pass them. In the front seat, Irvin was driving.

"Get in the back of the buggy. Quick! My boss is coming," Damaris said to Arabella. "I don't want him to see us together."

"In there?" Arabella pointed to the buggy.

"Yes." Damaris opened it for her and shoved her inside just in time. Irvin slowed his buggy down.

"Damaris? Are you all right? Are you having road trouble?" Irvin asked as his buggy stopped. "Why are you pulled over?"

"I'm fine," Damaris said, waving her hand. "I was just…um…picking some flowers." Damaris tried not to cringe, realizing her error as the words tumbled out.

"Flowers? It's autumn. There aren't any flowers," Irvin said, looking around.

"I thought I saw some. I was wrong. Oh well! Anyway, have a nice day." She climbed up into the buggy.

"Good day," Irvin said after giving her a confused look. He clicked his tongue to get his horse moving. As he drove away, she heard Arabella complaining in the back.

"Okay, can I sit up front with you now?"

"Yes. Come on," Damaris said with a laugh, helping her out. "I can teach you how to drive, but we can't let anyone see us together, or they will figure it out. I know a lot of people around here."

"Fine. Just tell me when, and I'll turn my face away," Arabella said as she climbed up onto the front seat next to Damaris.

"That was close. I can't believe I said I was picking flowers."

Arabella laughed. "He must think you're odd."

"That can't be helped. I think lots of people around here think I'm odd." Damaris shrugged. "I'll drive to town, then on the way back, you can try. Okay?"

"Okay," Arabella said slowly.

"This is how you hold the reins." Damaris showed Arabella the way she held her reins in her hands, then the vocal cues she gave Apple to get him to slow down, stop, or speed up. "Do you want to try?"

Arabella gave a nervous laugh. "No. Not yet. Like you said, maybe on the way back. We should go to the next town over so no one sees us together."

"You're right. I know a nice little café we can go to. You know, my best friend Ella Ruth might become suspicious while you're here. She knows me better than anyone, and she could help you while you're here. It would be good to have someone who knows to answer your questions and cover for you."

"Will she tell anyone?" Arabella asked.

"No. She can keep a secret."

"That's up to you then. You will have to teach me how to be Amish, and then I will teach you everything you need to know about how to be me," Arabella said.

What have I gotten myself into? Damaris wondered, growing more anxious with each moment. She shook her head as if to rid herself of the doubts. *Do you want to go to Germany or not? This is your only chance.*

After they arrived at a small café in the next town over and sat down at a table, they spoke in Pennsylvania Dutch so that Arabella could get used to the language.

"So, as you probably know, the Amish are known for their devout faith in God. Are you a Christian, Arabella? Do you have a relationship with God? I just think if we're going to switch places, it's an important question to ask," Damaris said, clasping her hands in her lap.

"Oh, yes," Arabella said, smiling. "My relationship with God is the center of my life. I don't know what I'd do without my faith. I'd be lost. My parents used to take me to church when I was younger, and they were also so devout back then. But as they became more consumed with running the business and keeping up appearances, always attending social events, they stopped going to church as much and put work first. I promised myself I'd never put work before God."

"I'm sorry to hear that," Damaris said. "But I'm glad you made that promise. So, what should I know about you in that regard? Where do you go to church? When do you read your Bible?"

"I go to a small church down the street every Sunday. I'll write down information about it for you, like how to get there. I also usually read my Bible every morning when I wake up."

"I read my Bible when I wake up too. I usually have to bake at five-thirty, so I get up around five to read my Bible," Damaris said.

"Five in the morning? Wow. That will take some getting used to. You know, you're right. I'm glad you asked me about this. It is an important question. If you read your Bible every morning and I don't, your family would probably notice."

"I also often sing hymns while doing my chores, and then my siblings often join in. Do you sing?"

Arabella laughed, her face turning red. "I mean, I can sing, but I don't sing in front of other people. Maybe I will just avoid singing altogether while I'm there."

Damaris scrunched up her face. "They might think that's odd. Singing is a huge part of our lives. We sing while we work, while we walk outside, and in church. Come on. You won't be able to avoid it the whole time. Can you just sing something for me? Our voices sound pretty similar when we speak, so maybe we have similar singing voices too."

Arabella rolled her eyes, looking around at the other people in the café. "Come on. Here?"

Damaris nodded. "Just sing quietly."

"Ugh. You are relentless." Arabella groaned. "Wait. I have an idea. I know it's hard to hear what you actually sound like when you speak and sing. Do you think our voices sound the same?"

"Well, actually, yes. I think we do. But how can we know?" Damaris asked.

Arabella held up her cell phone. "I can record us." She hit the record button. "See, we can speak and record ourselves, then compare and see if we sound the same."

"That's a great idea," Damaris said. "Then, we can record ourselves singing and see if our singing voices sound similar."

Arabella stopped the recording, then played it back.

"Wow, our voices do sound similar," Damaris said. "Now it's time to find out if we sound the same when we sing. Go ahead."

Arabella hit the record button again, took a deep breath, then softly began singing the words to Amazing Grace near her phone. When she finished, she looked up to see Damaris staring at her.

"Wow! You really can sing! I wonder if I sound like that," Damaris gushed. "I hope so."

"Okay, then, it's your turn. Now you have to sing it," Arabella said, grinning mischievously.

Damaris smirked, then her heart skipped as she looked around the people in the café nervously. Fortunately, no one seemed to notice them. Everyone else was wrapped up in their own conversations, and the din overshadowed Damaris' voice as she began to sing quietly. Arabella held the phone close to her.

When she finished the chorus of Amazing Grace, Arabella nodded. "Well, no wonder you sing all the time. You have a great voice."

"Thanks." Damaris blushed.

"Now let's see if we sound the same," Arabella said and played back the recordings. "Wow. You were right. We do sound the same."

"That's incredible," Damaris said.

"Tell me all about the Amish way of life."

Damaris explained the Amish customs and the details of her daily life, including the names and personalities of her family members, Arabella listened with rapt attention while jotting things down.

They discussed the differences between Pennsylvania Dutch words and German words, and Arabella found she recognized most of them and could easily keep up.

"My family speaks English most of the time," Arabella told Damaris. "Luckily, if someone speaks to you in German, I think you'll have no problem talking with them."

"It's important to know each Amish community has different rules," Damaris said. "Maybe you've read about the Amish in books or have seen TV shows about the Amish, but what you learned from that may not be true about my community. Many Amish communities ban bicycles, but we use them. There's even an Amish bike repair shop near my house. We are allowed to use buttons and zippers, like on our jackets, and the men use buttons on their shirts. We also use solar panels. Many Amish communities hold church services in homes, but we have our own church building. Some Amish communities don't have their own bishop, but some do. Some bishops are responsible for several communities."

"I saw on TV that bicycles are banned in Amish communities," Arabella said. "That's interesting. I also heard that engaged couples sleep together in the same bed with a board between them. Is that true?"

Damaris laughed. "No, we don't do that in Unity. Maybe other places do."

"And the Amish really can't have cell phones?"

"Well, midwives have them for emergencies. However, as I mentioned before, many of the Amish don't follow that rule and secretly have cell phones or use the internet. We also have the rule that Amish couples are not allowed to have any physical contact before marriage, but I've seen young Amish couples kiss and hold hands before their weddings when they thought no one was looking. Just because it's a rule doesn't mean everyone follows it."

Arabella winked at her. "Do you have a cell phone, Damaris?"

Damaris shook her head. "Actually, no. I don't have one. I've never had one. I do admit, though, that I'm curious. I think I'd like to have one."

"Well, when we switch places, you can use mine temporarily. So," Arabella leaned forward, placing her elbows on the table. "Do you have a boyfriend? Have you kissed anyone before?"

Damaris blushed, furiously shaking her head. "No. I don't have a boyfriend, and I've never been kissed. I thought I loved someone, but we're just friends. I don't feel that way about him after all."

"Oh? Who is he?"

"His name is Gilbert. He's a nice young man, and I thought I was in love with him for years. He was after my one of my best friends, Belle, for a while, but she ended up with someone else, and I was so happy when Gilbert wanted to go on a date with me. We went on a few dates, and I realized I'm not in love with him after all. I was in love with the idea of him, I think. Anyway, he felt the same way," Damaris explained.

"Is he cute?" Arabella asked.

Damaris chuckled. "He is good-looking and very sweet. I wish him the best. So, tell me what I need to know about your world."

Arabella taught Damaris everything about her parents and everything she knew about the bakery company. She told Damaris about Ms. Libby, the names of the other staff, and the duties Arabella did that contributed to the business. She taught her how to behave at formal social events, including table manners.

Damaris' head swam with the overload of information. How would she remember which spoon to use at dinner or remember all the information about the business, including where all the locations were?

She abruptly stood up and exclaimed, "I can't! I can't do this."

"Please," Arabella said, "I need this time here. You want to go to Germany, right?"

"Well, yes, of course."

"I can't get married without first having some time away from my life. I might never have this chance again, and neither will you. This is our one chance. Please. I need your help," Arabella pleaded.

Damaris gazed into her eyes, seeing a pain that mirrored hers. Maybe they had been brought together for a reason. There must be a purpose that God had not shown her yet. She heaved a sigh.

Chills coursed through her body, making her stand straighter. If not for herself, she had to do this for her new friend. At that moment, she realized that their connections ran deeper. She felt then that this was God's plan for her.

Damaris whispered, "I will do it." Then, a bit stronger, she repeated the statement. "I will do it."

"Step one. We need to give you a makeover, if you're still up for it," Arabella said with a smile. "Starting with clothing, then hair."

"Let's do it. I have to admit, I've always wondered what it would be like to wear clothes like yours." Damaris gestured to Arabella's leather jacket, jeans, sweater. "Even those silly high-heeled boots."

Arabella laughed. "Here." She held up a bag. "I brought some of my clothes for you to try. We're almost the exact same size, so I know they'll fit."

Damaris took the bag. "I'll be right back then. Hey, you should try on my Amish clothes. Want to?"

Arabella shrugged. "Sure. I have to admit, I'm curious to see how it looks on me."

They went to the restroom to change. It was a single bathroom, so Damaris went in first to put on the *Englisher* clothes.

In the bag, there was a pair of jeans, a sweater, a scarf, a hat, a denim jacket, and a pair of high-heeled dressy boots. She quickly dressed before she could change her mind. There was even a small pouch inside the bag with a long silver necklace. Damaris had never worn jewelry, even though she'd always wanted to. Giggling like a little girl, she put everything on and looked at herself in the mirror.

Her *kapp* was still on her head. She gingerly took it off, her hair still in a bun, and stared at herself in the mirror. The clothing looked very expensive and made her feel exposed, even though the sweater was very modest.

After being raised to have her prayer *kapp* on her head at all times, it seemed so strange to be in public with nothing covering her hair. She took the hat out of the bag and put it on. There. That felt a little better.

Damaris just stared at herself in the mirror, astonished at the beautiful girl that looked back at her. Wow. She had no idea she could look this good.

Arabella gasped when Damaris opened the door and stepped out. "Wow! Damaris, you look amazing."

"Thanks," Damaris said, smiling shyly.

Arabella tossed her hair over her shoulder dramatically, in a joking way. "If I do say so, you look just like me. Just wait till we are done with your hair. You will look even more gorgeous. Are you ready to cut it?"

Damaris finally tore her eyes away from the mirror. "Yes. Let's do it before I talk myself out of it. But first, you can put this on." Damaris handed Arabella her dress and prayer *kapp*. "Put it on, then I will help you with the straight pins."

"The what?" Arabella asked, raising one eyebrow.

"The dress is held together by pins."

"What? I won't be able to figure that out. Don't you ever poke yourself?"

"No, no. Come on, it's not that complicated. Just go put it on, and then I'll come in and help you." Damaris gave Arabella a little push toward the bathroom.

"Fine." Arabella went inside and changed. A few minutes later, she cracked open the bathroom door. "You can come in now."

Damaris stepped in and showed Arabella how to use the pins to hold the dress together.

"I can't believe you do this every morning," Arabella said with a laugh.

"Can't take much more time than doing makeup every day," Damaris said.

"True. Hey, I saw buttons and zippers on some of the jackets on the other Amish people at the store, and I saw buttons on some of the men's shirts. So, why don't you use buttons or zippers on your dresses?"

"It's just how things are done here. We've made our dresses the same way for so long. Many of the rules don't make sense to me either. In many communities, buttons and zippers are banned altogether." Damaris secured Arabella's hair into a bun and placed the *kapp* on her head, fastening it in place with a few bobby pins. "There. Done."

They stared at each other in the mirror.

"Wow. I do look Amish. I look like you," Arabella said breathlessly.

Damaris nodded. "*Ja.*"

"Now we test it out."

"What do you mean?"

"We should go somewhere where people know you and I can pretend to be you. We can see if they can tell it's not you. What do you say?" Arabella said.

"I mean, I guess so."

"Where?"

"I don't know. Not with my family or at work. Maybe the grocery store? There might be some people I don't know there as well. Do you think you're ready?"

"Sure. Come on."

"Now?" Damaris asked, but Arabella was already out the door. Damaris followed her out, and Arabella was halfway across the café. Just then, Laura, Lydia, and Mae walked in.

"Oh no," Damaris muttered, ducking behind a booth where an elderly couple were having lunch. What were the Millers doing here, the next town over? Damaris peeked over the booth to see Arabella sitting back down at the table where they'd been sitting before. She was too far away for Damaris to get her attention. What if the Millers saw her and tried talking to her? In her Amish clothing, Arabella stood out from everyone else.

Or worse—what if the Millers saw Damaris dressed in *Englisher* clothes? No, there was no way Damaris could come out from her hiding spot and risk being seen.

Damaris watched helplessly as Laura spotted Arabella and walked over to her.

Chapter Nine

Arabella tapped her foot on the floor, looking around. Where did Damaris go? She thought she was right behind her, following her out of the bathroom. Just then, a teenage Amish girl walked up to her. Her lively eyes could light up the entire café.

"Hi, Damaris. How are you?" she asked in Pennsylvania Dutch.

Who was this?

"Uh, good. How are you?" Arabella replied in Pennsylvania Dutch.

"Good. We were running errands, and I convinced *Maam* to let us stop here and have lunch. They have the best burgers. So, how is work going?"

Arabella tried to hide her confusion. "Good. Really good. I've been learning a lot at the bakery."

The girl cocked her head to the side. "I hope so."

"Yeah, the Millers have been teaching me a lot," Arabella blurted, then cringed. Was that their last name? Now she wasn't so sure.

The girl looked at her as though she'd sprouted green hair. "Uh... You mean my mother?"

Arabella's eyes went wide for one second, then she fought to regain composure. "Oh, yes. I meant to say Mrs. Miller. Of course. I mean, you've all taught me so much." Arabella's mind swam as she tried to remember the names of Mae's daughters. Lisa? Lena? Leah? Oh, what were they?

"Well, Lydia would like to take all the credit, but I won't let her." The girl chuckled. "Are you okay? You're acting weird."

"Weird? No, no, I'm fine." Arabella waved her hand, then suddenly spotted Damaris watching them from behind a booth. Arabella turned her

72

eyes back to the girl, whose name she still couldn't remember. Her mother and sister were talking with someone else they apparently knew, then started walking toward her.

Oh, great, Arabella thought. *I hope I don't blow it.*

Just then, a loud crash sounded from the back of the café where Damaris was. Arabella and everyone else looked over to see a waiter scrambling to pick up plates on the floor that had fallen off the tray he'd been carrying. A young woman was helping him, apologizing profusely.

It was Damaris. Had she bumped into him?

"What happened?" Mae asked, and they all continued to look.

If they looked any closer, they'd realize it was Damaris.

"Oh, my stomach!" Arabella cried, doubling over in mock pain.

The Millers all turned to her, concerned, completely forgetting about the fallen dishes.

"Are you all right, Damaris?" Mae asked, rushing to her.

"Ow," Arabella moaned, scrunching up her face. "It hurts so bad. I think I need to go to the hospital."

"Maybe your appendix is bursting," the girl put in. "I read about it in a book once."

"Not helping," Lydia said, shaking her head. "Come on, let's get her into the buggy."

The three of them helped her up and escorted her to the buggy. The whole way there, Arabella acted as though she could barely walk from the pain. As they hoisted her up into the buggy, she realized what was happening.

They were about to take her to the hospital, and she didn't even need to go there.

As she sat in the back of the buggy, she held up her hand. "Wait. Thank you for helping, but actually, I think I'm fine now."

"What? You were doubled over in pain a second ago," Laura said, squinting at her. "What's going on? You are acting really strange."

"Laura," Mae chided.

Laura. So that was her name. Right, she knew that. Now she remembered Damaris telling her.

"No, honestly, I think something I ate just disagreed with me. I'm sure it's only gas pains." She cringed again at her crude wording. "After a trip to the bathroom, I think I'll be just fine. In fact, I need to go right now." She burst out of the buggy and ran to Damaris' buggy. "Thanks anyway!" she called over her shoulder.

"You're welcome!" Laura called as she, Mae, and Lydia got out of the buggy and walked back to the café.

"You know, they have a bathroom in here," Lydia said.

"Are you sure you're okay?" Laura asked.

Arabella looked over her shoulder as she continued rushing down the sidewalk. "Oh, yes. Actually, I feel much better now. I should get going. Thanks again." Arabella climbed up into the driver's side of the buggy, hoping they'd stop looking at her, because she was definitely not about to start driving the buggy right then.

Finally, they shrugged and waved to her before stepping back inside the café. Hopefully, Damaris could sneak past them and get out of the café without them seeing her.

***

Damaris had been so focused on watching the Millers talking with Arabella, who they thought was her, that she didn't see the waiter right behind her. When she thought the Millers were about to see her, she

74

quickly spun around, about to dart away, when she ran right into the waiter.

The tray of plates filled with food that he'd been carrying clattered to the floor. Everyone in the café turned toward the deafening sound.

Her face burned with embarrassment. Now they'd see her for sure, but she couldn't just leave the waiter to clean this up all by himself. "I'm so sorry," she said, kneeling on the floor to pick up the mess, keeping her head down. "Oh, I'm so terribly sorry. I didn't see you there."

"It's okay, miss," the middle-aged man said. "It happens sometimes. Please, don't worry."

"Let me help you clean this up. It's the least I can do."

"We will take care of it. Please, don't worry about it."

Damaris helped clean it up anyway, feeling too guilty to get up and leave. Her eyes darted over to Arabella, who was acting as though she was suffering from kidney stones. Damaris stifled a giggle. Of course, Arabella would do something dramatic to keep the Millers from seeing her.

As Arabella and the Millers left the café, Damaris could focus better on helping the staff clean up the mess, even though they kept on reassuring her she didn't have to.

"Please. I'm glad to help. Again, I'm so sorry," she said. As she turned to leave, she looked around to see if the Millers were still outside. It looked as though they were getting in their buggy to leave. Relieved, she hurried toward the door.

She was about to walk out of the café when the Millers suddenly got out of their buggy and started walking back toward the café. What were they doing?

Damaris turned and bolted away from the door, sitting at a nearby empty table and holding a menu in front of her face. A waitress approached her.

It was the same waitress who'd just served Arabella and Damaris lunch.

"Can I get you anything?" she asked.

"Oh, no, thanks. I…uh…" Her eyes darted back toward the Millers, who were walking past her. Damaris ducked her head, turning her face away.

"Didn't you just eat here?" the waitress asked. She smiled. "Come back for seconds?"

"Ha," Damaris let out a fake laugh. "Actually, I was just waiting for my friend. We will be leaving in a minute."

"Oh, I see. Have a nice day then." The waitress walked away.

Damaris let out a breath of relief as the Millers sat down at a table in the back of the café.

"Finally," she muttered. She stood up and rushed out of the café.

Arabella was waiting in Damaris' buggy. "What the heck happened?" she demanded.

"I bumped into the waiter and made him drop all the plates he was carrying." Damaris shook her head, her cheeks burning at the mere memory of it. "Ugh, I feel terrible about it. What happened with you? I saw you faking a medical emergency."

"I told the Millers I had to go to the hospital." Arabella laughed. "Now I'm realizing how bad of an idea that was, but I panicked. I didn't know what else to do, and I had to think quickly. They were about to take me. I told them I was fine and ran off. They must think you're crazy now. Sorry. I just didn't want them to see you."

Damaris let out a nervous chuckle. "Thanks. Well, it worked. We should get out of here before someone else sees us together."

"Anyway. Off to the hair salon, then?" Arabella asked. "I'll have to change back into my clothes there. Do you know where one is?"

Damaris took a deep breath, trying to calm her nerves. "Yes. There is one downtown that doesn't require appointments. I've seen the sign in their window. Let's go."

***

At the salon, Damaris' heart pounded as she sat down in the hairstylist's chair. She'd never set foot in a salon before, and it felt so foreign to her, even though she'd always been curious. When running errands through town, she had sometimes stopped at the salon window to look inside and watch people having their hair done, wondering what it would be like to have someone color or cut her hair.

Now she was here, and it felt surreal.

"How can we help you?" the woman at the front desk asked as they walked in. She looked Arabella up and down, eyeing her Amish clothing.

"I need a color, and my friend needs a haircut, if you have availability," Arabella said.

"Of course. Have a seat and we will be right with you," the woman said.

First, Arabella went to the restroom and changed out of the Amish clothing and put on her normal clothing. When she walked out of the restroom, the receptionist stared at her, looking confused. Damaris held back a giggle at the sight.

A few minutes later, a stylist walked up to them. "Hi, I'm Ashley, and I will take care of both of you today. Come this way."

While Ashley applied the hair color to Arabella's hair, Damaris sat in an empty chair beside them. As the hair color processed, the stylist had them switch places.

Damaris' heart hammered as she sat in the stylist's chair.

"How much would you like me to cut?" Ashley asked. She put a cape around Damaris' neck and smiled at her in the mirror.

The stylist's hair was short with purple highlights, and anxiety shot through Damaris.

I hope she doesn't do anything like that to my hair, Damaris thought, eyeing the stylist's hair nervously.

"I'd like my hair cut to here, please," Damaris said, pointing to her elbow.

The stylist looked at each of them. "Okay, I have to ask. Are you twins? You look like twins."

"Well, no," Damaris stammered. "We just want to look alike. So, can you make my hair look like hers?"

"No problem. Let's take your hair down." The stylist carefully took Damaris' hair out of the bun it was in, then loosened it so it fell in long waves almost to the floor.

Ashley gasped. "Wow! I don't think I've ever seen hair this long that looks this healthy! Are you sure you want to cut it?"

"Yes," Damaris said. "My hair grows fast, anyway."

"You could definitely donate it. Do you want to?"

"What do you mean?"

"You can donate it to an organization that makes wigs for children who have lost their hair because of cancer treatments," the stylist explained. "It's easy. You just mail it. I can give you the information after."

"Sure, that would be great," Damaris said, smiling. She'd feel better knowing her hair was helping someone.

"They could make two wigs out of this," Ashley said with a laugh. "I'm going to brush it out and put it in a braid, then cut off the braid. You can mail it that way so it stays all together in the package when you mail it."

The stylist quickly braided it with an elastic on the top of the braid and the bottom. The top of the braid started below her elbows and extended almost to the floor.

"Now I'm going to cut above the hair elastic that's at the top of the braid," the stylist explained. "It'll look choppy and uneven at first, but I'll fix it after."

"Okay," Damaris choked out, panic suddenly shooting through her. What was she thinking? Was this a huge mistake? Maybe she should back out.

"Are you okay? Are you sure you want me to cut it?" the stylist asked, giving her a concerned look in the mirror. "You look a bit nervous."

"It's going to look great," Arabella added.

"Yes. I'm fine. I'm sure. Go ahead. Cut it." Damaris nodded with determination.

Chapter Ten

As the stylist picked up her shears and started cutting away at the hair above the braid, exhilaration shot through Damaris. This was probably the most outrageous thing she'd ever done and it felt...

Freeing.

"There it is," the stylist said as she held up the now severed braid. Damaris let out a nervous laugh and covered her mouth at the sight of all the hair that had been cut.

"It already looks great, Damaris," Arabella said in the chair beside her.

"It feels great," Damaris said, shaking her head. Her hair felt so much lighter now, and she loved the feeling.

What would her mother say if she were here?

"Now I will even out your hair." The stylist washed Damaris' hair in the sink, then clipped it up into sections, carefully evening out the ends of Damaris' hair. When she was done, she dried it with the blow dryer and used a large-barreled curling iron to style it with big curls. She finished with some hairspray and turned Damaris so she could see in the mirror.

"What do you think?" the stylist asked, removing the cape. "You can go closer to the mirror if you want." She turned to Arabella. "I can wash out your color now."

"Wow!" Damaris said, her eyes wide as she stared at herself in the mirror. She stood up, stepping forward to get a better look.

"Damaris, you look great!" Arabella cried as the stylist shampooed her hair in the sink.

Damaris ran her hands through her hair, which now felt so much healthier and fuller. She admired how it fell in waves around her shoulders, framing her face.

She'd never felt so…beautiful.

Yet, at the same time, she was filled with guilt. If her mother saw her now, she'd be ashamed of Damaris. If the church elders ever found out about this, she'd be in trouble. All her life she had been taught to never cut her hair, and now she'd cut over two feet off.

"Are you okay?" Arabella asked.

Damaris' eyes stung with tears.

"Oh no, you don't like it?" the stylist asked, putting conditioner in Arabella's hair.

"I love it," Damaris said, swiping away a tear. "It's not that. I've had long hair my whole life, so this feels so different."

"It's still so long," Ashley said. "It looks gorgeous on you." She finished washing Arabella's hair, wrapping it in a towel, and put the chair in the upright position.

"Thank you. I love it so much. This is the first time in my life I've felt…beautiful," Damaris admitted, her cheeks burning in embarrassment. "I feel like a whole new person. Thank you so much."

She spontaneously embraced the hair stylist in a hug.

The stylist hugged her back. "I'm so glad you like it. This made my day."

Damaris waited for Ashley to dry Arabella's hair. She also styled Arabella's hair with a large-barreled curling iron to match Damaris'. Arabella's blonde highlights were now gone, and her hair was now the same shade of light brown as Damaris' hair. When Arabella's hair was done, she stood next to Damaris in the mirror.

"Wow," Damaris said.

"Yeah. Wow." Arabella stared into the mirror.

"You sure you aren't twins?" Ashley asked. "You *have* to be related."

"We aren't. We are just friends," Damaris explained.

Arabella paid for their services, and they left the salon.

Standing on the sidewalk, Damaris asked, "Now what?"

"Now I need to teach you how to put on makeup. I've always worn makeup, and if I come home and stop wearing it, my family will definitely become suspicious."

"Makeup?" Damaris gulped. "I don't know anything about makeup."

"Oh, you will. I'll teach you everything I know. Come on. Let's go back to the inn where I'm staying," Arabella said.

They drove the buggy to the inn, and Arabella dumped out her makeup bag on the bathroom counter.

"This is eyeliner. This is foundation, this is concealer, and this is setting powder. This is eyeshadow." She held up a rectangular black box with different shades of bronze in it. "And this is mascara. Sometimes I wear fake eyelashes, but let's get to that later."

"Fake eyelashes? What?" Damaris put a hand to her head. "Wow. That's a lot to remember. But I've always been curious about makeup, wondering what I'd look like if I wore some."

"Let's find out." Arabella grinned. "How about if I put it on you and explain how to do it step by step, then it's your turn."

"Okay," Damaris said. She tried to remember everything as Arabella explained each product, but her head swam. When Arabella was done, Damaris looked in the mirror.

"Wow!" she exclaimed. "I look so different." She was shocked by how big her eyes looked, how long and dark her eyelashes were, and how perfect her skin appeared.

"You look great," Arabella said. "Never underestimate the power of makeup." She handed Damaris the makeup brush. "Wash your face. Now it's your turn to do it."

Damaris stared at the makeup brush as if it were a rat. "This is going to be a disaster."

"Come on. You'll need to get this right if you want this to work. I'll help you until you can do it on your own. I can even write down each step if you want."

Damaris nodded. "Okay."

After she was finished, she studied her reflection. Her eyeliner was crooked, her eyeshadow was smudged, and so was her lipstick. "Well, I tried."

"You'll get it next time."

It took several more attempts, but finally, Damaris got the hang of it.

"Now you look like me," Arabella said, hands on her hips. "I knew I was a good teacher."

Damaris laughed. "Sorry I'm such a terrible student."

"This is crazy," Arabella said quietly, still staring at their reflections. "We really look like the same person. You think anyone will suspect anything now?"

"No. As long as we can keep up the act, I don't think anyone will know," Damaris said. She wondered for the millionth time if she wasn't crazy for doing this. However, she decided to push all negative thoughts out of her head.

She would simply take it a day at a time and pray it all went well.

***

After a week of preparing each other to switch places, Damaris met Arabella behind the barn early in the morning. They'd practiced talking like the other, dressing and acting like the other. They'd memorized the names of family members and friends, daily routines, and everything they could think of.

Now, it was time to make the switch.

"Are you ready?" Damaris asked Arabella.

Was she ready for this? Arabella's hands smoothed over the prayer *kapp* on her head, which still felt so unfamiliar. She wore Damaris' lavender dress, which was covered with a white apron, and clunky black sneakers covered her feet.

"You'll get used to the clothing," Damaris said as if reading Arabella's mind. "Just remember everything we went over this past week."

"I don't think I can remember all your siblings' names," Arabella said in a panicky voice. "And you didn't even have any photos to show me which one is which."

"I call them the wrong names by accident all the time," Damaris said. "And so does my mother. Don't worry."

"What if I burn the house down with the woodstove? What if they can tell it's not you because I can't cook? What if—" Arabella rambled.

"You're overthinking it all!" Damaris said. "Remember, you can tell Ella Ruth what's going on, and she will help you. I'd tell her now, but I'm afraid she will talk me out of it." She looked around to see if anyone was nearby.

"You better go if you want to make your flight."

"Right. The cab will be down the street soon." They'd asked the cab to pick up Damaris away from the Amish homes so that it would be less conspicuous, even though Damaris was dressed like Arabella. "I better start walking. If you have an emergency, remember to call your cell phone, the one I'm taking with me, from your new phone. If I have an emergency, I will call you."

84

"Right. Okay." Arabella nodded, anxiety welling up in her at the thought of walking into Damaris' house pretending to be her.

"We can do this," Damaris said, as if to reassure herself most of all.

"Hey. Have fun in Germany. I hope Stefan doesn't bore you too much. You have your passport, right?"

"Of course, I have it." Damaris smiled. "Well, if Gilbert tries to talk to you, which I doubt, I hope he doesn't bore *you* too much. But he will probably avoid you since things might be awkward. Anyway, I hope you have fun here too."

"Thanks. Have a nice flight. Still nervous?"

"A little, but I'll be fine. I can't believe I'm finally getting to do this. Well, see you soon." Damaris waved and turned to walk down the lane, pulling along Arabella's rolling suitcase filled with her designer clothing.

Arabella waved. "See you soon." She watched Damaris make her way down the lane only to put off the chores she was about to do. Right now, Damaris' family thought Damaris was still outside doing her morning chores, when really, Arabella was taking her place in finishing them up while Damaris went to the airport. Arabella had come from the inn, and they'd switched clothes in the barn.

Arabella quickly fed the horse, Apple, hoping she was doing it right. She wrinkled her nose at the smell of the manure, then mucked out the stall as Damaris had taught her. She had to keep stepping outside, gulping in the fresh air, hoping to get the disgusting smell out of her nose.

Once that was over, she walked out of the barn and faced the house. It was time to meet Damaris' family.

Just then, a young man came down the lane toward her, waving. He looked so much like Damaris, Arabella knew instantly this had to be her older brother, Dominic. At least, she hoped so. Damaris had pointed out people as they had seen them around the community when they'd ridden in her buggy. Arabella had looked out the window, studying their faces, but Damaris hadn't had time to show Arabella every single person.

Without photographs of them, Damaris had only described the people she hadn't had time to show Arabella. Dominic was one of them.

"He looks so much like me, you'll know who he is right away," Arabella had told her. She was right.

"Good morning, Damaris," Dominic said cheerfully, but there was sadness in his eyes.

"Good morning. How are you?" Arabella asked, truly meaning it. She didn't know him, but something didn't seem right.

Dominic raked a hand through his hair. "I shouldn't lie. To be honest, Adriana and I aren't doing so well right now." He sighed. "She had a miscarriage a few weeks ago. She hasn't wanted anyone to know. She's having a hard time with it. I'm trying to comfort her, but I feel like I'm not doing a good job of it at all."

Arabella's heart went out to this man and his wife. She didn't have children of her own, and couldn't even imagine what his wife was feeling. "I'm so sorry. I don't even know what to say."

Dominic slowly nodded. "Thanks. She was about eight weeks along. She was so excited for our first baby. She was so distraught, and it's only gotten worse. She was in bed for days, just crying. She wants a baby so badly. Now she's angry, and she's taking it out on me. She's become bitter toward me, and it's been starting fights between us. I know she is just sad and it will pass, but it hurts. What should I do, Damaris? You always have the best advice."

"Uh…" Arabella froze. She had no idea what to say to him. She wasn't even married—she was not the best person to ask about relationship advice. "Have you prayed about it?"

"Oh, yes. So much. I guess I should pray more, right?"

"Yes. Always. I'm so sorry, Dominic. I wish I could be more helpful."

"That's kind of odd." He cocked his head to the side and studied her.

"What? What's odd?" She felt her face heat. Did he know? Why was he looking at her like that?

"It's just that you usually jump at the chance to give advice or put in your two cents. It's strange that you have nothing to say." He leaned toward her. "Are you okay?"

"What? Of course, I'm fine! I just feel so bad about what happened. I don't have kids or a husband, so I guess I can't relate. That's all." She scratched her neck, suddenly feeling itchy.

"Hmm." He shrugged. "I guess that makes sense, though you have given me marriage advice before. Well, I have to get going, but I think I'll talk to *Maam* about it soon. She's had so many years of marriage experience, and I know she's had three miscarriages."

"She would know exactly what advice to give you, I'm sure."

Dominic looked at her closely again, and she tried not to squirm like a bug under a microscope. "You don't really seem like yourself."

She gave a nervous laugh. "That's silly. It's just me."

"You're my sister. I know when something is going on with you. What is it?" He put his hands on his hips. "Come on, tell me. You're hiding something."

"What? It's nothing," Arabella insisted, taking a step back. Had he figured it out already? Maybe she should run and try to stop Damaris. Maybe everyone would see right through her instantly.

"Are you thinking of traveling somewhere?" he asked. "I knew one day you'd do it. Now you're nervous, afraid people will find out. Is that it?"

Arabella's heart raced as she tried to think. What should she say?

She threw her hands up in the air and sighed. "You caught me. Don't tell anyone, okay?"

"I won't." He looked around. "So, where are you going? I know you want to go to Germany, but that's way too far. Maybe New York City? You could take a bus, probably. That's not against the rules."

"Yes, that's it. New York City. I've always wanted to go."

"You're not going alone, are you? That's probably not safe."

"Uh, I don't know yet," she stammered.

"Well, I wish I could go with you, but I can't leave Adriana. I went a few times before I joined the church in my time away, and it can be overwhelming there. I just don't want anything to happen to you. Let me know before you go so I don't worry, okay?"

"Sure." She nodded.

Clearly satisfied, he turned and walked away. "I have to go, but say hi to *Maam* and the kids for me."

That was close. She took in a deep breath and slowly let it out. Now it was time to face the rest of the family. Would they suspect something, like Dominic?

She forced herself up the steps of the house, ignoring the way her heart pounded with each step. Before she could think twice, she grabbed the doorknob, turned it, and pushed open the door.

Chapter Eleven

The sound of chattering children greeted Arabella's ears.

"Where on earth have you been, Damaris? We've got to get breakfast on the table so the children can leave for school. Delphine helped me make the eggs," a woman said, out of breath, as she bustled into the entryway. A few of her wiry gray hairs escaped her prayer *kapp* in the front. So, this was Constance, Damaris' mother.

A German shepherd was curled up on a dog bed in the corner. Damaris had told Arabella about Coco, their German shepherd, who she said was very sweet and playful. Still, Arabella eyed the dog warily.

Coco stood up and stared at Arabella, letting out a deep, throaty growl.

"Coco," Constance chided. "It's only Damaris. What's the matter?"

The dog still snarled at her. It was obvious to the dog that Arabella was indeed a stranger.

"Come on, Coco," one of the boys, Danny, said, leading the dog outside. "Go outside and play. Maybe later you'll feel better."

"Are you all right, dear?" Constance asked Arabella. "You look frightened."

Arabella took in a deep breath, shaking off the dog's less than friendly reaction. "Yes, I'm fine. Sorry I'm late. I spilled the horse feed everywhere." She winced, not even knowing if that was what it was called.

Constance put her hands on her hips and gave her a skeptical look. "You were reading in the barn again, weren't you?"

"Uh…yes. I'm sorry," Arabella stammered.

"What did I tell you about reading in the mornings when we are in a hurry to get the children off to school? Oh, well, come on then, let's finish cooking." Constance bustled right back into the kitchen and Arabella followed her.

Sitting around the table were five children, Damaris' younger siblings. She remembered Damaris told her their names were Delphine, Danny, Dean, Daisy, and Desmond, oldest to youngest.

All of them stared at her as she walked into the kitchen.

"What's the matter? Are you sick?" Dean asked, then sneezed loudly.

"*Ja.* Why did you take so long in the barn?" Danny asked, crossing his arms.

Desmond mumbled something in Pennsylvania Dutch, rubbing his eyes.

"She was probably in the loft, reading again," Daisy said with a playful smile. "Am I right?"

Delphine said nothing as she finished slicing a loaf of bread.

"Well, yes. I was," Arabella said. "But then I talked to Dominic. He says hi. He didn't have time to come inside."

"I wish he would have. I haven't seen him in a while. Here, Damaris, come finish cooking this sausage." Constance called Arabella over to the woodstove.

Arabella gulped. Growing up with her food prepared for her by cooks, she'd never had to cook—and she had certainly never cooked on a woodstove. Sure, she could bake, but cooking was completely foreign to her.

Would her terrible cooking be a dead giveaway that she wasn't Damaris?

***

Damaris stared out the window of the airplane, trying to stop trembling. But it was no use. She trembled as she forced each breath through her lungs. The plane hadn't even taken off yet.

The woman sitting right next to her gave her a reassuring smile, asking, "Is this your first time flying?"

Damaris stared at the woman, unable to speak or even nod.

The woman gave a warm, endearing smile. "Don't worry; it's safer than driving in a car."

Damaris gazed into the woman's eyes and caught the compassion in them. She returned the smile and settled back into her chair.

I really need to get a hold of myself, she thought while willing herself to relax a bit.

It was important that she appeared composed, because according to Arabella, especially after getting off the plane, she had to play her role perfectly. They did look like twins, but their personalities were quite different, and this was displayed in their normal facial expressions.

Damaris took a deep breath, ignoring her pounding heart and nausea as the plane's engines roared. Soon, the plane was moving down the runway. As the plane ascended into the air, Damaris stifled a scream of terror. Her ears popped, and she gripped her armrests tightly.

"Here," the woman said beside her, handing her a stick of gum. "It helps with your ears popping."

"Thanks," Damaris said, gratefully taking the gum.

After the plane was in the air, Damaris tried to relax as she gazed out the window, willing herself to focus on the scenery as clouds and more clouds whizzed by. It was indeed quite beautiful from this height. The sun's radiance sparkled against the clouds, and its silent beauty was more satisfying. She finally closed her eyes, tuning out the chattering people and everything around her while praying that the ill feeling would go away.

Eventually, she fell asleep. This was going to be a long flight.

***

Damaris' hands shook as the taxi approached the Blackwood estate. She smoothed out imaginary wrinkles in her pencil skirt and fiddled with her hair, still marveling at how new and strange it felt. She wore Arabella's black heels, which still made her feet feel wobbly. What if she lost her balance and fell?

On the flight, Damaris had texted Arabella's parents, letting them know she was coming home. What would Arabella's parents say when they saw her? What if they took one look at her and knew she wasn't their daughter? Arabella had warned her that they'd be upset because Arabella had left, but what would their reaction be once she arrived?

To distract herself, Damaris looked out the taxi window to enjoy the scenery as they passed by. The town was more beautiful than Arabella had described. The lush gardens, the shops lining the streets, and the mountains in the distance enchanted her. It was a whole different world. Though she would be here for a short time, she already felt she would hate to leave it all behind.

After about forty-five minutes, the view outside changed from the bustling scenes of a town to lush expanses of fields and a wide river. The sun's radiance was reflected on the water as if the rays had been captured and brought to earth. Soon they came upon an enormous mansion which was more beautiful than Damaris could have ever imagined, surrounded by magnificent gardens.

Damaris gasped at the beautiful, architectural splendor. The architectural masterpiece sprawled out over a large estate which was meticulously manicured with ornamental shrubs, elegant fountains, and even statues. Tall towers spiraled up to the sky, giving the mansion a medieval look.

It was the closest thing to a fairy-tale castle that Damaris had ever seen. It was even more incredible than the castles she'd imagined in the books she read.

Knots of anxiety twisted in her stomach as the taxi drove up the front of the largest and most beautiful home she'd ever seen. Damaris got out of the cab before she could change her mind. She paid the driver, and he got her luggage out of the trunk for her.

A woman with her hair in a tight bun hurried out the mansion's large front door and down the front steps, adjusting her wire-rimmed glasses. "Arabella Blackwood, where on earth have you been this time? Your escapade has worried your parents sick. This was terrible timing."

This must be Ms. Libby. Arabella had told Damaris all about her.

"I'm so sorry. I had to get away before the wedding. I was hoping they'd understand. I'm back now, and we can continue as planned."

Ms. Libby took her suitcase and started taking it up the steps. "Well, let's go talk to them. You have some explaining and apologizing to do. Not only to them, but to the Castles as well."

The Castles were here right now? Helene and Henry must have invited them once Damaris had let them know she was coming.

Damaris bit back a groan and followed the woman up the steps as the cab drove away. Now she had to explain everything to them, too. More anxiety lodged in her stomach. What on earth would she say to these people?

As they set foot inside, Damaris could barely stifle a gasp. The marble floors shone, and a magnificent crystal chandelier sparkled above them. There was a staircase on each side of the room leading to a second floor, and oil paintings hung on the walls.

This was where Arabella lived? Wow, that girl was lucky.

"Don't just stand there, Arabella. Hurry now," Ms. Libby chided, and Damaris snapped to attention and scrambled to catch up to her. The woman was surprisingly fast.

"You there, take this luggage up to Arabella's room," Ms. Libby ordered a maid, who took the luggage up the stairs.

"Now," Ms. Libby said. "Let's go talk to your parents and the Castles. They're having dinner in the dining room. You should join them."

Arabella had told Damaris all about how Stefan had spilled soup on her, and Damaris hoped the incident wouldn't be repeated. She held back a nervous giggle as Ms. Libby opened two large doors. Why on earth was she laughing now of all times?

Ms. Libby announced, "Arabella wishes to join you."

"Oh, Arabella," a woman said, getting up from her seat at the table. Her blonde hair was done up in a French twist, and she wore a stylish knee-length navy blue dress. This must be Arabella's mother, Helene. She rushed over to Arabella and wrapped her in a tight hug.

"Arabella, we were so worried. How could you do this to us at a time like this? How could you?" Helene demanded.

Damaris stood motionless without returning the embrace, shocked by the raw emotions she witnessed from the woman, but she soon relaxed as it seemed apparent that her disguise was intact, at least for now.

"I am sorry, Mother," Damaris finally choked out.

"I see," Helene said, pulling away to look at her. Damaris tried not to cringe as the woman stared at her, but all Damaris saw was worry in Helene's eyes. Helene lowered her voice and leaned toward Damaris' ear and spoke softly. "Didn't you think about how much it would make us worry? And it was so embarrassing. Stefan and Philip were supposed to be staying here, but once you left, they went home. I invited them back today so you could apologize to them. I do understand there is a lot on your shoulders, but this was not the time to go on one of your escapades. This entire agreement could have fallen through."

"I'm sorry," Damaris choked out.

Then Helene stared at her more intently, taking a step back to look at her. "Your hair is different," she said. "It's brown again, like it used to be."

"I decided to go back to my natural color."

Helene continued to stare at her, and Damaris froze with fear, wondering if she had been discovered.

"It looks lovely. I'm glad you're back, my dear. Come sit down," Helene said, leading Damaris to the table.

Damaris let out a breath she didn't realize she'd been holding. Arabella's own mother hadn't realized that Damaris was not her daughter. Perhaps this was going to work after all.

Damaris followed Helene to the table, where she was seated between who she assumed was Stefan and Arabella's grandmother, Elizabeth.

Stefan only gave her awkward sidelong glances while Elizabeth tugged at Damaris' sleeve.

"Where did you go this time, my dear? I hope it was fun." The elderly woman's eyes twinkled, and Damaris could instantly tell this woman had an adventurous spirit of her own.

"I went to Maine, on the east coast of the United States," Damaris whispered back to her.

"Well, you scared us all half to death, leaving like that without telling anyone where you were going," Elizabeth said. "But I told that pig-headed son of mine that you could take care of yourself and you'd be back in time. I want to hear all about your trip later. Sounds fun."

Damaris looked into the warmth radiating in the eyes of the elderly woman, but she couldn't bring herself to breathe just yet. Arabella had warned her about her grandmother's uncanny eye for details.

Would she see right through Damaris' disguise?

"You seem as though you have come to terms with your future," Elizabeth added, nodding solemnly. "You're becoming more mature and responsible, I can tell." She leaned in closer and said in a quieter voice, "Just don't ever lose that sense of adventure. Remember, you don't have to do this."

Damaris smiled. She knew this was someone she could trust and who she'd like spending time with while she was here.

"Well, Arabella, what do you have to say for yourself?" the man at the head of the table boomed, whom Damaris guessed was Henry Blackwood, Arabella's father.

"I'm sorry I left the way I did. I hope you can understand why," Damaris said, pasting on her most apologetic expression. "I hope you can forgive me, especially you, Mr. Castle and Stefan." She bowed her head and stared at her hands in her lap, hoping what she'd said was convincing enough.

Henry stroked his short beard in thought. "Well, yes, I see why you might want some time away before the wedding, but you should have at least told us where you were going."

"I was afraid you wouldn't let me go."

"We thought you were backing out of the wedding," Philip Castle said. "We packed up and went home."

"No. The wedding is still on. I just needed time to reflect before beginning my new life." A pang of sympathy shot through her for Arabella. How could her parents ask this of her?

"We invite you to stay here for a few weeks as originally planned," Henry said to Philip and Stefan. "We'd love to have you here so we can all get to know each other better."

Philip nodded. "Very well, then. We will go home to pack later, then we will return. You have our forgiveness, and we will proceed as planned. I just hope you don't have any more surprises up your sleeve."

Damaris wanted to giggle again, but she nodded somberly as a server set a plate of food before her. She had no idea what it was. It looked like some type of roasted meat with vegetables. She started eating with everyone else and found it was absolutely delicious. After her long flight, she was ravenous, but she remembered the table manners Arabella had taught her and tried not to eat too quickly.

As Arabella's parents continued to talk with Philip, Damaris could see now the particulars of Arabella's family. They didn't seem to care very much about what she wanted. Damaris was deeply saddened and at the same time grateful that even though her father was gone, her mother and siblings treated her with more love and affection than Arabella's parents did.

As Henry and Helene talked with Philip about the business, Damaris listened intently.

"We are looking for a way to increase profits since our expenses are so high," Henry was saying.

"What is your biggest expense? Supplies? Paying employees? Marketing?" Damaris asked, leaning forward. "Maybe we can find a way to cut costs."

Henry's eyebrows shot up. Damaris then realized Arabella had probably not shown much interest in the business before.

"Well," Philip said as Henry just sat there, stunned. "You are indeed quite curious, aren't you?"

"Well, yes, of course. I want to learn as much as I can," Damaris said hesitantly. "Have you ever thought of using solar energy to reduce electricity costs?"

"That is a good idea," Henry said. "Actually, we've been considering switching over."

Then, as if she didn't exist, they began talking amongst themselves again.

Someone cleared their throat, and Damaris turned to Stefan. She'd almost forgotten he was sitting beside her.

"It is a good idea. Remember the other day when I said I've been researching alternative energy solutions that would cut our costs and increase profits? One of the options is solar power. You didn't seem interested in that at all before, to be honest," Stefan said.

"Well, you know, I realized I should be more involved and learning as much as I can. While I was away, I did a lot of thinking and realized things about myself," Damaris explained hurriedly, taking a drink of her sparkling water.

"What was New England like? Where did you go in particular?" he asked, his brown eyes widening with curiosity behind his black-rimmed glasses.

"I went to Maine," Damaris said, figuring she might as well tell the truth because she hadn't been to many other places. "It's beautiful there."

"I've never been to Maine. I've been to New York City and Chicago and big cities like that, but I'd die to see the coastline of Maine," Stefan said with a far-off look. "I hear the beaches are beautiful."

"Well, I wasn't exactly near the coast. But I have been there before," Damaris said. She'd gone there on a bus to Kennebunkport with her friends before. "I've been to Kennebunkport. The beaches and shops are lovely."

"Ever had lobster?" Stefan asked. "They're so creepy looking with their beady little eyes and all those legs, I just can't muster up the courage to try one."

Damaris laughed out loud and got a few odd glances. In a lower voice, she said, "I've tried it only once, and I am sorry to say I didn't like it. I agree, they are so funny looking."

"Well, then, we do have something in common after all." He gave her a warm smile. "I'm really sorry about spilling that soup on you and for babbling so much. I was so nervous about meeting you. I hope you can forgive me."

Damaris smiled back at him, taking in his high cheekbones, square jaw, and the endearing way his brown hair swept over his brow.

"Of course, I forgive you. Everyone makes mistakes." She shrugged.

He gave her a surprised expression. Oh no, maybe that was not something Arabella would have said.

"So, what are you reading?" Damaris asked to cover her blunder.

"The *Hallowed* series by Tony Graham. Well, now he goes by Cole Henderson. That's his real name. He's my favorite author. But I may have mentioned that before," Stefan said, looking away shyly.

"Really? I know Cole personally!" she exclaimed. "He's my favorite author too." Then her cheeks burned as she realized she'd spoken too loudly and enthusiastically. Besides, Arabella didn't like reading at all.

Get it together, Damaris, she chided herself.

"Hold on a minute," Stefan said, holding up his hand. He'd caught her in a lie, hadn't he?

He gave her a look of intense curiosity and interest as he leaned forward, his eyes sparkling with wonder like a child on Christmas morning. "You know him? As in, you've met him?"

Damaris let out a long breath of relief that she'd been holding. "Well, yes. He married my best friend, Belle. They live right next to my—" She cut herself off before she almost said her Amish community. She'd already said he'd married her best friend, and now she'd really said too much. "They live next to where I was staying in Maine. I got to know them. I mean, I say his wife is my best friend, but it's only because we got along so well when I was there that I felt like I've known her my entire life."

"Wow, he lives in Maine? Isn't it so strange why he used a pen name for so long and then only recently revealed to his fans who he really is?" Stefan asked.

"He only did that because he was afraid of what people would think of his scars," Damaris said. "He's a hero. He saved his comrades from an explosion in Afghanistan. For a while he was ashamed of how he looks, but now I think he's come to terms with it. Belle helped him through it. Actually, the Amish do not agree with serving in the military, but she left the Amish to be with him, since he's not Amish. She's one of the reasons why he went to that conference in New York City to tell his fans who he is. She told me all about it."

"Wow," Stefan said, propping his elbow on the table and letting his chin rest in his hand. Arabella had warned her not to put her elbows on the table, but Stefan didn't seem to care about manners at the moment. "That's amazing. I can't believe you actually know him. Do you know what he's working on next? Maybe a new series?"

"Well, yes, I do. But that's classified." She took a sip of water from her glass and gave him a mischievous look.

He laughed. "Seriously? You won't tell me?"

"Okay, I will, but you really can't tell anyone. The publisher hasn't announced it yet. He's working on a new series about Garret, about who he was before he got his powers."

100

"Wow!" Stefan said again. "He's my favorite character. I can't wait to read that. Hold on, you said before that you don't like reading. What changed?"

Oh, Damaris thought, *So he has caught me.*

Chapter Twelve

Damaris' heart tripped over itself as she fought for the right words. "Did I say that? I'm sorry. I don't know why I said that. I love to read. Every morning, I love to read my Bible, and I also love reading fiction. I guess when we first met, I was nervous and flippantly said I don't like to read. That's silly, isn't it?"

"I guess things aren't always what we expect." His eyes softened, and he looked at her again as if seeing her for the first time. "So, you read your Bible every day? I do too."

"You look surprised." Damaris gave him a small smile.

"Well, your parents didn't really mention that about you. So, I'm pleasantly surprised. It's important to me that the woman I marry also has a relationship with God. You know, you're a lot easier to talk to than I thought at first. Maybe we got off on the wrong foot."

"You too, and I think you're right."

Astonished, Damaris wondered why Arabella had described Stefan as nerdy, awkward, and clumsy. All she saw before her was a young man who seemed quite easy to talk to. To her, he was handsome—so much different from how she'd pictured him.

After dinner, the group retired to the sitting room.

"Arabella," Henry said, briefly touching her arm as they walked down the hall. They walked behind the group, and he spoke in a low voice so no one else could hear. "I was surprised to hear you asking questions about the business. You've never been interested in those types of things before. I'm glad you're wanting to learn all you can before taking over."

"Yes. Well, while I was away in Maine, I did a lot of thinking and reflecting."

"Maybe this trip was good for you. So, what do you think of Stefan?"

"He's nice. We get along well."

"I saw you were deep in conversation at dinner."

"We have more in common than I thought."

"Good. Who knows? You might be surprised and fall head over heels in love with him before you know it." Henry smiled at her, but her heart sank. She tried to hide her dismay with a fake smile.

Hopefully, he was wrong.

Of course, Damaris thought. *I'll be going home soon. That won't happen to me.*

They reached the sitting room and all sat down. Philip Castle, Elizabeth, and Arabella's parents continued discussing the business in detail. Damaris would normally want to listen in on the conversation about running the companies, but Stefan walked to the bookshelves lining the back walls, and she found herself following him.

"Will your mother also be joining us?" Damaris asked, then froze, realizing Arabella hadn't mentioned Stefan's mother. Was Damaris supposed to know something she didn't?

"Actually, my mother is no longer with us," Stefan said, putting a book back on the shelf. "My father doesn't like to talk about it, so I'm sure you didn't know."

Relief flooded through her. Good, she hadn't said anything she wasn't supposed to. "I'm sorry. If you don't mind, what happened?"

"She died when I was eighteen," Stefan explained, turning toward her. "She had a brain aneurysm. It was so sudden, and my father has never been the same since. He used to be a friendly, cheerful man. Ever since then, he's been a bit..." Stefan's voice trailed off as he glanced at his father. "He immersed himself into the business."

Damaris almost began to tell him about how her own father had also died suddenly of an undetected heart condition, but she stopped herself. As far as Stefan knew, her father was standing on the other side of the room.

No, she'd never be able to tell him about her father's death, how it had rocked the entire family, and how her mother had worked herself weary to take care of and provide for the family.

Oddly, she felt a brief pang of regret at the thought of never telling him.

"I'm so sorry, Stefan," Damaris said. "I can't even imagine."

Yet, she knew exactly how much it hurt, how the pain of grief became physical and cut so deep you could barely breathe sometimes. Time had made it more manageable, but she could only imagine how her mother had felt to lose the love of her life. Her parents had shared a special love that Damaris could only dream about.

"I wish you could have met my father before," Stefan said in a low voice. "He wasn't always so…cold. I'm sorry if he seems unfriendly. Really, he's a good man and a good father. He just wants what's best for me. That's why he wants me to marry you."

He means Arabella, Damaris thought in dismay. *Not me.*

"Of course," Damaris said. "You're blessed to have a father who cares so much about you."

"Your father cares about you too, doesn't he?"

There she went again. "Yes. Yes, he does," she stammered.

Her face burned, and she had to turn away to hide her embarrassed blush, pretending to be interested in one of the books on the shelves. Stefan certainly was nothing like she'd expected.

In fact, she looked forward to getting to know him better while she was here, but she had to be more careful about what she said around him.

104

The Amish attire made Arabella feel like a complete imposter, but she was more than eager to start this adventure. But first, she had to pass this test.

But what instantly made her drawn to Damaris' home was the laughter and peace that radiated through everyone. Even with their father passed away, the children seemed so happy and content, and they got along so well.

Damaris had explained to her that usually they would take turns making dinner—Damaris, Constance, and Delphine. That afternoon, Arabella stood alone in the kitchen after Constance had asked her to make dinner while she ran errands. She was completely confused about how to proceed with the cooking.

She quietly scanned the surroundings, even outside, to see if anyone was around. The children were still at school, so no one was home. Getting out the new cell phone she'd bought in case of emergencies, she did an online search for a recipe. She knew it was very risky, but there was really no other option.

After reading the recipe and directions, she proceeded with the cooking, which ended in a disaster. The online recipe app didn't exactly give instructions for how to make the meal in a woodstove.

First, she burnt her hand, then she accidentally dropped a bowl on the floor, shattering it. The food was much worse. The mashed potatoes were lumpy, and the vegetables and chicken she'd roasted in the oven had burned. Cooking with the woodstove had been even harder than she'd expected, especially without other modern appliances. She'd never cooked a full meal in her life. She'd never had to, with cooks always preparing meals for her and her parents.

With baking, she didn't mind not having the modern appliances, because a lot of the work was done by hand, anyway.

She stood, staring at the meal—her disastrous handiwork.

At dinner later that night, the children chattered on and on as they sat down to eat.

"Let's pray," Constance said, bowing her head. The children followed suit, and so did Arabella. This was the silent prayer Damaris had told her about.

After about twenty seconds, Constance looked up, and they began dishing the food onto their plates. The children continued talking as Constance helped the younger children with cutting up their chicken and vegetables, which were like rubber.

Everyone began eating and quickly fell silent.

Arabella squirmed in her seat, feeling her face heat in embarrassment at her failure. Should she come up with some excuse, giving a fictional reason why she'd let the food burn or why the mashed potatoes tasted like glue?

Instead, she sank lower in her seat, unable to think of any fake excuses. No, this food was terrible, and there was no lie she could come up with to justify it.

It was easy to see the horrified expressions of the entire family as they struggled to choke down the unsavory meal. No one complained. They simply ate the meal in silence, which was so much worse. Arabella kept her head down as she herself struggled to choke down her culinary failure.

"I'm sorry dinner didn't turn out so well," Arabella said apologetically, going to the kitchen counter. "I hope this makes up for it." She set a tray of pastries on the table that she'd baked after making dinner. They were her own recipe, one that she'd memorized and perfected. Feeling so guilty for ruining the meal, she had decided to make a special dessert for everyone.

"Wow!" several of the children exclaimed. The mood instantly changed from gloomy to enthusiastic as they reached with their small hands and grabbed the pastries off the table, devouring them.

"Damaris, what happened? I mean, you could bake pretty well before, but these are delicious," Daisy said, reaching for another one.

"Thanks. I've learned a lot working at the bakery with Lydia and Laura," Arabella lied.

Constance nodded in approval, taking a bite out of one of the pastries. "She's right, Damaris. These are very good."

"Thank you." Arabella smiled shyly. At least she'd done one thing right today.

After the meal, she cleared the table and washed the dishes. Mechanically, she struggled from one chore to another, trying hard not to think about how her entire body was beginning to scream at her for all the extra work. But strengthening her resolve, she completed the chores.

She finally finished cleaning the kitchen while Constance got the children ready for bed. Arabella wandered into the living room, barely upright.

As it got darker outside, Arabella lit the small gas lights on the ceilings, just as Damaris had explained how to do it. Delphine was humming to herself as she sewed in the living room. She glanced up at Arabella as soon as she walked in.

"*Maam* says we have to mend these clothes," she said, gesturing to the pile of clothes by her side. "Some have holes, and some of the boys' shirts are missing buttons."

Arabella stifled a tear that threatened to run down her cheek. The amount of work she had done was already telling on her physically; she was not sure she could do anymore. Damaris had warned her being Amish was not as simple as it seemed, but Arabella had no idea it was this hard.

However, determined not to cause a scene, she made a cup of chamomile tea, then sat down to begin her share of the mending. At least this was a job she could do. Her governess had taught her how to sew as a hobby when she was younger.

She noticed Delphine's glances at her, obviously because of the silence between them, but she was thankful that Delphine did not say anything. Damaris had told Arabella that Delphine was very shy.

Constance came into the living room, yawning. "They're all in bed. I'll help you finish up the mending." She sat down on the couch, weariness etched into her face.

Damaris' poor mother. It must be hard, raising so many children on her own. Arabella's heart went out to her.

"Dinner was…interesting," Constance said, picking up a shirt with a missing button. She grabbed some thread. "Did you get distracted?"

"As in, were you reading and lost track of time?" Delphine snickered and giggled.

Constance waved a hand at her daughter, smiling. "Well, I was wondering that too. What happened? Your cooking is normally so good. No offense, but this was not up to your usual standards."

"I know. I'm sorry. But yes," she said in a rush, grateful for Delphine's question. She took a sip of her tea to buy herself a few seconds to think. "I started reading halfway through the meal and lost track of time, so the food burned. I'm so sorry."

"And the potatoes? They weren't burned, but they were… What is the right word?" Constance asked, tapping her chin thoughtfully.

"Atrocious?" Delphine asked softly, smiling again as she kept her eyes on her sewing.

Arabella laughed at this supposedly shy girl's sense of humor. "Yes, they were atrocious. I must have been so distracted and tired, I just didn't put in the right ingredients and didn't mash them very well. I feel terrible you all ate it."

"We all have off days," Constance said. "Don't feel bad. Are you feeling well? Wait, is that tea? Are you drinking tea? You hate tea."

Uh oh. Damaris had failed to mention that. "Changed my mind. I like it now. I thought it might help me sleep better. I heard once that your taste buds change every seven years."

"Really?" Constance peered at her. "You just seem…not like yourself."

"No, I'm fine, really. I'll have to go to bed early tonight to make up for all those nights I stayed up too late reading recently. I'm sure that's all it is." Arabella's heart hammered. Could Constance tell?

"That must be it." Constance yawned again. "I don't think I can finish this tonight. I need to go to sleep." With that, she ambled down the hall.

After Arabella finished sewing, she headed to the bathroom and took a much-needed shower. Grateful the Amish here had indoor showers with hot water, she let it soothe her achy muscles. Afterward, she dressed in Damaris' nightgown and used a towel to pat the water from her hair.

Suddenly, the bathroom door opened. Arabella bit back a shriek, scrambling to cover her hair with the towel as Constance wearily stumbled in.

"Oh! I'm so sorry, Damaris. I must be so tired, I forgot to knock." The older woman rubbed her eyes.

"It's fine," Arabella said, using the towel as a turban and twisting it around her hair. Had Constance seen it? Or was she too tired to even notice?

Constance started to go back out the door.

"I'm done, actually," Arabella said, grabbing the dress she'd been wearing earlier off the floor. "Good night." She sidestepped around Constance and scurried down the hall to her room.

Phew. That was close, she thought, exhaling a long breath.

It was a good thing she had her own room. Otherwise, someone would have surely noticed her hair. She would have to shower at night, then go to bed with damp hair every time she washed her hair. Otherwise, someone would notice it was shorter than Damaris' had been. In the morning, she'd just put it up and put on her *kapp* before leaving the room.

When her head finally sought the comfort of a pillow, Arabella drifted into a deep sleep. Already, she dreaded the fast-approaching morning.

At least no one had figured out that she was not Damaris.

***

Before the sun rose, the rooster crowed loudly outside, jolting Arabella awake. As she looked around the dim, plain room, she wondered where she was for a moment. Where was her huge canopy bed and breakfast tray?

Then she remembered she was in Damaris' room, and now she had to get up to bake before making deliveries and working at the store in her place. She looked at the battery-operated clock on the nightstand. It said six o'clock.

Arabella bolted out of bed. She was supposed to be up and baking at five-thirty!

She hurried to get herself ready and dressed, which was an adventure itself because of the straight pins she had to fumble with that held her dress together. After poking her finger twice, she hastily put her hair up in a bun, put on her prayer *kapp*, and tiptoed quickly downstairs so she wouldn't wake the children.

"There you are, sleepyhead," Constance said with a chuckle as Arabella stumbled into the kitchen.

"I'm so sorry I'm late." Arabella took her place at the counter and opened the bag of flour.

"You seemed exhausted last night. I didn't want to wake you this morning. I got most of it done, but you'll have to leave soon to make the deliveries before the store opens."

110

"Thank you. I appreciate that. What's left to make?"

"Three dozen cinnamon rolls and four dozen blueberry pastries."

Simple enough.

Arabella set to work, quickly getting the baked goods on the tray and into the oven. Constance stared at her, clearly impressed.

"Good gracious. You have improved, Damaris," Constance said, wiping down the counter. "You're so much faster."

Was she being too obvious? Maybe she needed to tone it down a bit. "As I said before, I've learned a lot from baking with the Millers."

Constance seemed to believe her. Once the baked goods were ready and cooled off enough, she packed them into the buggy.

"Nice horse," Arabella said softly to Apple. "You'll be nice, right?" This was her first time driving the buggy on her own, and she hoped the horse wouldn't do anything out of the ordinary.

Arabella climbed up gingerly into the buggy, taking the reins in her hands. She clicked her tongue like Damaris had taught her, and the horse moved down the lane.

Now, hopefully she would remember the directions to the Millers' house.

As she reached the end of the road, Arabella froze. Had Damaris told her to take a right or left here? They'd only driven to the Millers' house once, and now Arabella couldn't remember.

Was it left? She hoped so as the horse began to turn to the left on his own. He'd probably gone this way so many times that he knew the route. As they continued down the road, cars whizzed by. While it didn't seem to bother Apple, it spooked Arabella, and she jumped every time a car passed.

She breathed a sigh of relief when she recognized the Millers' street and turned onto it. Fortunately, it was a very short drive. Soon she was pulling into the driveway, and a young woman came out of the house, smiling—Laura Miller.

"Running late this morning?" Laura asked with a wry smile.

"I'm so sorry. I woke up late."

"Up reading again past your bedtime?"

"No. I was just very tired. I hope I didn't put you behind."

"It's fine. *Maam* is finishing up some donuts for the market before we go, anyway."

"Oh. Good." Arabella helped Laura load the boxes into their buggy to take to the market.

"You seem weird today," Laura said, eyeing Arabella.

Arabella's stomach dropped. "What do you mean?"

"You just seem different. Everything okay?"

"Yes. Of course. I'm fine," Arabella stammered, getting into the buggy now that they were finished. "As I said before, I'm just tired. That's all."

"So, you're all better after what happened at the café? Do you know what was wrong with your stomach?"

"Oh, yes. I'm completely fine. Turns out it was just really bad gas pains after all." Arabella gave a sheepish smile, hoping it was convincing.

"Well, okay, then. If something is bothering you, you know you can talk to me about it, right?" Laura asked, concern lining her face.

"Thank you. I will. But really, I'm fine."

"You know what's funny? Remember when that waiter got bumped into and dropped his tray?"

Arabella felt the blood drain from her face. "Uh, yeah?"

"That woman who ran into him looked a lot like you." Laura raised her eyebrows and quickly shook her head. "It was so weird. Did you see her?"

"No, no, I didn't," Arabella stammered. "I was in so much pain, I hardly noticed."

"It was bizarre. I guess my mother and sister didn't see her either from where they were standing, and they were so focused on you, but I wish they'd seen her. It was like you could be twins! I mean, she was an *Englisher*, but I wonder if you wore the same thing if you'd look like twins," Laura said. "I bet you would."

"Well," Arabella gave a nervous laugh. "I heard once that even though each person is unique, chances are maybe one other person in the world looks somewhat like you." She'd never actually heard that, but she had to say something to get Laura off the scent.

"Really? Do you think that's true?"

Arabella shrugged. "Sure. Who knows, right? We can ask God when we get to heaven."

Laura laughed. "Definitely. I better go help clean up. Have a nice day, Damaris."

"You too." Arabella cued the horse to start moving, and she drove the buggy out of the Millers' driveway and to the Community Store, hoping she wouldn't be late.

After arriving, Arabella bolted into the store, glancing at the clock on the wall. Three minutes late.

"Good morning, Damaris," an older man said behind the counter. That must be Irvin, Ella Ruth's father.

"Good morning. Sorry I'm late. It won't happen again."

Irvin nodded. "Don't make it a habit."

"I won't."

"There you are. You're usually fifteen minutes early. I was starting to worry." A pretty young woman came out from behind the shelves, her white prayer *kapp* covering her dark hair.

"I slept late by accident. I'm sorry."

"Happens to the best of us." Ella Ruth shrugged. "Up late reading again?"

Why did everyone keep saying that? "No, I just needed some extra sleep, I guess."

The truth was, she wasn't used to waking up so early. An unavoidable yawn escaped her mouth.

"Well, come on. Let's get started."

As Ella Ruth taught her where merchandise went on the shelves and how to stock them, Arabella struggled to stay focused. How did Damaris do this every day—wake up so early to bake, go to work, then go home and take care of her family? Not to mention all her other chores.

It was utterly exhausting. Arabella had no idea how hard the Amish lifestyle would be.

Right now, she was really starting to miss breakfast in bed, having a maid do all her laundry, and a chef making her meals. She even missed Ms. Libby ordering her around.

Maybe this was a mistake.

"Damaris? Are you okay?"

Ella Ruth was staring at her, a can of beans in her hand.

"Yes. I'm sorry. I'm just out of it today."

Ella Ruth squinted at her. "You seem…different. Is something going on?"

Arabella looked around. Damaris had told Arabella that she could trust Ella Ruth and that she would help her through this. Right now, Arabella needed an ally.

Irvin was outside with a customer, and no one was in the store.

"Look, I have something to tell you. But you have to promise not to freak out. Okay?" Arabella whispered.

"What on earth is going on?"

"I don't really know how to say this, but I'm not Damaris."

"What?" Ella Ruth all but screamed. "What are you talking about?" She looked Arabella up and down. "This better not be a joke."

Chapter Thirteen

"I'm not joking. My name is Arabella Blackwood, and I'm from Germany. I saw you and Damaris on TV and I realized how much she looks like me. We switched places. She's in Germany, in my home," Arabella explained.

Ella Ruth took a step back, her hands up. "Okay, I don't know what is going on, but you're scaring me."

"Even you said I seem different. That's because I'm not Damaris."

"She always said she wanted to go to Germany…" Ella Ruth said. "But how is this possible? You look exactly like her."

"I know. It's uncanny how much we look alike. That's why we were able to switch places without anyone noticing. Yet."

"But why? Why would you want to stay here and pretend to be her?"

"Because I'm getting married to a man I don't know in a few weeks and I wanted to be someone else, just for a little while." Arabella sighed. "I just wanted to get away from my life. Back home, my face is on the bakery packaging, so people recognize me on the street. Here, no one knows who I am."

Ella Ruth gave her an understanding look. "So, why are you telling me if this is supposed to be a big secret?"

"Damaris told me you could help me. Clearly, I have no idea what I'm doing both with this job and the Amish lifestyle. Will you help me?"

Ella Ruth smiled. "Of course. But first, I want to talk to Damaris on the phone and make sure she's okay and that you didn't have her kidnapped or something. No offense."

Arabella thought Ella Ruth was joking, but judging by her serious expression, she clearly wasn't. Remembering the interview on TV about how Ella Ruth's sisters had been kidnapped, Arabella understood her concern. "Of course. You can call her now if you want. She has my cell phone."

"Thanks."

Arabella dialed the number for her and handed Ella Ruth the cell phone. She listened as Ella Ruth spoke with Damaris for a few minutes and kept asking if she was really okay. Finally satisfied, Ella Ruth hung up and returned the phone.

"She says she's doing well. Your parents weren't happy about you leaving, but the wedding and the business deal are still on," Ella Ruth said.

"Well, that's good, I guess." Arabella rolled her eyes. "At least no one has figured out she's not me yet."

The bell above the door rang, and both women turned to see who it was. A young Amish man with wavy brown hair walked in. He was tall with a smattering of endearing freckles on his face. When he turned to Arabella, his sky-blue eyes trained on her.

Arabella's heart crashed against her chest, and for a moment, she forgot how to breathe. Who was this devastatingly handsome man, and was he single?

"Gilbert," Ella Ruth said, glancing at Arabella awkwardly. "How can we help you?"

Gilbert? This was Gilbert, as in Gilbert Schwartz? What on earth had Damaris been thinking, ending things with this man? And why hadn't she emphasized how incredibly good-looking he was?

Clearly, Damaris didn't appreciate what had been right in front of her.

"Thanks, Ella Ruth. My mother sent me to get flour, and my younger siblings asked for donuts, of course," Gilbert said, sending a shy smile Arabella's way.

"Damaris made the donuts this morning. Here, Damaris. Will you pack some up for him?" Ella Ruth widened her eyes at Arabella, clearly trying to signal her. Arabella blinked, bringing herself to attention. Right. She needed to pack up some donuts, not stare at the dreamy Gilbert Schwartz all day.

As Ella Ruth walked to the back of the store to get the flour, Arabella went behind the counter to get a box. "How many donuts do you need?"

"A dozen," he said, looking at her intently. "You look lovely today, Damaris. Are you doing well?"

Arabella's cheeks burned as she avoided eye contact with him, knowing if she looked into those clear blue eyes again, she'd completely lose her train of thought and make a fool of herself. "We're not supposed to comment on outward appearances, remember?"

"I know. You won't tell anyone, will you?"

She looked up to see if he was serious or not, and he gave her a dashing smile. Her heart fluttered.

Oh, come on, Arabella, she scolded herself. *You're leaving soon to marry another man. Get a hold of yourself.*

"Of course not." She wrapped up the box of donuts and handed it to him. "One dozen donuts. Here, take one on the house. For the road." She handed him an extra.

He grinned. "Thanks." He quickly bit into it, then his eyes went wide. "Wow. These are so much better than last time. Did you change the recipe?"

Well, Arabella had made a few tweaks to the recipe. "Maybe," she said hesitantly, then lowered her voice. "But I don't want the Millers to know that. It's their recipe. They have taught me so much."

118

"They sure have." He was already taking his last bite and wiping his mouth with his sleeve like a little boy, leaving just a tad of powdered sugar on the corner of his lip. She stifled a giggle, looking away.

"What?"

"Nothing. You've just got some powdered sugar right there." She pointed to the corner of her lip.

He swiped at it again. "That was delicious. My sisters and brothers will love these. In fact, I'll take another dozen if you don't mind."

"Certainly." She wrapped up another twelve donuts in a box, then looked around. What was Ella Ruth doing? Was she purposely taking a long time to give them time alone?

Finally, Ella Ruth came out from the back of the store. "Sorry. I had to go to the storage room." She handed him the flour and gave him the total he owed.

"No problem. Thanks." Gilbert handed her the cash and smiled again at Arabella. Ella Ruth noticed, then made herself scarce again.

Gilbert leaned forward on the counter, looking right into Arabella's eyes. Feeling frozen by his gaze, she didn't move. "Damaris, I don't like the way things ended between us. I know it was mutual, but I was hoping we could talk again. Will you meet with me after work today?"

What was she supposed to do? Say no? Remind him it was over?

"Yes, of course," she heard herself say, then mentally kicked herself. Damaris would be furious with her.

But how could she say no to him, with the way he was looking at her like that?

"Great," he said with a smile, then walked toward the door. "I'll meet you back here when the store closes."

She could only nod as she watched him walk out. Arabella let out a breath she hadn't realized she'd been holding, feeling as though she'd been swept up by a whirlwind and set back down on her feet.

What had just happened?

***

Gilbert walked away from the store, holding two boxes of the most delectable donuts he'd ever tasted. Yes, Damaris could bake well before, but these were a hundred times better.

How had her baking skills improved so much overnight?

It didn't matter. Her donut recipe wasn't what had sent his heart into overdrive as he'd been talking with her. He'd never felt that way around her before, not even on their dates, so why now was his heart racing? She looked radiant, even more beautiful than ever, but that was not what had drawn him to her. For some reason, she seemed so much easier to talk to now.

Why, after all this time, was she suddenly so appealing and attractive? It made no sense.

Then he realized how much of a fool he'd been to let her go. What had he been thinking? He had to talk to her again. He had to fix this and convince her to give them one more chance.

He hummed a cheerful tune as he walked home, looking forward to when he'd see her again.

***

"You dolt! What did you just do?" Ella Ruth came rushing out from behind the shelves. "Damaris won't be happy about this. She broke up with him, remember?"

"I don't know what happened," Arabella said. "He's so handsome and sweet. What was she thinking, letting him go?"

"She had a crush on him for years, but after a few dates, she realized she didn't love him after all. They both said there was no spark. It was mutual. You've really gotten yourself into a tangled mess now. What if he asks to date you again? Or to court you?" Ella Ruth said.

"I…" She hesitated. Would she be able to say no to him when she so badly wanted to say yes, even after speaking with him for only a few minutes?

Why was she acting like such an immature schoolgirl?

"You'll say no, right?" Ella Ruth prodded, hands on her hips. "You are leaving soon, young lady. You can't tell him you'll date him then break his heart and leave Damaris to deal with the mess."

"I know. I know!" Arabella let out a frustrated sigh. "Maybe I'll just leave early so I'm not here when he arrives."

"No. You need to be forward with him and tell him there is nothing between you. Leave things the way Damaris left things. Don't make it complicated."

"I shouldn't have even talked to him," Arabella muttered, crossing her arms. "He's just so…"

"Yes, he's handsome, I know, and a good man."

"Why are you not interested in him?" Arabella asked. "I heard many of the single women are after him."

Ella Ruth shrugged. "I don't know. I just see him as a friend, like a brother, just as Damaris does. We grew up together. I kind of have the feeling my soul mate doesn't live in Unity, Maine." She gave a wry smile.

"Ella Ruth!" Arabella said in a teasing voice. "You're more adventurous than I thought! Do you ever wish you could travel and see what's out there, like Damaris?"

"Well, yes, but no one needs to know that." Ella Ruth's cheeks reddened as she straightened out things on the front desk. "We're supposed to be content with the way things are."

"There's nothing wrong with wanting to see the world," Arabella said.

Ella Ruth sighed. "Enough about me. You need to figure out what you're going to say to Gilbert later."

***

Damaris stepped outside, where Stefan was waiting. He looked so handsome in his coat, his cheeks a little pink from the chilly weather. He was holding a blanket and a cooler packed with their lunch, and he gave her an endearing smile when he saw her, and her heart fluttered.

You're supposed to be Arabella, who has no feelings for this man, she reminded herself, but it was hard not to be drawn to him.

It was their first date, and they planned on going horseback riding and having a picnic.

"Ready?" he asked.

She only nodded, following him to the stables, since she had no idea where they were. Arabella had told her about how afraid she was of horses, and since Damaris had grown up riding horses, she'd have to tone down her abilities.

When Stefan had asked her to go horseback riding, she'd agreed, since Arabella had asked her to spend time with him. He hadn't mentioned Arabella's fear of horses, and neither had she, so maybe he had no idea.

"You are so lucky, growing up with all these horses," Stefan remarked as they approached the massive, elegant stables. "You must have loved it. I had riding lessons as a kid, but we boarded our horses at another stable."

"I guess I took it for granted," Damaris said, her suspicions confirmed. He had no idea Arabella was afraid of horses, so she might as well ride as well as she knew how and enjoy this.

They stepped inside and Damaris inhaled the familiar scent of hay and manure. It was rather comforting to her, reminding her of home. How were *Maam* and her brothers and sisters? What was Arabella doing?

She shook her head, grabbing a saddle and bridle.

"Allow me, ma'am," a stable hand said. He hurried forward and took the saddle from her. "Let me saddle a horse for you." Then he said in a low voice. "I will get one of the gentler horses."

Damaris raised her eyebrows. "Thanks." She could have easily done it herself, and she didn't need one of the gentler horses, but she wouldn't object.

Damaris walked to the closest mare and stroked her nose. As she looked closer, she realized the mare was pregnant.

"She is due any day," the stable hand said as he saddled the horse Damaris would be riding.

"What a beauty." Damaris grinned at the horse, who whinnied.

Stefan was halfway down the stable hallway, talking softly to one of the horses. Damaris smiled as she watched him, speaking sweet words to the animal. He said something to one of the stable hands, smiling.

"It's a gorgeous day for a picnic," he said as he walked toward her. "And for a ride. The scenery here is beautiful."

That was certainly something she was looking forward to seeing. "Definitely."

After their horses were saddled, they mounted and rode out of the stable at a slow walk.

"Where to?" Stefan asked.

Damaris gestured to mountains in the distance, with hills sprawled out before them. "That way?"

He nodded.

"I'll race you." Damaris grinned and nudged her horse into a gallop. When she heard Stefan shout something behind her in a joking tone, she laughed out loud, the wind whipping at the French twist that Jamie had carefully done. She didn't care if it came out completely and looked like a wild mess, she just loved the familiar feeling of the horse sprinting beneath her combined with the new, breathtaking view around her.

As they rode, the hills grew closer, with tall and majestic mountains behind. The trees still had leaves in fiery colors, and she took in a deep breath, a part of her wishing she could stay in Germany forever. In the distance, she could see an old, regal castle beyond the mountains. All her life, she'd dreamed of seeing a real castle, and there it was.

I could get used to this, she thought.

Finally, she slowed the horse to a walk and Stefan rode right up beside her.

He laughed. "Well, I certainly was not expecting that. You didn't seem like the kind of girl who just takes off at a gallop. I thought we'd be doing a slow trail ride."

Damaris scoffed, patting her horse's neck. "Where's the fun in that?"

He raised his eyebrows and nodded. "I really did get the wrong impression of you, didn't I?"

"First impressions are often wrong," she said. "I may have done the same with you."

"Maybe we should start over."

She nodded, then froze. Would Arabella want her to be saying this? Well, Arabella was going to marry the man; he might as well think well of her.

"Good. This looks like a nice spot for a picnic, don't you think?" he asked.

"Yes, it does," she said enthusiastically and dismounted.

Stefan did also and untied the cooler and blanket from his horse. He unrolled the blanket and set it down on the grass, and they both sat.

For a moment, they were silent as Stefan opened the cooler and started unpacking it. Damaris took the containers he set down and opened them, revealing delicious-looking sandwiches, salads—and of course—pastries.

The awkward silence was growing more intense. Stefan finally spoke up. "Arabella, I want you to know I'm sorry about all of this."

"What do you mean?"

"I'm sorry our parents are making us do this. I wasn't any more enthused about this than you were when my father told me. Really, I feel terrible for even agreeing. I don't want to let my father down."

"I understand, Stefan. I don't want to let my parents down and see our company go under. This will help everyone."

"I just…" He sighed. "I don't want you to resent me. You know, after the wedding." He wouldn't meet her gaze. "I'm hoping we can at least be…friends. I'm not expecting anything more than that. I want you to know." He finally looked at her. "Unless, of course, your feelings changed, which I don't expect to happen either. I know I'm not much to look at, and I've been called nerdy and boring. I've never had a woman interested in me before, and I don't expect it to ever happen."

With each word he spoke, Damaris' heart broke for Stefan. How should she react? How would Arabella want her to react?

At that moment, she didn't care. All she could do was speak her mind.

"Stefan, I think you're underestimating yourself. I think you're handsome and kind, and I don't think you're boring at all. You have many interests and opinions, and I think it's crazy that no woman has ever been interested in you. I bet they have, but you had no idea." She laughed. "Sometimes men can be oblivious to things like that. Sorry. No offense."

"Really?" His cheeks reddened at her compliments. "And no, I'm pretty sure that's never happened."

"And of course, we can be friends. After the wedding, who knows? Sometimes people can learn to love each other."

Why was she saying these things and getting his hopes up?

Stop talking, Damaris, before you really dig yourself in a hole.

"You're saying that maybe one day...you think you might grow to love me? That you won't spend the rest of your life regretting marrying me?" he asked, staring at her intently, leaning closer as if anticipating her reply. She searched his dark brown eyes hiding behind his glasses, seeing so many questions and emotions. Once again, she admired his handsome features—his square jaw, his wavy hair falling across his forehead.

Why did Arabella think he was so nerdy, so annoying and clumsy, when all Damaris saw was a kind, interesting, handsome young man?

And how could she say no to him when he was looking at her like this?

"Yes. I mean, I think there's hope, Stefan," she said, her heart slamming into her rib cage. What if he tried to kiss her?

Why hadn't she thought of that before? What should she do? Arabella had probably thought he'd be too shy to even try it, but he didn't look shy now, not the way his eyes were searching hers and how his gaze was now dropping to her lips.

You're leaving soon, she reminded herself. *You're going back to Maine, and you'll never set foot in Germany again. Besides, Stefan is betrothed to Arabella. Stop this before you make a fool of yourself.*

She took in a deep breath. Her brain muddled, not knowing what else to do, she started taking the sandwiches out and setting them on plates. She handed him one. "Here."

He stared at it as if in a daze, just as confused as she was, then he reached out and took it.

"I know this is confusing for both of us," she said. "But I'm confident we will figure it out."

"You're right," Stefan said. "We both want the same thing, to make our businesses prosper and to please our families. At least for now we can get to know each other better, right?"

"Exactly. So, have you read any new books while I was gone?" Damaris asked.

"Yes. I read another Tony Graham novel. I mean, a Cole Henderson novel. I'm still getting used to his real name," Stefan said with a chuckle. "It's the newest one, *Captive Heart*."

"Oh, yes, I love that one! You know, Belle told me about it before anyone even knew the title," Damaris said, picking up a sandwich, about to take a bite.

"But that would have had to be at least a year ago, before it was released," Stefan said. "I thought you said you only just met Cole and his wife on your recent trip."

Damaris stopped mid-bite, caught in her lie, like a bug caught in a spider's web.

Oh no, what do I say?

"Oh… Well, don't tell anyone, but I've actually gone to Maine before. I've been known to go on 'escapades', as my parents call them. Please don't tell anyone." She cringed, hoping he couldn't see through her deception. At least now she wouldn't have to hide how much she knew about Unity.

"Oh, I see." Stefan slowly nodded. "I'm guessing you like to go there to escape the pressures of your life here?"

"Right. Out there, I can breathe. Here, I just feel suffocated sometimes, like I can't even make my own decisions. In Unity, in the Amish community, it's like stepping back in time. Life is lived at a slower pace. Things are simple there. A person can think out there. When I'm in Unity, I feel close to God. I love reading my Bible early in the morning, even before the sun is up, when the world is quiet and peaceful."

She stared off into the distance. Even though she was surrounded by scenery she had dreamed about seeing her entire life, she still found herself missing home—the smell of pastries baking in the kitchen, the sounds of her siblings chattering, and the loft in the barn where she often read after her morning chores—if she finished them early.

"It sounds wonderful. So, you mentioned you read your Bible every day. Truly, I'm so glad you and I are both believers."

Grateful she and Arabella had discussed this, Damaris nodded. "Oh, yes. My relationship with Jesus is everything to me. When I talk with Him, I feel as though I am talking to my best friend."

"Same for me," Stefan said with a wide grin. "Studying the Bible and my relationship with God are the most important things to me, and I was hoping my future wife would also be a Christian. I just don't see why your parents didn't really say much about that."

Damaris nodded. "My parents believe too; they're just not as vocal about it. I guess that's why they didn't mention it."

"I know the Amish are also very devoted in their faith. I would like to learn more about the Amish. Is that why you go there? Do you miss it there?"

Damaris blinked. "Oh, yes. I hope to go back soon. God is central to their way of life. Everything they do is to honor Him. That is why I love it there so much. Without all the worldly distractions, they can focus on Him so much more."

"That sounds incredible. I would like to go there someday. You know, when we're married, I won't mind if you want to travel and take time off from the business. In fact, I'd like to go there with you one day." Stefan gave her a crooked smile. "You should have the time to do what you want. If you want to do things or go places without me, that's okay too."

"Really?" Damaris' eyes widened in surprise. She hadn't expected that.

"Of course. I like a woman who thinks for herself and has her own opinions and interests."

Damaris blushed. Was he talking about her or Arabella? "You know, I would like to take you there one day. You'd love it."

"I'd love to visit an Amish community and learn about their culture. I've always been a bit fascinated with them." Stefan looked at the sandwich in his lap shyly. "To be honest, I'd really love to meet Cole Henderson. I know he lives a very private life, but since you already are friends with him, maybe…"

"He does like his privacy, and he hates it when people ask for his autograph," Damaris warned. "But maybe, just maybe, I could arrange that one day."

What was she saying? Of course, she couldn't promise that. She'd probably never see Stefan again after she left here unless she and Arabella stayed in touch. By then, Arabella would be married to Stefan.

Damaris cringed.

But it was too late to take back her words now. Stefan's eyes lit up with hope. "Wow, that would be amazing."

"So, what did you think of *Captive Heart*?" she asked, changing the subject.

Stefan smiled at the woman before him, wondering just how on earth he could have thought she was cold and rude the first day he'd met her. Like him, she'd just been nervous, and now she was being herself. "I loved it. Have you read it?" he asked.

"Yes, a while back, actually. I got an advanced copy."

"Really? Wow. You're so lucky."

"It's fun. I read the book, make notes, and give Cole feedback. He likes to make sure it's the best it can be before he submits it to his publishers. I'm not the only one. He has other people he sends advanced copies to. I think many authors do that."

"Well, it makes sense to have several people read it before publishing."

"I told him some things that were unrealistic about the farm in the book. He was way off track. I hope I didn't embarrass him too much." Damaris smiled and took a bite out of her sandwich.

"How do you know so much about farms? Did the Amish teach you?"

"Yes, they taught me about farming there."

"So, you actually stayed with Amish families? That's incredible!" Impressed, he hadn't expected her to do anything like that, since she had seemed like the type of woman who couldn't go one day without her cell phone when he'd first met her. Again, he'd been totally wrong. He admired that she made the effort to learn about other cultures. "What's it like?"

"Well, it was a lot of work. There are so many chores, it takes all day. As you probably know, they don't use electricity. So we—I mean, they— wash dishes by hand after every meal. Many of the families have several children, so that alone can take up a large portion of the day."

"And they don't use phones or indoor toilets?"

She laughed. "Of course, they have indoor toilets. Well, in Unity they do. Maybe in some other Amish communities in other states they don't. They are all different. They don't have phones in the houses, but they do have them in businesses and there are phone shanties everyone shares."

"Wow." Stefan reached for a pastry. "I'd love to go and learn about the agriculture, the farming, and the different types of businesses they have."

"They do have many different businesses. Many of the families own their own businesses. They don't go to school past the eighth grade, but they are very knowledgeable. I just get annoyed when people think the Amish aren't educated and make all these other assumptions about them."

Her face reddened a bit with irritation at the injustice, and Stefan had to smile. He admired how much she loved to learn about the Amish, how she loved to travel, and how she was an independent thinker. The sunlight made her long, light brown hair shimmer around her shoulders, and he admired her intense eyes and lilting mouth.

She was beautiful in every way. How had he not seen it before? How had he not felt this before? When he'd first seen her, why hadn't he been knocked off his chair by how stunning she was?

Clearly, he'd been blind and was only now opening his eyes to the truth about who she really was. Now he felt fortunate to spend the rest of his life with her. In fact, he was looking forward to it, which was something he'd never expected to want.

He found himself brushing the powdered sugar off his fingers and reaching forward for her hand. She jumped in surprise and stared up at him with her big brown eyes.

"Arabella, we're getting married soon anyway, so I don't see any reason for me to hide this from you. I'm not so good with words or talking to people, but I find it easy to talk to you. I think you're interesting and admirable. I think you're beautiful. I just want you to know, I'm actually looking forward to marrying you. I don't expect you to say the same about me, but I just wanted you to know."

His cheeks burned furiously with an intense blush. Embarrassed about pouring his heart out to her, he snatched his hand back and continued eating, pretending that hadn't just happened.

Why had he said all of that to her? She probably didn't care about him in the slightest, not the way he cared about her.

No, it was more than caring. He had feelings for her.

"Stefan," she said. He looked up. Her eyes were filled with…what? Pity? Disgust?

Or was it something totally different? If he didn't know any better, he might even say her eyes held longing and…something more.

His heart pounded.

"I'm glad you said that. I admire you too. I was wrong about my first impression of you, and I'm so happy we are getting to know each other. I think we will make a great team when we run the company together." She gave a polite smile and continued eating.

Disappointment filled him, lodging an ache in his chest.

No. She didn't have any romantic feelings for him. She saw him as a future business partner, an obligation, nothing more. Of course, she did. He was the nerdy, annoying, clumsy kid who got picked on in school. Why would a beautiful woman like her want him?

How was it possible that only after this short amount of time knowing her, he was already falling for her? He'd never felt this way about anyone before.

Stefan's heart wilted as he realized the truth.

He'd spend his entire life loving someone who didn't see him as more than a business partner.

Chapter Fourteen

After the picnic's awkward ending, Damaris fought with herself the entire ride back to the mansion, which was a slow walk compared to their rambunctious race earlier.

Oh, Lord, what have I done? What should I have said? Damaris asked God for the fifth time since they'd left the picnic spot.

She'd frozen when Stefan had poured his heart out to her, not having any clue how to respond. What would Arabella want her to say? She'd have to call her and ask. Deciding to play it safe, Damaris had given him a reply that did not indicate she had any feelings for him.

But the truth was, she did feel something for him. When he looked at her, her entire being came alive and her heart raced. Why did she feel this way? She'd never felt this way about anyone before, and she'd only just met him. What was wrong with her?

Must be the jet lag still messing with her head.

There was no missing how Stefan hung his head on the ride back, how embarrassed and disappointed he seemed, and how badly he hid it. Once they got back to the stables, Damaris made an excuse and hurried up to Arabella's room to call her.

Just as she was dialing the phone number, there was a knock at her door. She answered it to see a maid.

"Miss Emily is here to see you," the maid said. Damaris wondered if the maid might curtsey, fighting back a giggle. Of course, she wouldn't.

"Great. Send her up," Damaris said.

Oh, good. Arabella's best friend was here. Arabella had told Damaris she could trust Emily with their secret, and Damaris was dying to talk to someone about it.

The door opened, and Emily sashayed in. "Hi! How are you? I want to know all about your trip to the Amish. Why didn't you call me? I need details. Did you meet any hot Amish guys?" Emily plopped onto Arabella's bed. "Spill it."

Damaris was so stunned by all her questions for a second, she just stared at the lively redhead. Arabella had described her as talkative, but that didn't do her justice.

"What's wrong? Are you okay?" Emily asked.

"Yes. I'm fine. Sorry. It's just that a lot has happened." Damaris closed the door and turned to Emily. "I have something to tell you."

"You did meet a guy. Who is he?" Emily's eyes widened, and she bounced where she sat.

"It's not that. Well, sort of." Damaris chuckled. "You have no idea."

"Well, come on! Tell me."

"Okay. First, you have to promise me you won't tell anyone."

"That's obvious. How many secrets have you told me and I've never told anyone?"

Damaris raised her eyebrows. "I have no idea. Anyway, I don't know how to tell you this, so I'll just tell you. My name is Damaris Kauffman. I'm an Amish woman from Unity. Arabella stayed in Unity and took my place, pretending to be me. She wanted to be someone else before getting married and starting her new life, and she offered to pay for my trip here. I've always dreamed of traveling to Germany. So, we switched places and no one knows."

Emily just stared at her. "That is the weirdest thing you have ever said. It's the worst joke you've ever tried to play on me. You're going to have to do better than that to fool me, Arabella."

"Come on, I'm serious. Look, we can call Arabella right now, and she will confirm everything I said."

Emily burst into laughter. "You're kidding, right? You can't be serious."

"I'm serious. She told me I could trust you with our secret. You won't tell anyone, right?"

Realization crossed Emily's face. "Wait, you are serious, aren't you? Arabella did want to see the Amish, but I didn't ever expect her to stay long. She's pretending to be you, an Amish woman?"

"Yes."

"You're telling me Arabella is wearing a bonnet and dress, not using electricity or her cell phone or internet?"

"Well, it's called a prayer *kapp*. Yes, that's true. I mean, we do have one outlet for charging our rechargeable batteries, but she's not using her phone except for emergencies. She's doing all my chores and working at my jobs for me, which is baking and working at a store."

Emily laughed again, slapping her leg. "I wish I could see that! So, what did you mean about the guy you met? Or did you mean she met an Amish guy?"

"I was talking about Stefan. He's...nice. He's sweet—nothing like how she described him. Why doesn't Arabella like him?"

Emily widened her eyes. "Hold on. Do you *like* him?"

Guilt flooded through Damaris. "It's horrible, I know. He's engaged to Arabella. But I just don't see why she thinks he's some bumbling nerd. He's so much more than that. I just hope she takes the time to get to know him. He's..." Her face burned with embarrassment and she threw up her hands. "I didn't mean to start falling for him. I've made a huge mess of things."

"Didn't you just meet him?" Emily asked.

"Yes! So, it must be this trip and this whole whirlwind that's getting to my head. I'm feeling things that aren't real. When I go home, I'm sure I will forget all about him."

Wouldn't she?

"Well, you better hope so. Because Arabella is marrying him in a few weeks. We should definitely call her." Emily took out her cell phone.

"Wait! Maybe we shouldn't tell her about that. I just need to ask her what I'm supposed to say when Stefan pours his heart out to me, basically telling me he got the wrong impression of me and now he likes me."

"Hold on. He likes you? As in you, Damaris? Or Arabella?" Emily shook her head in confusion, her red curls bouncing.

"I don't know! I think he meant me. He only met Arabella once, that time he spilled soup on her. I think they were together just during that dinner and that's it. After that, it was me."

Emily let out a mirthless laugh. "This is bad. What do we do? What if she's angry and comes right home?"

Damaris' stomach sank. Could that happen? Could this trip be over just like that? "Just call her. You have to call her other cell phone because I have her cell phone here, since I'm pretending to be her. We bought a second phone for us to use to contact each other." Damaris rattled off the phone number she'd memorized.

Emily dialed the number, giving Damaris a furtive glance.

"Damaris?" Arabella said when she answered the phone.

Emily put the call on speaker so they could both hear. "Hey, it's Emily. Damaris is here, too," Emily said.

"Oh, hi! Wow, it's great to hear from you. First of all, Damaris, I have a question for you. Why didn't you say anything about how gorgeous and sweet Gilbert Schwartz is?" Arabella gushed.

Damaris laughed out loud. "Oh, wow. Great. This is just great. I can see where this is going." She paced the room.

"About that," Emily said while Damaris continued to pace nervously. "We have a bit of a situation here. Stefan is falling for Damaris, thinking she's you."

"What? Seriously?"

"I was just pretending to be you," Damaris said in her defense. "So, what do you want me to say to Stefan when he says sweet things to me?"

"What kind of sweet things?" Arabella said.

"Like how he thinks he admires me and is looking forward to marrying me. I mean you." Damaris covered her face with her hands and sat on the bench at the end of the bed.

"What did you say?" Arabella demanded.

"I told him I thought we'd make great business partners. I kind of panicked."

"Well, that's good, I guess. If it happens again, you should say that sort of thing. I don't want him to think I'm falling for him and then find out I have no feelings for him at all after we're married. He'd be so disappointed," Arabella said.

"Of course. You're absolutely right," Damaris said. "I'm sorry."

"You better not fall for him, Damaris. I'm sorry, but I have to be the one to marry him to save our business," Arabella warned.

"I know. I know. I'm leaving soon. I don't have enough time to fall for him, anyway. So, what about you and Gilbert? You're not falling for him, are you?"

"Well, he is devastatingly good-looking," Arabella said. "And thoughtful."

"You mean dull? A bit boring?"

"Dull? Boring? No!" Arabella sounded offended. "He, uh, asked to talk to me later. He wants to talk about how we ended things."

"As in he's regretting breaking up?" Damaris snapped. "What did you say to him? Did you flirt with him?"

"No," Arabella retorted. "I packed up two dozen donuts for him and talked with him. That's all. I don't know what happened."

Emily looked at Damaris, tilting her head down and raising her eyebrows, unimpressed. "She flirted with him."

"Stop it, Emily," Arabella retorted.

Emily just laughed.

"Well, if he wants to get back together, you have to say no. Okay?" Damaris said.

Arabella hesitated.

"Arabella! You can't tell me not to fall for Stefan, then date my ex-boyfriend, pretending to be me."

Emily laughed out loud again, clearly enjoying the drama. "Sorry. This is too funny."

"Not helping, Emily," Arabella said, sounded annoyed. Damaris imagined her rolling her eyes.

"Both of you calm down," Emily said. "You need to make sure you remember you're switching back soon and not fall in love. Got it?"

Damaris crossed her arms. "Fine. I can do that."

"Me too," Arabella said.

"Good. We are all in agreement," Emily said. "You two are getting tangled up in something that's so much more complicated than you realized. Maybe you should just switch back now before things get worse and someone gets hurt."

"No," Arabella said. "I can't come home now. I need more time away before the wedding."

"And I'm loving it here," Damaris said. "Not yet."

"Fine. But I think you might both regret this." Emily shook her head.

"Where's the spontaneous, carefree Emily I know?" Arabella asked.

Emily sighed. "I just don't want to see either of you get hurt."

***

After Arabella's shift at the store ended that afternoon, she stepped outside to see Gilbert leaning against his buggy, waiting for her behind the store. All the customers had left, and the only people around were Ella Ruth and Irvin, who were now getting into their buggy and driving home. Ella Ruth gave Arabella a curious glance as they rode away.

Arabella and Gilbert were completely alone.

Her breath froze in her chest when she saw him standing there in his black wide-brimmed hat and black jacket. It was a look she might have made fun of in the past, but now she found it extremely appealing. His arms were crossed over his chest as he watched her walk toward him, and a slow smile spread over his handsome face. Butterflies exploded in her stomach.

Then, all too quickly, she remembered what Damaris had made her promise to do—to tell him they couldn't get back together.

The butterflies were replaced by rocks in her core.

"Thanks for agreeing to meet with me," he said, still smiling.

She took a deep breath. "I can't stay long. I have to get home to help make dinner."

"Always thinking of others. That's what I admire about you."

139

Her heart sank even more. Wasn't he talking about Damaris? She liked to think she always put others first, but did she really? Yes, she was considering marrying a stranger to help her parents, but other than that…

The longer she was here, the longer she realized how long she'd been self-absorbed, ignorant of what was going on in the world outside of her own life.

Arabella wanted that to change.

Yes, she'd traveled to places all over the world, but nowhere had ever impacted her like this in such a short amount of time. Here, this was the way life was meant to be—faith, family, and friends were the most important things in life, not designer handbags and trips to Paris.

She was so deep in thought, she'd looked at the ground. When she looked up, the way he looked at her made her heart swell, so she had to look away to keep her composure before she said something foolish.

"What do you want to talk about with me?" she asked.

"I'll get right to the point. I don't like how we ended things. I thought I didn't have feelings for you, but I was wrong. I don't know why, but I realized today that I do. I want to be with you, Damaris. Do you feel it too? If you do, will you give us one more chance?" he asked, his blue eyes pleading with hers.

He was so close now, she could feel his warm breath on her face and see each individual freckle on his nose and cheeks. She wanted to stand there and count them. She shook her head, backing away, chiding herself for thinking such silly thoughts.

He grabbed her hand and she stopped, then slowly turned toward him.

"I can see it in your eyes. You feel it too. So why are you walking away?" he asked in a low voice, sending chills down her spine that wasn't from the cold weather. The feeling of his warm hand holding hers was a feeling she wanted to savor, so she couldn't bring herself to let go.

"If you don't want to give us another chance, then walk away, and I won't bother you again," he said, finality in his voice.

Instead of rejecting him, like Damaris had asked her to do, she found herself stepping closer to him and looking up into his eyes.

"Is this a yes?" he whispered, leaning his head down near hers so his lips brushed her ear. His arm wrapped around her, pulling her closer. She leaned her head against his chest, welcoming his embrace.

Walk away, she told herself, but her feet wouldn't move. *Damaris is going to kill me.*

This was the exact opposite of what she was supposed to be doing.

Instead, she let him hold her as the leaves fell from the trees and swirled around them, like a picturesque scene from a romance movie.

Arabella knew that for the rest of her life, she'd never forget this moment.

"I want to kiss you," Gilbert murmured.

Oh no. That would really cross the line. As though she'd been stung by a bee, she jumped out of his arms.

"We shouldn't," she blurted.

"You're right. We aren't supposed to until marriage," he said, frowning. "I'm sorry."

She gave him a smile. "It's okay. I wanted to do it, too."

He gave her a crooked grin. Her insides melted.

"I better go before someone sees us," he said, reluctantly turning toward his buggy.

"Me too. To make dinner." She tripped over her words, backing away.

"I'll see you soon, Damaris," Gilbert said. He climbed up into the buggy and drove away.

Her soaring heart crashed and burned at his final word. Damaris.

In his eyes, she was Damaris. What would he say when he discovered the truth about who she really was?

***

Gilbert rode away, not bothering to hide the wide grin on his face.

That was by far the most blissful, romantic moment of his life. Sure, several of the young women in the community were interested in him, and he'd been on a few dates, but he'd never felt like this before about anyone.

How on earth had he not seen her this way before? How had he known her for so long and not realized the beautiful, kind, and godly woman right in front of him?

"God, I have been such a fool," he murmured. "Please help me get it right from now on. Is she the one for me, Lord?"

He looked up at the sky as if expecting words to be written there, but there were only a few fluffy clouds being chased away by the autumn breeze. A feeling of peace washed over him, and the sound of the breeze filled his ears like the playful whisper of a child.

Maybe she was the one for him. He grinned again, remembering the way her body had melted against him as he held her, how he'd wanted to kiss her so much, but he knew they shouldn't before marriage. Of course, Amish couples didn't always follow the rules.

This was so much more difficult than he'd anticipated, especially when she'd admitted she'd wanted him to kiss her.

Yet, even though she'd said that, and she'd let him hold her, something about her seemed—hesitant. Unsure.

Even...regretful.

Had he just been imagining it, thinking it was too good to be true? Maybe she'd just been nervous like he had.

"Well, Lord, I am putting this in Your hands. Thank You for revealing this woman Damaris to me, for opening my eyes. I trust it was in Your perfect timing. Show me the way, Lord. Please, guide me. I don't want to mess this up."

***

Arabella went inside Damaris' house, shut the door, and leaned against it. She smiled up at the ceiling, then frowned.

Oh, how heavenly those few moments with Gilbert had been. Sure, she'd been kissed before, but she'd never felt butterflies exploding in her stomach like this, and they hadn't even kissed. But it had been close.

What would Damaris say? How could this possibly end well?

Even if she had a chance with Gilbert, she knew she wasn't good enough for him. She wanted to be more caring, thoughtful of others, and selfless. This place made her want to change.

He made her want to change.

"Well, are you going to make dinner or stand there all day, Damaris? It's your turn today." Constance said, chuckling to herself as she whisked by with a broom, sweeping the floor, only giving her a quick glance.

"Oh. Yes. Sorry." Arabella yanked off her shoes and jacket, then went inside. Tonight, she would be making taco casserole with a cornbread topping. She'd had no idea the Amish even ate taco casserole, but this place surprised her every day.

"It's a family recipe," Constance said as Arabella studied the recipe on an index card. "One of my favorites."

Arabella gulped. Hopefully, she wouldn't botch it too badly.

Over an hour later, Arabella pulled the creation out of the woodstove and set it on the counter, staring at it. It didn't look bad. In fact, it looked…good. She leaned closer and took a big whiff. It smelled good too.

143

"Mmm. My favorite," said Daisy as she plopped down at the table, followed by the other children.

"Wow. That smells good," Danny said. "And I smell something else. Cinnamon?"

"Maybe." Arabella smiled.

"At least you didn't burn the food this time," Dean said with a smirk, playfully elbowing Danny.

Arabella bit back a retort as they all sat down to eat and shared a silent prayer.

Please, God, change my heart. I want to be a better person. I'm not sure how or what to pray, but I know you can help me, Arabella prayed.

As they all dished the food onto their plates and began eating, it was silent at first, and Arabella watched, unable to even move.

"This is good," Daisy said as she put more on her plate.

"Mmm." Desmond smiled and rubbed his tummy.

Arabella wanted to laugh out loud. Finally, she had made a good meal! Hopefully, it wouldn't be the last. Had she just gotten lucky, or was her cooking improving a bit? She hadn't been there long enough for it to improve significantly, but at least she could manage making this one simple recipe without ruining it.

As they finished eating, she stood up, opened the oven, and pulled out a tray of homemade cinnamon rolls—one of her specialties.

The children all exclaimed their delight, which was a huge reward for her efforts. Yes, the Amish way of life was so much work and more difficult than she'd expected, but maybe by the time she left here, this place would have a more lasting positive effect on her than she'd ever expected.

***

After thinking about Gilbert and her predicament all night, Arabella dragged herself out of bed the next morning at five-thirty. It was market day, so she had to go to the market and help the Millers sell their baked goods. But first, she had baking to do.

Today, since they had a much larger amount to bake than usual, Arabella drove the buggy to the Millers' house so she could bake with them there while Constance stayed home with the children.

Her mind had been whirling with so many questions and thoughts of Gilbert last night, she felt as though she hadn't slept at all. So when she walked into the Millers' house and smelled coffee brewing, she breathed a sigh of relief, grateful the Amish here drank coffee.

"Good morning," Laura said, waving her inside. "Coffee?"

"Oh, yes, please. I really need it this morning."

"Reading again all night?"

"No, no. Just couldn't sleep." Arabella rubbed her eyes, for once not having to worry about smudging her mascara and eyeliner. She ambled into the kitchen, and Laura poured her a mug of the warm liquid and handed it to her.

"Thank you." Arabella practically gulped it down.

Mae bustled into the kitchen. "Well, let's get a move on. We've got a lot to do." She grinned at Arabella. "Good morning, Damaris."

"Good morning."

Lydia also came into the kitchen and greeted her.

"You know, I was thinking today we could try one of my new recipes," Arabella ventured.

All three women turned to look at her.

"One of...your recipes?" Laura said, twirling the ribbon on her *kapp,* giving her mother a doubtful look.

"Yes. I've been working on this one for weeks on my own and I've really perfected it. Trust me. I know it'll be a hit." Arabella nodded.

"We're known for what we bake now," Lydia added. "Why change it?"

"I know, everyone loves shoofly pie and cinnamon rolls and donuts, but why not add something new? It could bring new customers," Arabella said, bouncing on her toes. "Why not give it a try?"

Laura piped up, "So many people at the store have commented on how much better Damaris' baking is. She's drastically improved. I say we give her a chance."

"What is the recipe for?" Mae asked.

"Cherry tarts," Arabella said, hiking her chin.

Mae looked to her two daughters. "I am willing to try it. Let's get to work. I've got several jars of cherries I canned last winter. Lydia, come help me carry them."

Lydia gave her mother another skeptical glance, but Mae just shrugged and smiled as they walked out of the room.

"Since when have you been working on recipes?" Laura asked, sidling up next to her. "And why has your baking improved so much in so little time?"

Arabella spread flour over the counter and began gathering ingredients. "You have taught me a lot since I've been working here."

"No one improves this much overnight."

"Well... I don't want to sound prideful, but maybe I have." Arabella's hands shook. Was Laura suspicious?

Suddenly, Arabella's phone vibrated in her jacket pocket hanging by the front door. She froze, her eyes wide. She must have forgotten to put it on silent that morning. Panic set in as Laura gasped.

"What on earth was that? It almost sounded like a…" Laura looked at Arabella, studying her. "Like a cell phone."

Arabella's heart fell as though it dropped to the floor.

Chapter Fifteen

"What? A cell phone? Why would you have a cell phone in the house?" Arabella stammered, clumsily knocking over one of the measuring cups.

"We sure don't. But your jacket is over there with ours." Laura put her hands on her hips. "Damaris Kaufmann. You said you would never own a cell phone, that it would cause too much temptation."

"Maybe it's Lydia's," Arabella ventured, but even the words sounded ridiculous to her own ears.

Laura laughed out loud. "My sister is the most boring person I know. She'd never break a rule. You, on the other hand…" Laura wiggled her eyebrows playfully. "Did you get one secretly? I know people get them secretly."

There was no hiding the unmistakable sound of another text notification. Arabella cringed, then hurried over to her jacket to silence it before Lydia and Mae returned.

Laura gasped again, following her like a curious child. "You little badger! You do have one!"

"Shh!" Arabella whispered, shoving the phone back into the jacket pocket. "Promise you won't tell?"

Laura waved her hand and laughed. "Oh, come on. Do you know how many of the Amish teens secretly have cell phones, even the adults? You're not the only one."

"Seriously. Promise?"

"Of course, I promise. What, do you think I'd tell on you?" Laura shook her head and went back to the kitchen. "I'm just surprised. It doesn't seem like something you'd do."

"Look, I just wanted it for emergencies. With my father not around anymore, and my brother moved out, I worry about my mother and my siblings when I'm not home. I wanted them to be able to get a hold of me quickly," Arabella blurted.

Laura's face softened with understanding, and she nodded. "So, your mother knows?"

Arabella squinted her eyes shut, realizing her error. "Well, not yet. Don't mention it, okay? I will have to tell her."

"Of course you're worried about them. I understand. Personally, I don't see what is so wrong about having a cell phone as long as you only use it when you really need to call someone, especially for emergencies," Laura said, mixing ingredients into a bowl. "Just don't tell anyone I said that."

"Oh, you rebel." Arabella laughed and flicked some flour at her friend. "Don't worry, I won't tell."

"Hey!" Laura flung some flour back at Arabella.

"You two are no more mature than five-year-old kids," Lydia said dryly as she carried a box into the kitchen, followed by Mae.

Mae smiled. "Oh, Lydia. So serious all the time."

Arabella just smiled, relieved they hadn't overheard anything.

Mae set down the box she was carrying. "Let's get to work. We have a lot of baking to do before going to the market."

After the cherry tarts came out of the oven and had cooled, they each tried a bite.

"This is scrumptious!" Laura cried.

"It is absolutely delicious, Damaris. This was a good idea. I think the customers will love them," Mac said.

Even Lydia agreed. "They're good." She gave a curt nod.

When they were finished with the baking, they loaded up the merchandise into the buggy and drove downtown where they would set up their baked goods in a booth at the local farmers market. This was the busiest day of the week for the bakery.

After Arabella stepped down from the buggy, she slowly turned in a circle, taking in the atmosphere of the farmers market. Various vendors set up their booths selling products varying from homemade soaps, flowers, jams, vegetables, and cheese. Some of the vendors were Amish, but many were *Englishers* like her.

She inhaled deeply, taking in the scent of the homemade candles in the booth beside theirs. It was still early, so only the vendors were milling about, but soon she imagined this place would be busy with customers.

"Come on, Damaris. Quit gawking and help us set everything up," Laura said, smiling as she poked Arabella in the ribs playfully.

"Sorry. I just love this place."

"Just wait until the customers arrive. The day will go by quickly, as always."

Arabella lifted a box out of the back of the buggy and brought it to their table. Mae was covering the table with a homemade Amish quilt and placing boxes underneath it to add height to the display. Arabella watched with fascination as Mae and her daughters made the table beautiful, even adding their business cards and small Amish decorative items such as an Amish doll and a prayer *kapp* to make their table unique. In front of the table, Lydia hung a sign that said *The Millers' Bakery*.

Arabella helped them unload the tarts, pastries, donuts, and cinnamon rolls. Soon, they were finished, and they each took a seat behind the table.

Now she guessed they would wait for the customers to arrive.

The first two hours sped by rapidly as Arabella tried to keep up with serving customers. She bagged their orders, took their payments, and answered questions. Soon, there was a lull, and they sat back down.

"Sometimes this happens," Laura said. "Hopefully more customers will come."

Arabella sighed and looked around, then her heart leapt when she saw Gilbert walking past some of the booths across from them. He stopped and bought a bag of produce, then slowly turned. When their eyes met, he smiled at her, and she grinned back at him. As he walked closer, she stood up, her heart slamming against her rib cage at the way he was staring at her as if she was the only person around.

"Good morning," he said. "I was here to get some produce from the Yoders. They have the best apples around. How is business today?"

"It was busy earlier, but now things have slowed down a bit," Arabella explained.

Gilbert surveyed the display of baked goods. "Well, I'll take a cherry tart and two dozen donuts to take home to my siblings. They raved about those donuts so much last time. I'd like to surprise them again."

"That's wonderful," Mae said. "Damaris' baking has improved, *ja*?"

"*Ja*. Definitely." He grinned at her.

Arabella's heart warmed at how thoughtful he was to surprise his family with treats. She placed the goods in a paper bag and told him the total. He handed her cash.

"Keep the change," he said, digging the cherry tart out of the bag and taking a bite. His eyes widened. Was that a good sign or a bad sign? Though she didn't think it was possible, her heart raced even faster.

"These are delicious!" he cried. "Are they new?"

"Yes," Laura piped up. "They're Damaris' new recipe. We made them for the first time this morning."

"This is the best thing I've ever eaten," he cried.

Arabella gave a nervous laugh. "Oh, don't be silly."

"I'm serious. This is wonderful. You should make a sign for them. That will get customers' attention." He took several more bites, quickly devouring the tart before wiping his mouth on his sleeve like a little boy. He raised his eyebrows and nodded. "I'll get the word out."

"Thank you, Gilbert," Mae said with a smile. "We'd appreciate it."

"Well, I will see you later." He nodded to each of them, but his gaze lingered on Arabella the longest. "Have a good day."

"Thank you," Arabella said, watching him turn and walk away.

"I'll make that sign," Laura said, taking a piece of cardboard from one of the boxes. She wrote *New: Cherry Tarts* in bold letters and hung the cardboard on the front of the table near their bakery sign.

"I have an idea," Arabella said. "On the sign, we should write *Post about us on social media for a free donut.*"

"What? Why?" Mae asked, flabbergasted.

"Don't underestimate the power of social media," Arabella said.

"I'll say. That's why we don't use it," Mae quipped.

"Well, Englishers do, which make up a large part of your customer base. Trust me, they will be happy to share about our baked goods online, which will let their friends know about us. This can work. Why not try it?"

"What if they lie? Or what if they post about us, take the free donut, then delete the post?" Laura asked curiously. Mae and Lydia gave her stern looks, and Laura shrugged innocently. "What? I've heard people talk about it."

"We can ask them to show us the post if you want."

"No. No, thank you. I don't want to be looking at cell phones," Lydia said, shaking her head.

"I'd rather not," Mae added.

"Well, then we will just have to take their word for it. About them deleting it, that is possible, but I think most people won't delete it. People love to post about food online. They do it all the time," Arabella explained.

"How do you know so much about social media all of the sudden, Damaris?" Lydia asked suspiciously.

"I...uh..." Arabella wracked her brain for an excuse. "Like Laura said, I just overhear people talking about it when I'm out and about, like at the Community Store."

"Hmm." Mae put her hands on her hips, looking around. She nodded. "Okay. Let's try it."

"Mother," Lydia argued.

"It's not like we are using social media ourselves. They are. I think it's a good idea, Damaris," Mae said with a smile.

"Really? Thanks," Arabella said. She turned to Lydia. "Want me to add that to the sign?"

Lydia reluctantly handed her the sign. "Fine."

Arabella took a black marker and added *Post about us on social media for a free donut* to the cardboard sign.

She looked up and noticed Gilbert leaving. Before he reached his buggy, he stopped to talk to several people. A moment later, those same people walked up to their booth.

"We heard your cherry tarts are divine," a woman said. "I'll take six, please. A dozen donuts. I heard those are good, too."

"Thank you. We are running a special today. If you post about us on social media, you get a free donut," Arabella told her.

"Really? I am happy to!" the woman said, whipping out her phone. "I'll do it right now."

As Mae bagged her order, two more people who Gilbert had talked to got in line behind the woman. They also bought cherry tarts along with some of the other types of sweets and were willing to post about the bakery on social media. They ambled away, stopping and chatting with people they seemed to know.

Soon, a line was forming at the Millers' booth. Everyone wanted cherry tarts and a free donut, and almost everyone bought at least one other type of item. Many people bought multiple other items, even a dozen baked goods or more. The line only got longer as people noticed a crowd forming and came to see what all the commotion was about.

"We're going to sell out of tarts soon and run out of donuts," Laura said as they scrambled to cash out the customers. "We should have made more!"

"We've sold so much of everything today," Mae added enthusiastically.

Sure enough, they sold out of cherry tarts, but customers kept coming to buy the other goods. They also ran out of donuts, but many people told them they would still post about them on social media, anyway.

By closing time, Mae collapsed in her chair and let out a long breath.

"That was the best day we've ever had here!" she cried, fanning her face. "Thanks to you, Damaris, for your new recipe and your social media idea. And to Gilbert for spreading the word."

Arabella's face heated. "I'm just glad it worked."

"We need to make more next time," Lydia said. "Maybe twice as many. We should do the social media special again and make even more donuts, or maybe give away something else instead. Maybe cinnamon rolls."

"Wow! I'm exhausted. I can't believe we almost sold out of everything!" Laura exclaimed, also falling onto her chair.

"I have to admit, Damaris, that was a good idea. I'm sorry I doubted it at first," Lydia said with a small smile.

Arabella smiled, grateful for the rare compliment from her. "Thanks, Lydia."

Arabella was also worn out, yet she felt the satisfaction of a hard day's work. But she wasn't done yet. She still had to go home and help Constance with cooking, doing chores, and taking care of the children for the rest of the day. She inwardly groaned, just wanting to go to bed and rub her tired feet.

But this was where she wanted to be—here in Unity. She never wanted to leave.

Chapter Sixteen

The next morning, Arabella awoke early with the rest of Damaris' family for church, which would start promptly at nine. She wasn't looking forward to sitting on a backless bench for three hours singing slow hymns and listening to long sermons.

After getting dressed, helping the younger children get ready, and helping make breakfast, they piled into the buggy. The children chatted happily, talking about which friends they were looking forward to playing with after church at the potluck lunch.

As Constance drove, Arabella sat beside her in the front and held a tray of her homemade donuts in her lap, not trusting herself to cook anything for the lunch.

Less than ten minutes later, they pulled into the church lot. Damaris hadn't had time to show Arabella the church but had taught her about all the customs and how the service would go. The Amish were normally known for having church services in people's homes, but here in Unity, they'd decided to build a church building instead.

As Arabella watched families file into the two-story wooden structure that also doubled as the school, her stomach tightened. What if people saw right through her? What if she accidentally did something stupid— or worse—offensive? What if she stood at the wrong time or knelt at the wrong time? Then they would know for sure she wasn't Damaris.

"Are you okay, Damaris?" Constance asked, glancing at Arabella.

"Of course," Arabella stammered. "Just tired. And no, I wasn't up late reading last night."

"For once." Constance chuckled and stopped the buggy, then climbed out to hitch up the horse. Arabella set her tray down on the seat so she could help the younger children climb out.

As she lifted Daisy out of the buggy and set her on the ground, another pair of larger hands reached for Desmond and lifted him out of the buggy as well.

Arabella turned to see Gilbert. Her heart leapt at the sight of him.

"Good morning," he said, smiling at her before spinning Desmond around. The boy giggled loudly, and Gilbert set him down. The children hurried off to see their friends, and Constance was already making her way inside the church.

"Thank you so much for telling those people about the cherry tarts," Arabella said. "It was so busy after that, we sold out of the tarts and almost everything else!"

"Wow! That's wonderful. I'm glad to help."

"Mae says it was the best day they've had at the market so far."

"It wasn't me, Damaris. It was your incredible baking skills. Also, the Millers told me about your social media special. I think that was a great idea, and it sure sounds like it was worth it. You're good at what you do, Damaris."

Her cheeks burned at his compliment, and she gave a shy smile.

Gilbert grinned, then leaned forward. "I've been thinking about our meeting behind the store," he said in a low voice, looking around to see if anyone could hear them. "I thought about it all night."

All night? Her cheeks burned again. Guilt rushed through her, but the feeling was overpowered by the way her heart soared whenever he was near.

"Me too," she whispered.

"May I see you after church?"

No. Of course not.

"I think so."

157

"Good morning!" a bright voice called.

They turned to see an older couple walking toward them.

"*Maam. Daed.* Good morning," Gilbert said to them, giving his mother a hug.

These were his parents? Arabella couldn't remember their names or if Damaris had even told her. She smiled at them, forgetting to speak for a moment. "Good morning," she said, guilt suddenly railing into her.

She was lying to their son, letting him think she was someone she wasn't.

"How are you, Damaris?" his mother asked.

"I'm good, thank you."

"I hear you've been busy at the bakery. Ernie here had two of your donuts and loved them." Gilbert's mother chuckled, nodding toward her husband.

"Hannah, how could I resist? I have a terrible sweet tooth. Those donuts were delicious," Ernie said.

Hannah and Ernie, Arabella thought, storing the names away in her memory. "Thank you. Glad you liked them."

"Well, we better get inside," Hannah said, and the couple walked away.

"See you after church." Gilbert gave Arabella another heart-melting grin before tipping his hat and walking away.

Arabella sighed, watching him go.

"Um...what just happened?"

Arabella spun around to see Ella Ruth standing behind her with wide eyes. "What exactly happened when you talked with him about not getting back together?"

"I...uh..." Arabella stammered, twisting the skirt of Damaris' dress in her hands.

"You told him no, right? That you can't get back together with him? Why did he look so happy just now?" Ella Ruth asked, her brows knit together in confusion. Realization lit up her face. "No. You didn't. You told him yes, didn't you? Why did you tell him yes?"

"I didn't say yes or no, technically." Arabella threw her hands up. "He wrapped his arms around me and I let him."

"Why?" Ella Ruth drew the word out. "Why didn't you say no?"

"I couldn't! I didn't want the moment to end. It felt so nice. Haven't you ever felt drawn to someone like that before? Well, I never have until I met him. I couldn't turn him down."

"No, I haven't. Not yet." Ella Ruth looked down at the ground.

"When you do, maybe you'll understand."

Ella Ruth met her eyes. "But you're leaving soon. How will you explain this to him? He's going to figure it out when Damaris comes back and wants nothing to do with him, and you're married to someone else."

A pang of guilt stabbed through Arabella's heart again at the thought of her deception and how she'd have to leave Gilbert and everyone here behind, probably never seeing them again.

How could she explain this to him? Should she tell him the truth now or later, when it was time for her to leave? Maybe she should tell him now, before things got too out of hand.

No matter how she looked at it, someone was going to get hurt. Maybe Emily was right. Maybe this was a terrible idea and they should have never done it.

"I don't know what I'm going to do, Ella Ruth. Do you think I should just tell him the truth now?" Arabella asked.

"I have no idea," Ella Ruth said. "But I do know the truth will set you free."

"Even when you know it'll hurt someone?"

"If you wait until you leave, you'll only hurt him so much worse."

"I know."

"Look, church is about to start. Let's go." After Arabella grabbed the tray of donuts from the back of the buggy, Ella Ruth looped her arm around Arabella's, and they hurried inside. When they walked through the door, several of the women greeted them, and Arabella just smiled and nodded, not having any idea who they were.

Many people were taking off their jackets and setting them on a long table in the back of the church. This half of the building clearly doubled as the schoolroom on weekdays, with the academic charts and children's artwork on the walls. There was a collapsible room divider pushed back against the wall, making the whole top floor one large room. Arabella imagined they used the divider on the weekdays when school was in session.

"Come on. Let's bring your donuts downstairs." Ella Ruth led Arabella down the steps to another open room with several large tables covered in food. There were sandwiches, pies, casseroles, salads, and more.

Arabella set her donuts down with the other desserts.

"Damaris, I heard your donuts are even better than they were before," a young woman said, grinning at her.

Who was this?

"Maria, that is so sweet of you to say," Ella Ruth said, glancing at Arabella to make sure she got the hint.

"Yes, thank you, Maria," Arabella said, glancing at Ella Ruth. "I've been learning so much from Laura and Lydia while baking with them."

"That's right," Laura said, sashaying up to Arabella. "Your baking has improved so much. It's almost like it improved overnight!"

The women laughed, but Arabella could only let out an unconvincing chuckle.

Another young woman joined them. "I heard you and Gilbert might be getting back together."

"Don't believe everything you hear, Charlotte," Ella Ruth said.

"I don't know why you let him go in the first place," Laura said, fanning her face. "He's so handsome."

"Shh!" Maria swatted at her playfully. "Not in church. You're too young for him, anyway."

Adriana, Damaris' sister-in-law, spoke up. "You two seemed like such a perfect couple. What's going on with you two?"

What should she tell them? Arabella bit her lip.

"Well?" Charlotte asked Arabella.

They looked at Arabella, who shrugged. She felt her face heating in a furious blush as she glanced around. When she saw Gilbert smiling at her from across the room, she couldn't help but smile back.

Adriana looked at her, then Gilbert. "Well, I guess that answers that question."

"No, no," Arabella protested. "I don't know exactly what's happening with us yet."

"You better tell him that," Adriana said. "Because from the way he's looking at you, you're not on the same page."

"Come on. Let's go upstairs and sit before the service starts," Ella Ruth said, taking Arabella's arm again and bringing her upstairs. They approached the benches, and she followed Ella Ruth to where her family was sitting, which was right next to Damaris' family, near the front. She would have rather sat in the back where no one could see her if she made a mistake.

They sat down as a man came to the front of the room and opened the service with prayer.

Arabella's mind kept wandering to the situation with Gilbert and what Ella Ruth had said about telling him the truth. Inwardly chiding herself for letting her mind wander, she concentrated on the service.

This was going to be a long three hours.

Ella Ruth handed her a book, the *Ausbund* songbook. Everyone opened their books and began singing hymns without any instrumental accompaniment. Even though there were no drums, no piano, no guitars, the music touched Arabella in a way she'd never been impacted before.

She understood most of the words of the German songs, though some of the Pennsylvania Dutch pronunciations sounded a little odd to her ears. Still, she felt the sincerity and the love for God from the congregation's voices.

Arabella closed her eyes and sang. Though she was usually shy about singing, at that moment, she just felt free. She let the music surround her, calm her, letting her know everything would work out.

Her parents had brought her to church when she was younger, but as the business took over their lives, they stopped going. Arabella had enjoyed church and the singing, reading the Bible, and listening to the sermons. It had filled her with a peace she hadn't known for years, and she longed for that again.

God, if you're there, can you show me what I should do? How can I make this situation right?

Arabella didn't really know how to pray, so she didn't know if she was doing it right, but she sent her silent prayer up with hope.

After several more hymns, a man who Arabella assumed was the bishop began to speak.

"The truth should always be told, even when it's uncomfortable," he said. "We should always put our trust in God that he will work things out for good."

Was he talking directly to her? Arabella looked around, wondering if she was the only one who felt that way.

God, is this you saying I should tell Gilbert the truth? Arabella prayed. *I know I've never prayed much before, but being here has opened my eyes. Please show me what I should do.*

***

That evening at dinner, Damaris once again sat between Arabella's grandmother and Stefan. Damaris wore a knee-length black dress with a real pearl necklace, so different from her normal attire.

"Everything is in place for your engagement dinner party tomorrow night," Helene said to her and Stefan.

Damaris almost choked on her salmon filet. "Tomorrow night?" she squeaked, then regretted saying anything.

"Did you forget, Arabella?" Helene demanded, and Stefan was looking at her with a perplexed look on his face.

"No. Of course not. The time just got away from me. That sounds lovely." She took her cloth napkin and dabbed at the corner of her mouth.

How had Arabella completely forgotten to mention this engagement dinner party?

"Good. Your dress is ready. I had it sent up to your room," Helene added.

"Thank you." Damaris nodded. If it was a formal gown, that could only mean it would be a formal party, and Damaris had no idea how to act at such an event. Sure, Arabella had taught her the basic table manners, but how had this event slipped her mind?

"Are you all right, Arabella?" Stefan asked. "You look a bit pale."

"Yes, I'm fine, really." Damaris continued to eat, hoping she was somewhat convincing. Elizabeth looked at her suspiciously from the corner of her eye.

She could see right through Damaris, couldn't she?

"Arabella has a lot on her shoulders," Elizabeth piped up. "It would be understandable even if she did forget the date of the party."

Damaris gave her a grateful smile.

After dinner, Damaris hurried up to Arabella's room. A long, formal gown was hanging in her room on the curtain rod. It was gold with elaborate beading on the bodice and a full tulle skirt.

Definitely for a formal event.

A knock sounded on her door.

"Come in."

Elizabeth opened the door and sauntered in.

"Tell me who you are and what you've done with Arabella," the elderly woman demanded, shaking a wrinkled finger at her vehemently.

Was she kidding? Or was she serious?

"You haven't been acting like Arabella at all. She wouldn't have forgotten the engagement party, and for some reason all of the sudden you like to read novels, something other than your morning devotionals. I know something isn't right," Elizabeth added. "Who forgets their own engagement party?"

"Fine, I'll tell you." Damaris quickly shut the door. "You're right. I'm not Arabella. My name is Damaris. I switched places with Arabella because she wanted some time away before her wedding."

The elderly woman stared at her, mouth agape. "I didn't literally mean that I thought you weren't Arabella, but this is quite interesting." She sat down on the bench at the end of Arabella's bed and patted the spot beside her. "Tell me everything right now."

Damaris explained the entire situation, and to her surprise, Elizabeth didn't interrupt her but listened intently the whole time.

"So, Arabella is in your Amish community pretending to be you? I should have known she'd do something like this. She's been known to go on escapades, but this one takes the cake." The elderly woman let out a loud laugh. "Well, I'm glad she's doing something for herself before marrying Stefan. Personally, I don't think her parents should have placed the fate of the company on her shoulders by asking her to marry a stranger. So, I think this switch is a wonderful idea, and I want to help."

"Really?"

"Of course. I won't tell anyone your secret."

Damaris let out a deep breath, relieved to have another person she could confide in who would keep her secret.

"You have no idea how to conduct yourself at a formal party with socialites and government officials in attendance, do you?" Elizabeth asked.

Damaris shook her head. "Not at all. I need your help, Mrs. Blackwood."

"Please, call me Elizabeth. I used to run Blackwood Bakery, you know, before I passed it on to my son. I've been to many social gatherings in my time, so I can teach you everything you need to know."

"But we only have one day," Damaris said. "How can I possibly learn everything?"

"We better get started then." A twinkle glimmered in Elizabeth's eye. "Just look at your posture. It's a dead giveaway that you're not Arabella."

"I have bad posture?"

"Not terrible, but it can be improved." Elizabeth walked to a nearby shelf and grabbed a book. "Here. Walk with this on your head. Once you get that, you can try it with your high heels on."

"That sounds nearly impossible."

"So does the story you just told me. Here. Do it."

Well, well, this woman was bossy. Damaris took the book and placed it on her head. Not even two steps later, the book fell.

"Oh, dear. I haven't even mentioned dancing."

"Dancing? Oh, no. I don't dance."

Elizabeth shook her head and clicked her tongue. "We have a lot of work to do."

***

After lunch at church, families stayed to mingle for a while before eventually packing up their food and children and going home. As Constance started gathering up Damaris' younger siblings, Gilbert walked over to them.

"Are you ready to walk home?" he asked.

Arabella turned to Constance. "Do you mind if I walk home with Gilbert?"

"Of course not," Constance said, waving her hand. "You two go on ahead."

Arabella was almost hoping Constance would say no so she wouldn't have to tell him what she was about to tell him.

They walked out of the building, and she followed him to the trees, where he started down a path through the woods. Maybe it was a shortcut.

"Your donuts were a hit at church." Gilbert chuckled. "All my friends were raving about them."

"Thanks." Arabella pulled her jacket tighter around her.

The path through the trees was embellished with the warm, fiery colors of the leaves, but Arabella barely noticed as she searched for the right words to tell Gilbert the truth.

"Are you okay, Damaris?" Gilbert asked, reaching for her hand.

"Yes," she said, smiling when his hand found hers. "There's something I have to tell you, Gilbert. I'm so sorry for what I'm about to say."

He stopped and turned to her with a pleading look in his eyes. "Are you breaking up with me? Because if you are, I don't think I can bear that again."

"It's not that," Arabella blurted. Was she? What was even happening between them, really? "I have to tell you that I'm not who you think I am."

"Of course, I know who you are. We grew up together. You're Damaris Kauffman. You're the girl who'd rather read a book than sneak out and could always climb a tree better than any of the boys. You're the one I always saw as a friend until I realized how blind I was." He ran a thumb over her knuckles, and she shivered.

If only he was talking about her.

She took a deep breath and blurted out the words before she could change her mind. "I'm not Damaris. My name is Arabella Blackwood."

Chapter Seventeen

Gilbert just stared at Arabella, so she continued in a rush, before she lost her nerve. "I look just like Damaris, so we secretly switched places. I live in Germany, and I'm supposed to marry a man I don't love in a few weeks. I don't want to marry him, but I have to in order to save my family's bakery company. I just wanted to be someone else before I started my new life." She sucked in a breath, slowly turning away, expecting him to storm off. Would he call her a liar? Would he hate her?

Gilbert dropped her hands. "What?"

"I never meant to hurt anyone, especially you, and I didn't expect to fall for you, but I am. If you never want to see me again, I understand," Arabella said, staring at the ground.

"I see."

"That day in the store when I packed up the two dozen donuts for you was the first time we met."

"Who else knows?" he asked softly.

"No one else knows except Ella Ruth."

Gilbert sighed and slowly nodded. "I need some time to think about this, but your secret is safe with me."

As he turned and walked away, Arabella felt as though a buggy had fallen on top of her. Did he hate her? Would he ever want to speak to her again?

What if he exposed her secret?

***

Arabella's maid Jamie helped Damaris dress for the engagement party, for which Damaris was grateful. It would have been nearly impossible to get the huge gown on all by herself, especially buttoning it in the back. At least it had sleeves and wasn't a strapless, because Damaris would have refused to wear a dress that showed her shoulders.

"You look beautiful, Miss Blackwood," Jamie said with a grin as they both stared at Damaris' reflection in the mirror. She barely recognized herself in the gold gown as she ran her hands over the intricate beadwork. Jamie had curled and pinned up her hair into an elegant updo with a few curled tendrils framing her face. She'd borrowed one of Arabella's necklaces, but used pieces of her hair to cover up her ears, which weren't pierced.

"How about these earrings?" Jamie asked, holding up a pair of earrings that matched the necklace.

Oh, no. Damaris shook her head. "No, thanks."

"Oh, but it would look so nice." Jamie pushed back the hair that had been covering one of her ears. "Your ears... Did the piercings close up?"

"Uh...yes. I guess they did," Damaris stammered.

"But it hasn't been that long since you've worn earrings. How is that possible?"

"I don't know. Weird, isn't it?" Hopefully, no one else would notice.

"Hmm. That is strange. Do you need anything else?"

"No, that's okay. Thank you, Jamie, and for your help. I couldn't have gotten this dress on without you." Damaris chuckled.

"My pleasure, Miss Blackwood."

"You can call me Da—I mean, you can call me Arabella." Damaris bowed her head, hoping her blunder hadn't been too obvious.

169

"I'm supposed to call you Miss Blackwood, but thank you." Jamie checked the clock on the wall. "It's time to go down. If you don't need anything else, I'm needed downstairs."

"Of course. Thank you." Damaris nodded and Jamie hurried out. Just then, Elizabeth burst into the room, followed by Emily. They both gasped when they saw Damaris.

"Wow! You look amazing!" Emily cried.

"Just lovely," Elizabeth said, clasping her hands together. "You are a vision."

"You don't think it's too much?" Damaris touched her hair self-consciously. "I feel so...not me."

"Nonsense." Elizabeth waved a hand. "Everything is perfect. Besides, you're not you. Tonight, you're Arabella."

"And don't forget it," Emily added.

"Remember everything I taught you," Elizabeth said.

Damaris put her hands to her temples, her head swirling with the manners and dance steps Elizabeth had taught her. "I don't know if I can do this." She sat down in the chair in front of the vanity, feeling slightly nauseated. Maybe the dress was too tight, cutting off her oxygen.

"Don't worry. You have us to help you. Now let's go. They're about to announce you as a couple," Elizabeth said, taking her hand and helping her up. Before Damaris could protest, Ms. Libby bustled in.

"Time to go," Ms. Libby said, waving her hand toward the door without a smile. "You don't want to be late to your own engagement party, Miss Blackwood."

The three of them whisked Damaris out of the room and down the stairs.

As Damaris walked toward the ballroom, she felt like a lamb being led to the slaughter. What if she made a complete fool out of herself, making Arabella look terrible?

As they turned a corner, the large ballroom doors appeared, and Stefan waited in front of them. He was dressed in a regal black suit and tie with his brown hair combed back. Damaris' heart felt as though it might burst at the sight of him. He looked so incredibly handsome.

"I'm needed in the kitchen to make sure everything is in order," Ms. Libby said, then hurried down the hall.

At that same moment, Elizabeth and Emily both turned and walked away swiftly, smiling at her over their shoulders.

She was alone with Stefan.

"You look absolutely beautiful, Arabella," Stefan said, coming toward her. He bent and took her hand, gently kissing it. Pleasant sparks seem to shoot up her arm at his touch, and she wished more than anything he'd take her into his arms and kiss her.

But he wouldn't really be kissing her—he would think he was kissing Arabella.

"Thank you," she managed to utter. "You look handsome yourself."

A furious blush crept up his neck, and he tugged at his collar. "Thank you. I'm so glad to be here with you tonight. I'm really looking forward to this."

No. She couldn't do this. She had to tell him the truth, before everyone here was led to believe they were a happy couple about to enter wedded bliss. Before she continued to deceive him in front of everyone.

"Stefan, there's something I need to tell you—" she began, but just then, the doors opened.

Stefan just smiled and took her hand. "We can talk about it later. I promise."

171

She nodded, feeling bile creep up her throat.

"The future Mrs. and Mr. Stefan Castle," a loud voice announced, and Damaris let Stefan lead her through the wide double doors. Dozens of guests greeted them with enthusiastic applause, with Arabella's parents and Stefan's father right in the front, beaming.

And there were news crews there with cameras flashing. She should have realized the media would be there, covering the story of the two largest bakery companies in Germany merging.

How could she tell Stefan the truth now, with everyone here? She'd just have to get through tonight and tell him after the party.

Dinner was announced, and everyone was seated at round tables except for Damaris, Stefan, Mr. Castle, Elizabeth, and Arabella's parents, who were sitting at one long table in the front of the room.

The first course was brought out, and Damaris felt as though she was in a fog as they ate. Many people came over throughout the meal to offer their congratulations, and she didn't know any of them. Fortunately, Elizabeth was seated next to Damaris. Elizabeth often gave Damaris cues, like nudging Damaris if she ate with the wrong fork, which Damaris was grateful for.

After the meal was over, the dancing began, including old-fashioned formal group dances. Elizabeth had done her best to teach Damaris the steps, but they were only mixed up in her head. She fumbled throughout the first dance and almost ran off the dance floor in embarrassment. Stefan tried to guide her throughout the dance, but it was no use.

When the music finally ended, Damaris hurried away and sat down. Stefan went over to the band and spoke with them for a moment, then joined her.

"Are you okay?" Stefan asked. "Did you forget the steps?"

"Yes. I'm sorry. I just can't focus because of everything going on. I hope I didn't embarrass you too much."

"Not at all. Don't worry." He sat down next to her. "That's completely understandable."

"When this party is over, I have something really important to tell you."

"Okay. But for now, I have something very important to say to you." Something glimmered in his eyes—hope and anticipation—as he reached into his pocket, pulling out a small black box.

Damaris wanted to shout for joy, but her heart sank to her toes. Was he really about to officially propose to her, right in front of all these people?

He stood up and nodded to the band, who stopped playing. Stefan cleared his throat and began speaking.

"Can I have everyone's attention?" he said, suddenly seeming nervous as she noticed his hands shaking.

Everyone stopped talking and dancing and turned to him, staring at both of them.

He took her hand, and she got up from her chair, standing beside him. Damaris' heart raced, her palms sweating as she realized just exactly what was about to happen. She wanted to dart out of the room, but it was too late now, with everyone watching.

"I want to thank you for coming to our engagement party. I'm not so good with words, so I'll keep this short," he said, swiping a hand across his suddenly sweaty forehead. "As many of you know, Blackwood Bakery and Castle Cakes will be merging when Arabella and I are married. As some of you may have noticed, Arabella isn't wearing a ring yet. That's because I haven't given it to her yet. I've been waiting for this special moment and also to officially ask her."

Stefan turned to Damaris, and her heart lurched. She felt as though she was floating as he got down on one knee in front of her and took her hand in his, yet at the same time, her deception made her sick.

"Arabella, I admire you, I care for you, and I love you. Will you marry me?"

Chapter Eighteen

Damaris gulped as Stefan's eyes pleaded with hers, but they were filled with such sincerity and—was that love?

Could it really be love? Did he really love her or the idea of Arabella Blackwood, socialite and local celebrity heiress?

If he knew who she was—just a simple Amish woman from Maine who had no company, wealth, or status—would he still love her?

Damaris' eyes wandered from Stefan's face to the people, especially Arabella's parents and Stefan's father, watching them expectantly, waiting for her to say yes.

They thought she was someone she wasn't—especially Stefan. But if she ran out in tears, like she wanted to so badly, she'd let everyone down and the business agreement might fall through. She couldn't be the reason Arabella's family lost their company.

Though the tears threatened to overflow, she gave a fake smile and said as confidently as she could, "Yes."

The room erupted in applause as Stefan slipped the ring on her finger, wrapping her in his arms. At the comfort of his warm embrace, she couldn't keep the burning tears at bay any longer, and they ran down her cheeks. Hopefully, everyone would think they were tears of joy and not tears of guilt.

As several people came up to them to congratulate them, all Damaris wanted to do was run out and find a place where she could be alone and cry, but she couldn't find a way out past the people without making a fool of herself.

Stefan squeezed her hand. "Are you okay, Arabella?"

She wiped her eyes. "Yes. I'm sorry. I was so surprised. That was lovely."

"I hope I didn't embarrass you by putting you on the spot like that."

She shook her head. "No. Actually, it was really sweet." She hoped one day, her soulmate would propose to her like that, but since she was Amish, there would be no public proposal and there certainly wouldn't be a ring involved.

At the thought of another man besides Stefan proposing to her, her gut twisted. She didn't want anyone else to propose to her except for him.

And he was the one man she couldn't ever have.

At that realization, the overwhelming urge to run overtook her. She let go of his hand and darted away, apologizing as she made her way through the crowd of people toward the door.

Once she got through the large ballroom doors and saw no one was in the hall, she ran as fast as she could in her high heels toward the closest door that led outside. The chilly night air assaulted her as she gulped in deep breaths, feeling as though she'd been suffocated.

Just breathe, she told herself. *Somehow, everything will work out.*

As she heard footsteps coming down the hall, panic rose within her, and she turned and bolted toward the stables. Hopefully, no one would look for her there. Once she got inside, she leaned against the wall and took in more deep breaths.

A distressed whinny came from a nearby stall. She walked closer. Was that the pregnant mare?

Damaris peered into the open stall to see the stable hand next to the mare.

"What's going on? Is she okay?" Damaris asked.

"She's in labor," the stable hand said. "The veterinarian is really sick, and the other nearby veterinarian is on vacation. The next closest one is hours away. I don't know what to do." The young man seemed to be only about eighteen or nineteen years old and looked worried as he stroked the horse's neck.

"What's your name?"

"Zack," said the stable hand.

"Well, Zack, I'm here to help." She grabbed the pair of long medical gloves that he was holding. When she put them on, they reached her elbows.

"I mean no disrespect, ma'am, but do you know anything about delivering foals?" Zack asked.

She smiled. "On my last trip, I stayed with Amish families, and they taught me about this. Don't worry. I know what I'm doing."

***

Stefan felt completely abandoned as his fiancée ran out of the room, and when everyone looked at him with concern and questions in their eyes, he felt his face burning red.

Why had she run out like that? Maybe he shouldn't have proposed to her in front of everyone. He thought it would be romantic, like he'd read about in novels.

"What's going on?" his father asked him. "She looked upset."

"I don't know."

"You should go after her," Helene said. "I'm sure it was just the attention that overwhelmed her. She'll be fine."

"I hope so," Stefan's father said with a grunt. "I hope she isn't having second thoughts." He shook his head disapprovingly.

"I'm sure it's not that, Dad," Stefan said, but in his heart, he wondered if that was exactly what it was. Why else would she have run off crying like that?

177

"Go," his father urged, shooing him away. Stefan walked to the doors and went into the hallway. She was nowhere in sight. Maybe she'd gone up to her room. He ran to the staircase. Concern filled him. Was she really just overwhelmed, or could she be regretting saying yes to him in front of everyone?

After checking her room and asking several of the staff if they'd seen her, Stefan still hadn't found her. An idea struck him, and he felt like a dolt for not realizing it before.

The stables. She was probably in the stables.

With newfound energy, he dashed back down the stairs and out the door. When he reached the stables, he heard talking and commotion in one of the stalls. He walked closer to see his fiancée in her ball gown with gloves that reached her elbows, covered in blood and who knew what else, smiling and laughing with the stable hand as the mare nuzzled her newborn foal.

"What... What just happened?" Stefan asked, cautiously coming closer.

"She delivered the foal," the stable hand said. "Great work, ma'am."

"Thank you," she said with a nod. She knelt beside the foal and took off the gloves. "Thanks for keeping the mare calm."

"I didn't do anything," the teenage boy said with a laugh.

"Arabella, how did you know how to do that?" Stefan asked.

Just then, several footsteps sounded at the door of the barn. Stefan turned to see the camera crew headed right for them.

Oh no.

They crowded around the stall, snapping photos of his fiancée, who was still kneeling beside the foal in her ruined ball gown. When she saw the photographers, she covered her face and turned away.

"Arabella, did you deliver the foal?" one reporter asked.

"Why did you run out of the ballroom?" another asked.

Several more of them assaulted her with questions before Stefan took her hand and pulled her out of the stall, shoving past any of the reporters who stood in his way. They had no right to bombard her like that, especially if she didn't want her photo pasted on every local tabloid and newspaper.

Ms. Libby hurried into the barn, then gasped in horror. "Arabella! What on earth happened? How dare you run out of the party like that? Now you've ruined your gown."

Enough is enough, Stefan thought. He pulled on her hand, leading her away.

They burst out of the barn and ran across the field, down the hill. Out of breath, they finally stopped and sat down by a tree, hidden by the hill.

"Wow. Thank you. That happened so fast," she said, her frown finally faded and replaced with a smile.

"How on earth did you know how to deliver a foal, Arabella?" Stefan asked once he caught his breath.

"From the Amish families. They deliver foals on their farms all the time," she explained. "Thanks for getting me out of there. It was overwhelming."

"I could tell you were upset. Those reporters shouldn't have done that. I'm sorry I couldn't get you out sooner. I'm sure your photo will be in tabloids and in newspapers tomorrow, not to mention all over social media. Our parents won't be happy about it."

She shrugged. "Nothing we can do about it now." She let out a laugh.

"What's so funny?" He chuckled.

She looked down at her ruined dress, which now also had hay sticking to it. "I look terrible. Ms. Libby was right—I completely ruined my dress. But it was totally worth it to deliver that foal." She smiled.

His heart swelled with admiration for her. "That's why I love you, Arabella. You always think of others first, even baby horses."

Her smile quickly faded.

"What's wrong? Why did you run out of the ballroom?"

"Oh, I'm so sorry about that. I was just feeling so overwhelmed. Everyone was talking to us at once, and I started to feel claustrophobic. I had to get some air. I hope you understand," she said apologetically.

He nodded, filled with relief. "Yes, of course. You said you had something important to tell me. Can you tell me now?"

She turned away. "Oh, it's nothing. I just…I've been really enjoying spending time with you." Her cheeks turned red, and he smiled at the pretty sight.

"The ring looks lovely on you," he murmured, taking her hand in his. She slowly looked up at him.

"I meant what I said in the ballroom, Arabella. I love you. I didn't expect to ever feel anything for you, but you've shown me what love is. I hope one day you'll feel the same way about me. Do you think you ever could?"

He knew he was asking a lot, but still, hope rose up within him. Why would a beautiful woman like her love someone like him? He didn't deserve her.

Yet, why was she looking at him like that, with longing in her eyes? Why was she leaning closer to him, letting her gaze fall to his lips?

The realization that she was about to kiss him ignited electricity through his veins. He wanted to pull her into his arms suddenly, but he didn't want to scare her away. Instead, he slowly leaned toward her, closer and closer, until her lips touched his.

She was sitting beside him; she was turned to face him and lifted her hand to hold the side of his face. He wrapped his arm around her waist, pulling her closer as he kissed her. This was his first kiss, and he had no idea if he was doing it right, so he pulled away to look at her face. Her eyes still closed, she was smiling, so he figured he wasn't doing too terribly.

More confident, he reached up to comb his fingers through her hair, which had fallen down while they had been running from the stables. It was just as soft and silky as he'd imagined, and he let the strands glide between his fingers as she let out a sigh.

He pulled away. "That was my first kiss," he whispered.

"Mine too."

"Really? I find that hard to believe."

"It's true." She blushed.

"Maybe it's old-fashioned, but I've always wanted to save my first kiss for the person I'm going to marry. So, I've been waiting a long time."

"That is so sweet," she said with a sigh. Her smile faded again. "I'm sorry. I shouldn't have kissed you."

"Why are you sorry? We're engaged." Why was she doing this again—acting as though she loved him one minute then pushing him away the next? "Arabella, why are you so confusing? You act like you're falling in love with me, but then you apologize for kissing me. How do you really feel about me, right here, right now? I want to know."

She turned to him, tears in her eyes.

This was the most confusing woman he'd ever met.

"Do you want to marry me, Arabella? I mean, do you just want to save the business, or do you actually want to spend the rest of your life with me at all?" Stefan asked, more persistent.

"Ugh!" She let out a frustrated growl and stood up. "I can't."

"You can't what?"

"I can't keep doing this," she muttered, barely above a whisper.

"Arabella, what are you talking about? What is going on? You just kissed me like you love me, and it was amazing. Now you're acting like you don't want to marry me. I'm really confused here," he said, frustration causing his voice to crack. "If you don't love me, I understand. I just want to know."

She burst into tears, stood up, and sprinted away, her gown trailing behind her.

Stefan shook his head and let his head fall into his hands. He still had no idea how she felt about him.

God, why is she acting like this? Does she love me, or am I just fooling myself? he prayed.

Yes. She was truly the most confusing woman on earth.

***

Arabella was doing chores in the barn when she heard a knock coming from the open doorway. She looked up to see Gilbert standing there, giving a small wave.

"Do you have time to go for a walk?" he asked.

"Of course." Anxiety shot through her. Would he tell her it was over, that he never wanted to speak to her again? That he would tell the whole church her secret?

They left the barn and began walking through the woods. Arabella asked, "Are you mad at me for keeping the truth from you?"

"No, I'm not mad. I understand why you did it. You didn't want anyone to know. I'm sure you didn't want Damaris to get in trouble."

Arabella let out a long breath, relieved. So, he didn't hate her after all. "Yes. That was a big part of it."

"I don't care that you're not Damaris. I want you, the woman I met who sold me the best donuts in the world."

"Really?" Arabella smiled up at him. He took her hand and gently squeezed, making her heart race.

"I knew something was different when I first met you in the store. No offense to Damaris' baking, but your donuts are out of this world. But it wasn't just the donuts. I knew the moment I saw you that you were the most beautiful woman I've ever seen, inside and out. I couldn't figure out what was different. I just want to get to know you better."

A blush tinged her cheeks. "Thanks."

"First, I have an important question to ask. I value my relationship with God above everything else, and so I have to ask you... Do you also have a relationship with God, Arabella?"

"Yes, I do, and I'm so glad you do too. That is also very important to me."

"Oh, good." Gilbert let out a sigh of relief. "So, this man you're betrothed to...you don't want to marry him?"

"No, not at all. My parents expect me to, though. We don't know how else to save the company. His father promised to pay our debts as our wedding gift."

"What if we found another way?" Gilbert asked. "You shouldn't marry someone else if you don't want to."

"I don't think I have a choice."

"Of course, you have a choice. Do you want to be with him or me?" He stopped walking and took her by the arms and pulled her close to him, then wrapped her in an embrace. She closed her eyes, taking in his sawdust smell.

"I want to be with you, Gilbert," Arabella whispered. "And I don't want to leave here."

"Then we will find a way, Arabella."

She smiled when he said her name—her real name. It sounded like smooth velvet on his lips, caressing her ears, and she savored it like the last bite of a chocolate cake.

Arabella didn't want it to end.

All too soon, they reached Damaris' house. Arabella smiled as she watched Gilbert walk away, leaving her standing in Damaris' driveway.

The children were playing in the yard, so Gilbert had only quickly squeezed her hand and said a quick goodbye. She wished he had kissed her.

She approached the front door and was about to turn the handle when she heard voices. She stopped.

"I have no idea what's going on with Damaris lately," she heard Constance say. "The other day she told me she only saw Gilbert as a friend, and now she seems like she's in love with him again."

"Well, people change," she heard a woman's voice say. "Maybe she's realized how much of a catch he is and is finally committed to him."

"She's old enough to be married by now, but I don't want to rush her. But the Lord knows with my husband passed away and Dominic married, I want to make sure Damaris is well taken care of. I want my children to be well taken care of. I'm not getting any younger."

"Of course, Constance. That's understandable."

"Another thing is her cooking is suddenly terrible while her baking has greatly improved overnight," Constance said, and Arabella imagined her shaking her head. "It is so strange. She just doesn't seem like herself at all."

Arabella backed away from the door. Was it obvious? How long before Damaris' family figured it out?

She walked away from the house, toward the woods, so she could check her phone. She gasped when she saw she had five missed calls from Damaris. Immediately, she called her back.

"Arabella?" Damaris said when she picked up the phone.

"Damaris! What's wrong?"

"So much has happened. At your engagement party, Stefan proposed and gave me the ring. When everyone crowded around us, I ran out because I felt so terrible about lying to him. Then, I kissed him. I'm completely falling for him. What is wrong with me?" A sob escaped her.

"Oh, wow. Okay, Damaris, calm down. We can figure this out."

"I should come home before I completely ruin everything, including the business agreement. I can't keep this up much longer. I can't hide my feelings for him, especially when he's so open with me. If your parents or Stefan's father find out, there's no way they'll want to proceed with the wedding and merging the companies," Damaris said.

"Well, you've got a point there," Arabella said, a knot forming in her stomach. "But I don't want to come home."

"What?" Damaris retorted. "Why?"

"Because… I told Gilbert the truth and he was so understanding. We want to be together."

"Oh, my goodness," Damaris said with a groan. "But how would that ever work when you're betrothed to Stefan, the one I'm falling for? This is so much more complicated than I could have ever imagined." She sighed.

"I know. I don't know what to do. All I know is I don't want to leave, not now, after I've told Gilbert everything and he still wants to be with me." Arabella turned when she heard children's voices coming closer. Damaris' siblings were running right toward the woods, where she was standing. "Your siblings are coming. I've got to go."

185

"Arabella, wait!"

Arabella ended the call and shoved the cell phone into her jacket pocket right before the children burst through the trees, laughing and chasing each other.

Chapter Nineteen

Damaris threw the cell phone on the bed with an angry growl of frustration. Now what? There was a knock on the door, and Damaris opened it to see Emily and Elizabeth.

"Oh, thank heavens," she said, ushering them inside.

"What on earth happened? Why did you run out of the ballroom like that?" Elizabeth asked.

"And why is there blood and straw all over your gown? Did you get hurt?" Emily asked.

"I was just about to change. I'm fine. I delivered a foal in the stables." Damaris turned to grab some clothes out of the closet.

"What?" Emily cried. "Okay, you need to tell us everything."

"I will, but help me get out of this dress first, will you?" Damaris turned around so Emily could undo the buttons in the back. Afterward, Damaris grabbed a change of clothes and changed behind the closet door while she explained. When she came out from behind the door, Emily and Elizabeth were staring at her.

"You kissed him?" Emily asked.

"Well, yes."

"Then you ran away again," Elizabeth added.

Damaris nodded sheepishly.

"Poor guy. He must be completely confused with your mixed signals." Emily shook her head.

"I know." Damaris fell on the bed. "This is a disaster, and it's all my fault."

A knock sounded on the door, and Emily went to answer it.

A maid stood at the door, bowing her head. "Stefan is downstairs and wishes to see Arabella."

Damaris gave Emily a panicky look. Emily shrugged.

"Tell him I'm not feeling well and I can't see him," Damaris said.

"Yes, ma'am." The maid nodded. Emily closed the door and turned to Damaris.

"Sorry. I can't see him now. Not after ruining everything. I should go before I make more of a mess. I am falling in love with him, and I can't show it because when Arabella comes back, she won't love him at all. She has no idea what a wonderful man he is. I don't think she will ever appreciate him." Damaris sat up to see both women giving her sympathetic looks. "What should I do? Arabella doesn't want to come home yet. She wants to be with Gilbert. She told him the truth, and he's fine with it."

"What can you do? If you leave again before she comes back, Stefan's father might think Arabella has cold feet and call off the agreement. You have to wait until she wants to come home," Elizabeth advised.

"But what if she doesn't ever want to come back?"

Emily said, "I know Arabella. She will do the right thing."

"What if the right thing for her is staying in Unity with Gilbert?" Damaris asked.

"I don't think she'd want to let her parents lose the entire company so she can be with her Amish man in Maine," Emily said with a chuckle. "She will realize her duty and return home."

"Damaris, dear, right now all you can do is keep up the charade, or our family will lose everything. Can you do it for a little longer? Please? If you leave or tell the truth now, everything will fall through and the company will go under." Elizabeth took Damaris' hand as she pleaded with her. "Please. I know it's hard, but it is only for a bit longer."

Damaris took a deep breath. Seeing the desperation in the older woman's eyes, she couldn't refuse her. "Of course. Of course, I will."

There was another knock at the door, and this time it was much louder.

The three women glanced at each other before the door was opened by Helene Blackwood. Damaris' stomach lurched at the sight of Helene's angry stare trained right on her.

"We will let you two talk," Elizabeth said, giving Emily a look before they both hurried out. Damaris watched them go, desperately wishing they'd stay, but from the look on Helene's face, she wanted to speak with Damaris alone.

Helene shook her head and sat down on the bench at the end of the bed. "Arabella, you've made a royal mess out of everything tonight. Why did you leave the party, running out like that? Then I heard you were in the stables, delivering a foal. What on earth? How do you know how to do that, first of all? I heard the paparazzi and camera crews found you."

Did she know about the kiss? Damaris wasn't sure, but she wouldn't mention it.

Damaris took a deep breath. "I'm very sorry. I just needed some air at the party. Everyone was crowding around us, congratulating us. About the foal, the veterinarian was sick and it was an emergency. I learned so much farm work when I was staying with the Amish. I didn't mean for my photo to be taken. That was the last thing I wanted. After my dress was ruined, I couldn't return to the party."

"Well, I'm sure it will be in the papers and tabloids. You must have looked a fright." Helene clicked her tongue. "And there are still guests downstairs. Why are you dressed like that?" She waved a disapproving hand at the casual sweatpants Damaris was wearing.

"I wasn't even thinking about the party. Do you want me to go back down? I'm not sure I can face everyone again after running out like that. They must think—"

"Yes, there are many rumors flying around. Most people are thinking you're having second thoughts about Stefan. Poor young man. He told me he tried to see you a few minutes ago and you refused. Tell me, Arabella. Are you having second thoughts?"

"No, that's not it at all. I just didn't want to see him because I was so embarrassed."

"Well, I think that he thinks you're about to back out of the wedding. Are you? If you are, you should tell me now, before we embarrass ourselves in front of the entire country." Helene set her hands in her lap, giving Damaris a cold stare.

"You said it was my choice." That was what Arabella had told her. "But it doesn't seem that way at all. Even if I did back out, would you support my decision? Would you still love me?" She had to know, for Arabella's sake, what would happen if Arabella backed out of the agreement.

"What a preposterous question." Helene looked away.

"Please, tell me the truth."

Helene slowly turned back to her. "Arabella, your father and I will always love you, no matter what. Yes, we would be hurt personally and financially if you back out, but we don't want to force you into marrying Stefan. We would support you either way, but it would be a huge embarrassment and devastating loss if you backed out."

"You're putting so much pressure on her."

Damaris cringed. Thankfully, Helene didn't seem to notice Damaris' blunder. "I mean…on me," she added quickly. "You say I have a choice, but I don't, really." Damaris let the words spill out, not knowing if Arabella had already spoken these things to her mother before.

"We don't have any other options, Arabella. I'm sorry." Helene looked truly defeated, staring down at her lap. "If we lose the company, we lose everything."

"Not everything. You'd still have your daughter."

Helene faced her. "Of course. We'd have each other. But we'd have to sell this estate, the vehicles, let go of the staff—everything would have to go. This company has been in the family for generations. I'd hate to see it go under."

"Me too. But an arranged marriage?" Damaris shook her head. "Maybe it's not worth it to sacrifice your daughter's happiness and entire future."

Helene looked at her lap again, biting her lip, as if contemplating Damaris' point of view. Was she reconsidering?

"I just need to know if you still plan on marrying Stefan so I know what to tell his father, Arabella," Helene said coldly without looking at her.

What should she do? Refuse? Say yes? What would Arabella want her to say?

"Yes, of course. The wedding is still on," she said in a panic.

"Thank you. Now, you have a very distressed fiancé pacing around downstairs. I suggest you put on a nice dress, speak with him, then join us again at your engagement party." Helene went into the closet and came back out with a light blue formal gown. "You wore this to last year's New Year's Eve ball, but it will have to do." She handed her the dress, gave a curt nod, and left the room as swiftly as she had come.

What a cold woman. Damaris shivered, wondering what it would be like to have a mother like that instead of the endearing, caring mother she had at home.

Poor Arabella. She didn't deserve this, to be forced to marry a stranger. No one deserved that.

Damaris put on the long, shimmering blue gown. She checked her reflection in the mirror. Her hair had come loose from its updo, but was now falling around her shoulders in loose curls. It was good enough. She ran a hand through it, put on some heels, and hurried downstairs.

Stefan was pacing in the hallway, as Helene had said. When he saw her, his face lit up, but he wasn't smiling. "Arabella? Are you going to return to the party?"

"Yes. My mother asked me to. I should, after leaving the way I did. I don't want people thinking I'm having second thoughts."

"Are you?"

"No, Stefan, I'm not. I'm sorry I've been so confusing. My parents are putting a lot of pressure on me, and with the paparazzi and all the people here tonight, it was too much." She shook her head, staring at the toes of her shoes.

Stefan gently touched her chin and lifted her face so she was looking into his warm brown eyes. "I understand, Arabella. I just want you to be honest with me and tell me exactly how you feel about me."

Damaris glanced around. No one was in sight. Apparently, everyone was still in the ballroom.

She took in a deep shaky breath. No, she couldn't hide her feelings from him any longer. "You want to know how I feel about you? I feel like I'm floating when you look at me. I want to be with you all the time, and I have never felt so at ease talking to someone before. I am falling in love with you, Stefan."

His hand found its way into her hair again as he pulled her head closer to his, bringing his lips down to touch hers. He gently kissed her once more, filling her entire being with sparking electricity, reaching to the tips of her fingers and her toes, even though they were crammed into high heels that were a bit too small.

When she pulled away, she smiled. "I'm glad we have that cleared up."

"Me too. Let's go in there and reassure everyone this wedding is still on." He grinned, offering her his elbow. She took it, and though she wanted to forget everything else but him, the worry and guilt still niggled at her.

Was she making the mistake of a lifetime? Would he ever speak to her again after this?

Before she could reconsider, the ballroom doors opened, and a hush fell over the room as they walked in together, arm in arm. After a moment, everyone resumed talking, but many of the guests kept on glancing over at them, as if talking about them.

Stefan seemed to sense it too. "I can see the rumors spreading now. Maybe we should put their minds at ease." He gave her a mischievous smile and bent down to kiss her, right in front of everyone.

Damaris forgot about everyone else in the room—all she was aware of was how Stefan's surprisingly strong arms felt around her, how sweet his lips were on hers. When he pulled away, everyone began clapping.

"I think that worked," she said breathlessly.

He took her hand, beaming as they made their way around the room, thanking everyone for coming and accepting congratulations.

Philip walked up to them after several minutes. "I was a bit worried there, Arabella. Your mother explained to me that you needed some air and ended up delivering a foal in the stables. I'm sure you understand it seemed like you were having second thoughts when you ran out. I'm sorry I jumped to conclusions."

"I understand, Mr. Castle. I do apologize. I was feeling very overwhelmed with so many people. I am very introverted."

"I see. Well, I am glad to see you two together. You seem very happy." He smiled.

"We are," Stefan said, grinning down at her.

Philip looked surprised. "Well. That is good news. Enjoy the rest of your evening."

Another group of people approached them, and Damaris pasted on her party smile. This was going to be a long evening.

***

The next morning, Arabella woke up and quickly checked her phone before getting dressed and doing Damaris' chores. Her eyebrows shot up when she saw several panicky texts from Damaris.

I can't do this anymore. I told Stefan I'm falling in love with him and kissed him again, then he kissed me in front of everyone at the engagement party. We need to switch back before I ruin everything!

Please answer as soon as you can. I know you don't want to leave Gilbert, but if we don't fix this soon, the whole business agreement will fall apart and your family will lose the business, and it will be my fault.

Arabella! Text me back! I'm panicking over here!

Arabella sighed and rolled her eyes. Damaris didn't seem like a drama queen in person, but she sure did over texting. Arabella dialed her number and Damaris picked up right away.

"Finally!" Damaris snapped. "What took you so long?"

"There is a time difference, remember? And I'm not able to check my phone much here."

"This is an emergency! I can't keep this up much longer. We have to switch places again. How long did you think we could do this for? Doesn't my family suspect anything?"

"I think your mother is starting to suspect something, with the whole Gilbert situation. Plus, everyone says your baking improved overnight." Arabella couldn't help but smirk.

"Oh, please. I delivered a foal in the stables, and everyone kept asking how on earth I knew how to do such a thing."

194

Arabella scoffed. "Ha, well, they're right. There's no way I'd know how to deliver a baby horse."

"It happened during the engagement party. The paparazzi came in and took photos of me in my ruined gown... I'm sorry."

"What? Everyone thinks I did that? In a ball gown? Oh, great. How am I going to explain that I know nothing about horses when I get back?" Arabella asked.

"That is the least of your problems. What about Stefan? And Gilbert?"

"I have no idea." Arabella heaved a heavy sigh. "I don't want to leave Gilbert, but I don't want my family to lose the bakery company. I am so confused about what to do. I just want to stay here and create new recipes for the bakery and be with Gilbert. I just wish that were an option."

Suddenly the door flung open.

Arabella flew off the bed in surprise, landing on the floor with a thud. Constance was standing there, red-faced with her fists on her hips.

"What was that?" Damaris' voice was faint coming from the phone, which was now on the floor beside Arabella.

Constance was starting hard at Arabella, her eyes squinted as she scrutinized her. "Who are you?" she asked slowly.

Chapter Twenty

"What do you mean?" Arabella choked out, knowing it wasn't convincing at all.

Stepping around the bed, Constance bent down and picked up the cell phone. "Hello?"

There was silence on the other end.

"Who is this? I demand to know who this is," Constance persisted.

Arabella heard Damaris' voice, but it was hard to make out what she was saying.

"Damaris?" Constance's eyes went wide. "Where are you? And who is this person in my house who looks so much like you?" Damaris' mother turned to Arabella, training her eyes on her again, which were now wide in shock. "You need to explain to me what is going on right now."

Constance continued to listen to what Damaris was saying. After several long moments, Constance nodded her head slowly. "I see. Well, you need to come home immediately. Please, Damaris. The thought of you so far away is terrifying. I can't believe you flew on an airplane! You could get in serious trouble with the church for this."

Damaris said something else, which sounded like protesting.

"I can't believe you deceived me like this, Damaris. You need to come home as soon as you can get a flight. Understand?" Constance turned to Arabella. "And you, I want you to go home today too, or as soon as you can. Understood?"

Arabella sighed. "Yes. I will."

Constance said into the phone, "This woman—Arabella—is flying back today."

"When I get back home, we will have some explaining to do and make things right with my parents and Stefan's father. Can she stay for that?" Arabella asked.

"Fine," Constance said into the phone. "Do what you need to do in Germany and make amends, then come home. I'll see you soon, Damaris."

Constance hung up the phone and turned to Arabella again.

Arabella gulped, feeling as though her heart was lodged in her throat, wondering if she'd be able to speak at all.

"How dare you? How dare you pretend to be my daughter, stay in my house with my children, and deceive us all?" Constance demanded between gritted teeth. Her intense gray eyes seemed to flame with indignation and outrage. Gone was the quiet, meek woman Arabella had come to know. When it came to protecting her children, Constance turned into a mother bear.

Arabella hung her head in shame. "You're absolutely right. I am sorry I deceived you all. Damaris wanted to go to Germany so badly, and I just wanted to be someone else, and swapping places with her seemed perfect. I thought it might be nice to live as an Amish woman for a little while before going home and taking over the entire bakery company and marrying a man I don't know." Arabella sighed. "Maybe Ella Ruth was right. Maybe this was a terrible idea."

"Ella Ruth knew?"

Arabella nodded. "And I told Gilbert."

"Gilbert! You love him, don't you? That explains so much. What are you going to tell him when you leave to marry someone else? You're going to break his heart, aren't you? He is a good man. He doesn't deserve to be treated like that." Constance shook her head. "This is a disaster."

"I know. It's my fault. This was my idea. I talked Damaris into it. Please don't be too hard on her. I think a big reason why she did it was to help me," Arabella pleaded.

Constance sighed heavily, placing her hand on her heart as she looked out the window. The farm fields stretched out before them, framed by the fiery colors of the few leaves that still remained on the trees. Winter was coming soon.

"I will love her and forgive her, no matter what. She has always longed to travel to the places she reads about in her books. Part of me is glad she got the chance to do it before she joins the church," Constance said.

"Will she get in trouble with the church?"

"Not too severely. She hasn't officially joined the Amish church yet."

"Will you tell anyone about this?"

Constance turned to Arabella. "I… I don't know. I should, I suppose, and Damaris should too. People will most likely hear about it eventually."

"I'm sorry again, Constance. I had the experience of a lifetime here. I learned about what family and faith and life should truly be like. Damaris is so blessed to have a family like yours and a mother like you. I wish my mother was half as understanding and warm as you."

"Oh? What is she like?" Constance asked with concern.

Arabella's eyes welled with tears as she looked away. "My mother was always too busy to spend much time with me, and she expects perfection from me. I feel like I'll never live up to her expectations."

Constance touched Arabella's hand. "I'm sorry, Arabella. Maybe after all this has happened, this will change her perspective."

Arabella let out a humorless laugh. "If you think my parents won't still want me to marry Stefan when I return, I doubt that. When I get back, things will just go back to the way they were. I'm sure of it."

***

Damaris ended the call with her mother and rubbed her thumb and forefinger over the bridge of her nose. Well, her mother had taken that surprisingly well.

But now she really had to return home. Guilt filled her at the thought of causing her mother worry.

Damaris sat under the tree where she and Stefan had set up their picnic, which was far enough from the mansion where no one would be around to hear her conversation. The day of their picnic seemed like so long ago now. She relived her time here with Stefan over and over in her mind.

"Is it true?" she heard a voice say behind her.

Stunned, Damaris jumped to her feet and whirled around to see Stefan standing there.

How much of her conversation on the phone had he heard?

She sucked in a deep breath, her heart sinking farther and farther down until she felt as though she might collapse from the weight of this entire situation.

"How did you know I was out here?" she asked.

"I didn't. I was taking a walk and decided to come here. This place is special to me."

"Me too."

"Really? I just heard you explain to someone on the phone that you switched places with Arabella. Is that true?" he asked in a pained voice, taking a step closer. "If you're not Arabella, who are you?"

Damaris sighed heavily. She'd been caught. There was no denying it now.

"Yes, it's true. Arabella wanted some time away before the wedding, and I've always wanted to travel here to Germany, so we secretly switched places. My real name is Damaris Kauffman, and I am not Arabella, but an Amish woman from Maine. I never meant to hurt anyone," she told him, clasping her hands in front of her, the guilt overwhelming her. "Please, let me explain."

"I heard you say you couldn't keep this up much longer." His voice cracked with emotion. "Did you mean pretending to love me? You can't keep up the act anymore?"

Damaris threw her hands up. "No! That's not at all what I meant. I meant—"

He turned away, tears reddening his eyes. "I knew it. I knew no woman as beautiful as you could ever love me. I should have known."

"But Stefan, I do love you!" Damaris cried out, running toward him.

He jerked away from her, turning to leave.

She reached out and grabbed his arm. "That was not part of the lie. Everything between us was real. I had to hide my feelings for you because Arabella asked me to. She didn't want to come back and have you wondering why her feelings had changed so suddenly. She doesn't love you, but I do."

He slowly turned, and a tear had now spilled onto his cheek. She slowly reached up and wiped it away with her thumb, surprised that he let her. Behind his glasses, his eyes were filled with questions and pain.

Did he believe her at all?

"Please, Stefan," Damaris said, now realizing tears were coursing down her own cheeks. "Why would I lie about this now?"

He threw his hands up. "I don't know. I just don't see how I can trust you after lying about all of this."

"Elizabeth knew and asked me not to tell you. I wanted to tell you. At the engagement party when I said I had to tell you something important. When you proposed and I ran out like that, it was because I felt so horribly

200

guilty for lying to you. I realized I'd never be able to be with you because Arabella is marrying you." She shook her head, swiping at the tears on her face. "I wanted to tell you the truth, but Elizabeth said if I did, your father might back out on the business agreement and Arabella's family would lose the business. I didn't want to be the reason for that. I'm so sorry, Stefan. I wanted to tell you."

"You could have trusted me," Stefan retorted.

"I do trust you. I was doing it because Arabella and Elizabeth made me promise not to tell." Damaris hung her head. "I was so confused."

Damaris took off the diamond engagement ring and held it out to him. "Either way, I don't deserve this. It wasn't really meant for me."

She heard Stefan take in a deep breath. He slowly reached out and took the ring from her, then put it in his pocket. To her surprise, his hand gently touched the side of her face. She looked up into his eyes.

"So, you really do love me?" he whispered.

"Yes, Stefan. I love you. I wish it was me who was engaged to you," she blurted, but she didn't regret speaking the words. "I wish there was some way we could fix everything."

"Maybe if we talk to my father—"

"No! He can't know. Arabella and Elizabeth are convinced he'd back out if he knew."

"But I want to be with you, not Arabella. Clearly, she doesn't want to marry me."

"She's in love with my ex-boyfriend," Damaris said, unable to hide a chuckle at the irony. "I wouldn't even call him that. We only went on a few dates. But no, she doesn't want to marry you."

"Maybe there is some way we can still save their business and be together," he said softly, leaning his head closer to hers so his breath lifted away the few hairs that were brushing against her neck. She sighed, wishing the moment would never end.

"I don't see how. My mother wants me to go home as soon as possible. But maybe I should try to make things right first. She would understand if I did."

"If you did leave your Amish community, would you be shunned?"

"No. I never officially joined the Amish church."

"Oh, good. Wait." He held up a finger, then touched his chin. "My father agreed to pay off Arabella's debts as a wedding gift, right?"

"Yes. The wedding gift was meant for Arabella, not me."

"Well, he could still do it for me."

Damaris' mind swam with questions. "Do you think there is a chance? I don't think it will be easy, trying to change his mind. He seems a bit…"

"Stubborn? Cold?"

Damaris nodded slowly. "Well, yes. What if he's so outraged that he calls the entire thing off? Maybe he should never know I switched places with Arabella."

"I think we need to tell him the truth and take that chance."

Damaris was about to protest, but Stefan pulled her close, making her forget what she was about to say. She breathed in the scent of him—he smelled a bit like the stables and the grass of the meadows.

"I will talk to him. Trust me, Damaris." His eyes smiled when he said her name, and so did her soul.

She reached up and threw her arms around his neck, tugging him closer until his lips met hers.

Damaris pulled away for only a moment, saying, "Arabella is flying back. When she gets here, the three of us should tell him together, then tell Arabella's parents. I don't know when she will get here. Maybe tomorrow."

"Yes. Sounds like a plan."

The wind swirled around them, rustling the leaves on the tree and tangling her hair. All she was aware of was how close he was to her and how she never wanted to leave him.

God, please let this work out for good...somehow, Damaris prayed silently.

***

Arabella grabbed a suitcase out of the closet and started throwing in the few things she'd kept with her here. Damaris had taken the rest to Germany when she'd left, and Arabella had been using most of Damaris' things during her stay.

A knock sounded on the door, and Arabella answered it. Constance stood in the hall, wringing her hands together in front of her apron.

"I'm sorry about how I reacted," she said. "I was upset at the thought of a total stranger living here this whole time under the same roof as my children. But more than that, I was angry at myself for not noticing—for not noticing that you were not Damaris. How did I not notice?"

Arabella smiled. "We look a lot alike. You have five other children to care for. You're busy. Don't worry, no one will hold it against you."

"But she's my daughter. I should have known. Especially with your terrible cooking." Constance stifled a laugh. "Sorry."

"It is pretty terrible," Arabella said with a chuckle. "I'm not so good at being Amish, I guess. I wish I was."

"You could improve with practice."

"My parents would never allow that."

"I am sorry about your situation with the arranged marriage. I hope everything works out for you."

"Thank you."

"I think many people assume the Amish participate in arranged marriages, but we don't, at least we don't here in Unity. I just can't imagine marrying a stranger." Constance sighed. "I loved my husband very much. Not many people experience that kind of true love. I hope you will have that one day, too."

Arabella slowly shook her head. "I don't think that will happen for me, but thank you. Well, I better get going. I have a very long flight ahead of me. What will you tell the children?"

"I think it would be best to explain everything to them once Damaris returns. For now, I will say Damaris is visiting a friend, which is true."

"Well, I had a really wonderful time here. I will never forget it. You showed me how life should be, and that will always stay with me. Thank you." Arabella took Constance's hand as tears filled her eyes. "I hope one day I can come back here."

Tears welled in Constance's eyes as well. "I hope so too."

Arabella said goodbye, picked up the suitcase, and walked out of the house. Some of the children were in the kitchen, talking and laughing, and barely noticed as she walked out of the house. She looked at them longingly before heading out the door, hoping one day she would see them again.

Now, she had to find Gilbert. She hurried down the lane toward his house and arrived there only a moment later.

As she walked up the porch steps, Arabella's heart twisted in her chest. Would she ever see Gilbert again, or would her parents forbid her to ever leave the estate again?

Arabella lifted her hand to knock on the door, then hesitated. Maybe this would only make things more painful by saying goodbye. Maybe she should just—

"Arabella?"

She spun around to see Gilbert coming out from behind his house. His hair was slightly tousled, and he wore a black jacket and black hat. "I was in the back yard and saw you coming. What are you doing here so early?"

Just the sight of him, just the thought of maybe never seeing him again made her eyes burn with a thousand unshed tears. One spilled onto her cheek, and she quickly swiped it away.

"What's wrong?" He rushed over to her and looked at her bag. "Wait. Are you…leaving? Already?"

She nodded. "Constance heard me on the phone with Damaris. I have to go back, and Damaris is coming home. I don't know what will happen after this, Gilbert. I'm going to try to work everything out with my parents and Stefan's father, but I have no idea what will happen…or if I will ever be able to come back here again."

"We have to figure this out somehow. Maybe if Damaris tells them she's in love with Stefan, they will change their minds."

"But really, it's up to Stefan's father if our company collapses or not. If he finds out I want to back out of the wedding, we could lose everything."

"Do you want to spend the rest of your life wishing you married someone else? Is that really worth your family's company? Yes, I know it's important, but so is your entire life and your happiness." Gilbert ran his thumb gently along Arabella's jawline. "I just want you to be happy, and your parents should too."

Arabella sighed. "I wish it were that simple."

"I want to be with you. Promise me you'll come back," he whispered, drawing her into his warm embrace.

There, in his arms, she couldn't say no when she so badly wanted to say yes. "I promise."

She sniffed, wiping away more tears that had escaped down her cheek. She grabbed the handle of her suitcase, forced herself to turn away from Gilbert, then walked down the lane, pulling her suitcase behind her like the weight of the promise she'd just made.

Could she keep her word?

***

Arabella stepped out of the taxi and let out a deep breath. She was back at the mansion, which strangely didn't feel like home anymore.

Unity felt like home now. Unity was her home now.

After getting the suitcase and paying the driver, she walked up to the side door and called Damaris, who met her there and let her in.

"I'm so glad you're here," Damaris said, looking like she was on the verge of tears, her eyes red-rimmed. "I am so worried about how we will tell everyone the truth." Her fingers fiddled with a button on her blouse.

Arabella shook her head. "Don't worry. This is my mess. I talked you into it, and I'll deal with my parents. It's my family's company on the line, not yours." Arabella touched Damaris' arm. "I'm so sorry everything got so out of control."

"I'm not sorry I came here and met Stefan. I love him, and I'm going to fight to be with him."

"That's the spirit. Come on. Let's go meet up with Stefan and speak with his father, then we will have to see my parents after waiting for his decision." With every word Arabella spoke, Damaris looked more and more tense, so Arabella grabbed her friend's upper arms. "Listen. Whatever happens to the company, none of it is your fault. This was my idea, so it's my responsibility. Got it?"

Damaris nodded.

206

"Good. Now let's go."

The two women quietly went inside and down the hallway, where Stefan was waiting. Arabella set her rolling suitcase upright on the floor and faced him.

"Wow," he said, eyes wide. "It's incredible how much you look alike, especially with your hair the same."

"Did Damaris tell you her hair was down to her knees before I made her chop it off?" Arabella asked with a chuckle.

"No, she never mentioned that. Really?" Stefan asked.

Damaris nodded. "It would have been a dead giveaway. Besides, I like it better like this. It was so long, it used to get snagged on things sometimes when I would wear it down at home."

Stefan chuckled. "I have a lot to learn about you, don't I?"

"Well, you can play twenty questions later. For now, we need to speak with your father, Stefan," Arabella said.

***

As Damaris, Arabella, and Stefan walked toward the room where Philip Castle was staying, Damaris' heart twisted in her chest. Stefan seemed to sense her anxiety, because he squeezed her hand.

"How should we do this?" Stefan asked when they reached the room.

"I should go in with you to help explain," Damaris said. "Then we can bring in Arabella so we can explain first."

Arabella nodded. "Sounds good."

"Okay. Let's get this over with." Stefan knocked on the door, and they heard a gruff voice tell them to come in.

Stefan slowly opened the door. "Dad? I need to talk to you."

"Come in, son. Hello, Arabella." He was sitting at the desk and beckoned them inside, so Damaris and Stefan entered the room.

"Have a seat." When Philip saw their serious expression, his smile faded. "What is this about?"

"We have something to tell you," Stefan said, his voice wavering a little. "This will come as a shock to you, but please, I ask you to hear the entire explanation before you react."

Philip's eyes were skeptical. "I see. Well, then, go on and tell me, I suppose."

Stefan turned to Damaris, a desperate look on his face, as if at a loss for words.

"Mr. Castle, I'm not Arabella. My name is actually Damaris Kauffman."

"What? That is preposterous." Philip threw his hands up. "Is this some kind of joke?"

Stefan opened the door, and Arabella walked in. Philip's eyes went wide as he glanced back and forth between Damaris and Arabella.

"Are you…twins? What is going on here?" Philip demanded. "Why didn't Helene and Henry mention they have two daughters?"

"We're not related," Arabella said. "I'm Arabella. This is Damaris, from the United States. We only met recently. I talked her into switching places with me. I take full responsibility for all that has happened, and we didn't mean for anyone to get hurt."

As Arabella explained the entire situation, Mr. Castle listened intently, his face growing redder and redder with each word. After she explained, she added, "Again, we never meant to hurt anyone, and we never meant to jeopardize the business agreement or the company."

Mr. Castle just stared at them with hard eyes, taking in rapid, deep breaths. Was he about to explode? Call the whole thing off?

"Dad, I love Damaris. I want to be with her, not Arabella. Arabella is in love with someone else. If I were to marry Damaris instead, wouldn't you still pay off the debt of Blackwood Bakery as your wedding gift to me and join the companies?"

Philip said nothing, but turned and walked to the window to stare out of it.

"Have you told Helene and Henry about this?" he asked, facing away from them.

"Not yet. We wanted to tell you first," Arabella said.

"And what about you, Arabella? What will you do?" Philip asked.

"I want to stay in Maine, working for a small bakery. I've been creating new recipes for the company. If I stay there and continue to make new recipes, Stefan and Damaris could run the business here together," Arabella said.

"I would take Arabella's place, and the three of us would be much happier," Damaris added, hopeful.

Philip slowly turned to face them. "You deceived us, Damaris, or whatever your name is. You expect me to just proceed with paying off Blackwood Bakery's debts like nothing ever happened?"

Damaris' heart lurched. She glanced furtively at Stefan, who looked pale, then looked to Arabella, who bit her lip.

"I am so sorry for deceiving everyone." Damaris hung her head.

"She wanted to tell the truth, especially to Stefan, but my grandmother and I asked her not to. We were afraid you'd back out of the agreement. We are taking a leap of faith by telling you now."

"I see. I need you to get out—now." Philip ran a hand over his balding head.

"Dad? Won't you please—"

"Get out now, so I can think." He shooed them toward the door, and Stefan, Arabella, and Damaris backed out of the room. Once they were in the hall, the door slammed in their faces.

"What… What just happened?" Arabella asked.

"I'm not sure," Stefan said slowly.

"Do you think there is any chance he will consider what we asked?" Damaris asked.

"He's my father, but still, it's hard to read him. I honestly have no idea." Stefan sighed and turned to her. "Should we tell Helene and Henry now or wait for his answer?"

"We should wait to hear what he decides. That way we can tell my parents when we explain everything to them," Arabella said.

"So, I guess for now, all we can do is wait," Damaris said.

***

Arabella suggested that the three of them go for a walk while waiting to work off some of the tension they were feeling. Arabella told Damaris and Stefan about her time in Unity, and Stefan enthusiastically addressed several questions about the Amish to both Arabella and Damaris.

Not even a half hour later, Arabella's cell phone rang, which was still in Damaris' pocket. Damaris handed it to Arabella, seeing the call was from Helene.

Had Philip gone and told them everything without them? That was not the plan.

This could be bad. Very bad. Her stomach clenched as she stared at her mother's face on the screen, then she forced herself to answer the call, putting it on speakerphone.

"Hello?"

"Arabella? Or is this Damaris?" Helene demanded.

The three of them looked at each other, their unspoken words reflecting on each of their faces.

"Get back here right now and meet us in the sitting room. You two have some explaining to do," Helene ordered. She hung up.

"My father went and told them? We told him we would tell your parents everything after we heard his decision. How could he do this?" Stefan said, his hands in fists.

"I'm sure he's upset," Damaris said.

"Yes, but now he's made things go from bad to worse." Stefan shook his head.

"We better go," Arabella said, and they hurried inside.

Once they reached the sitting room, they walked through the doors to see Henry, Philip, Elizabeth, and Helene waiting for them and quickly rose from the chairs they'd been sitting in.

"How dare you do this? Both of you!" Henry shouted, and Damaris cringed.

"Father," Arabella said. "Don't yell at her. This was my idea. I convinced her to do it."

"But it was my choice, Arabella," Damaris insisted.

"You are both to blame for this deception," Helene said in a shaky voice. "Arabella, you knew what was at stake, and you risked it all for a trip to the United States? And now I hear you've fallen in love with an Amish man from Damaris' Amish community? This is an outrage."

Arabella stood taller, hiking her chin. "Yes, I have, and he is wonderful. You would like him if you gave him the chance—if you gave us a chance."

"We will talk about that later," Arabella's father said with a warning look.

Stefan held up his hands. "Hold on. Back up. Dad, you weren't supposed to go and tell them like this. We told you we planned on telling Henry and Helene once you made your decision."

"I have made my decision. I am backing out. If you marry Damaris, there is no business agreement. I don't see the benefit of our bakeries merging any longer," Philip said, waving his hand. "You would not be marrying into the Blackwood family."

"Everyone needs to take a breath and calm down," Elizabeth said from the couch, raising her hands. "Let Damaris and Arabella explain."

"Thanks, Grandma. This could still work," Arabella said, nodding to Elizabeth. "I want to stay in Maine and create and develop new recipes for the company. Mother, Father, you know I am terrible with the business side of things. Damaris is so much better at that than I am. It's been her dream to run a business, and she wants to take over the company with Stefan. They can run it together while I continue to create more recipes for new products. I could marry who I want, and Stefan and Damaris can be together." Arabella took in a deep breath after rushing to get all the words out before she could be interrupted. She looked at her father, her mother, and Philip, trying to read their expressions.

"It's absurd!" Philip cried, throwing his hands up.

"Dad, won't you at least consider what we are proposing?" Stefan pleaded.

"You know, this could work," Helene said, and everyone turned to her. "Maybe it was wrong of Henry and me to put so much pressure on Arabella to agree to an arranged marriage."

Arabella rolled her eyes. "You think?"

Elizabeth nodded. "It was. I tried to tell you."

Helene held up a hand. "If we agree to what you say, everyone would be happy." She looked to Henry and Philip. "Why not consider it?"

212

Philip's face only grew redder, and Arabella expected steam to burst from his ears at any moment. She hid a smile at the thought of it.

"It was not the original agreement, Helene," Henry snapped.

"Things have changed! It's time you consider what your daughter wants for a change," Elizabeth snapped at Henry and Helene. "What comes first—business or family?"

"She's right, Henry." Helene turned to Arabella, her eyes soft for once. "Arabella has taken initiative. She wants to bake and create recipes, not run the company. Damaris does want to run the company and be with Stefan. To me, it works out. As long as you still want to merge the bakeries, Philip." She looked at him expectantly. "You don't want your son to marry our daughter when he loves someone else, do you?"

Elizabeth crossed her arms, her eyebrows raised, clearly impressed with Helene's change of heart.

Arabella smiled at Helene, feeling proud of her mother for standing up for them.

Philip nervously looked from Helene, to Henry, then Stefan. He sighed heavily. "I do want you to be happy, Stefan. But I also want you to have a wife who can help you run the company once we all retire. Arabella has been trained in the business her whole life. She's an expert."

Helene laughed. "That may be a bit of an exaggeration, Philip."

"She's right. I'm terrible at it. I'm not the right person for the job. Damaris is. You can teach her everything," Arabella said, touching Damaris' shoulder.

"I am a fast learner." Damaris smiled. "I vow to do everything I can to help Stefan run the company and make it successful. I've always wanted to run a business."

Stefan smiled down at her, and the look that he and Damaris shared warmed Arabella's heart. They were perfect for each other.

"How can you refuse, Dad?" Stefan asked Philip.

Philip stepped forward, closer to Stefan. For a long moment, he clasped his hands together and stared at the floor. When he looked up, he had tears reddening his eyes, to Arabella's surprise.

"You love Damaris, you say? You want to marry her?" Philip asked.

"Yes. If she will have me." Stefan looked down at Damaris, who grinned and nodded.

"Well, then. You're right, Stefan. How can I refuse?" He raised his hands, palms up, smiling. "I want you to be happy, my son. I agree to pay off Blackwood Bakery's debt after the wedding as your wedding gift and proceed with merging the two bakery companies."

"Oh, that is wonderful!" Helene cried, shaking Philip's hand. "Thank you."

"As long as you are sure," Henry said, approaching Philip.

"Yes. I am sure. I have not seen my son this happy since... Well, this is the happiest I have ever seen him, I suppose." Philip beamed at his son.

"Well, then, thank you, Philip." Henry firmly shook Philip's hand.

"Yes. Thank you, Dad." Stefan threw his arms around Philip, who looked stunned for a moment, then wrapped his arms around his much taller son.

As Stefan and his father spoke, Arabella's parents and Elizabeth walked over to her.

Well, here goes nothing, Arabella thought grimly.

"So, what's this about you wanting to be with an Amish man?" Helene asked.

"Is he handsome?" Elizabeth asked with a sly grin.

"Well, yes, he is," Arabella replied, returning her smile.

"And you want to move to Maine?" Henry added, not amused.

"Yes. His name is Gilbert. He's so kind and honest and hardworking. You would love him. After I move to Maine, I want to join the Amish." The second half of the sentence she blurted out quickly before she lost her nerve.

Chapter Twenty-one

Arabella watched as her mother's face turned a shade of light gray. "What?" Helene cried. "Why?"

"I love their way of life. They live at a slower pace, savoring each moment. They put God and family first, and I want to live like that. Also, I wouldn't be able to be with Gilbert unless I join the Amish church," Arabella explained.

Henry's hands balled into fists. "Arabella, why would you want to give up this life for...*that*?" her father spat out. "They don't even use electricity, right? Do they even have indoor toilets? Why trade this luxurious lifestyle you're used to for such a primitive one?"

"It's not primitive," Arabella retorted. "And yes, they do have indoor toilets. They live a simpler life. Without all the distractions of modern technology, it allows them to truly value what is most important."

"I think it sounds splendid," Elizabeth piped up.

"Helene, please talk some sense into her," Henry said, throwing his hands up. He walked away and paced the room, and Elizabeth also backed up to give them some space.

"Your father is just worried you'll regret your decision," her mother said calmly, taking Arabella's hand. "And frankly, so am I. What if you're really just joining for this young man, and if things don't work out, what will you do then?"

"I'm not joining just because of Gilbert. I want to be Amish. Even if things don't work out with Gilbert, I still want to join the church," Arabella explained. "If you went there, you'd understand."

Her mother chuckled. "Me? Travel to an Amish community?"

"Why not? You're going to have to if you want to come to my wedding and see your future grandchildren someday. I'd love to show you around. Maybe you and Father would finally see what I love about it so much there."

"Well, maybe, dear. But I think you need to think long and hard about this first," Helene said.

Henry walked back over and let out a deep breath. "I'm sorry, Arabella. You have to understand this is a lot for us to take in. We only want the best for you. We want to make sure you won't regret your decision. You know, if you did, you can always come home. Right?"

"I won't regret it, Father. I want to do this. I've never been more sure about anything in my life." Arabella hiked her chin and stood up taller.

"She wants us to go there with her," Helene said to her husband. "To show us why she loves it there."

Henry sighed. "Well, if it truly is that important, then we should."

"I'm glad you're finally respecting my wishes," Arabella blurted. "I feel like my entire life you've been grooming me to take on the business, but you never listened to what I wanted. I was willing to even marry a stranger to save the company, but it's time now that I choose my own path for my life. So, thank you for trying to understand." The words that she'd been wanting to say for so long rushed out of her so quickly. She took in a sharp breath, expecting a horrified reaction from her parents.

"We are trying to understand now," Henry said, touching her shoulder. "We're so sorry, dear. Truly, we only thought we were doing the right thing."

"We thought that you inheriting the company would be the best thing we could give you, no matter the price you had to pay," Helene said. "I'm sorry we didn't listen to what you wanted."

"I know," Arabella said. "And I'm grateful for everything you've done for me. Thank you."

217

Arabella's heart felt as though it would burst with joy as her mother pulled her closer and hugged her.

"I am so sorry for pressuring you into marrying Stefan," Helene said. "And for being so cold toward you. I wasn't always there for you growing up, and I am so sorry for that. Now, suddenly, I blink, and you've grown into a mature woman who knows exactly what she wants. You deserve a better mother, Arabella."

"No," Arabella said, taking her mother's hands. "I would never want anyone else for a mother. Thank you for standing up for me and what I want now."

"This is what you want? You're sure? To move all the way to Maine and be with this man?" Henry asked.

"Well, even if it doesn't work out between the two of us, I still want to live in Maine and bake with my Amish friends." Arabella nodded. "Yes, it's what I want. It's everything I've been dreaming of."

Helene squeezed her daughter in a hug once more. "I'm proud of you, Arabella. We will go to Maine and meet him, but we're not making any promises about approving this. Right, Henry?"

Arabella released her mother and looked up to see her father.

"Your mother is right. You've grown into a mature woman, and yes, it was wrong of us to ask you to agree to an arranged marriage. I'm sorry, Arabella. Perhaps you switching places with Damaris was for the best all along. Otherwise, we would have never realized what a colossal mistake we were making. We may have come to regret it the rest of our lives," Henry said, and Arabella hugged him also, shocked at her father's apology. He was not usually one to admit he was wrong, so Arabella savored the moment.

"Thank you, Father. I know you were trying to do what you could to save Blackwood Bakery."

"Your happiness and how you spend the rest of your life is more important," Henry said, his voice cracking with emotion. "We shouldn't have asked you to choose between the two. And I do agree with your mother. I can't give my blessing until I get to know this man—Gilbert."

"I'm sure you'll both love him once you meet him," Arabella said. "All is forgiven. I love you both."

Behind him, Elizabeth winked at Arabella. Arabella gave her a grateful smile.

***

"Well. That went better than I expected," Stefan said bluntly, and Damaris laughed out loud.

He loved her laugh. He wanted to hear it every day for the rest of his life.

They walked hand in hand to the stables, saddled up, then went for another ride to their spot—the tree in the meadow.

The closer they rode to the meadow, the more nervous Stefan became. He felt as though his heart was beating as fast and as hard as the horse's hooves pounding the ground beneath him.

Once they arrived, Stefan unrolled a blanket and set it down on the grass. Damaris sat beside him, resting her head on his shoulder. He wrapped his arm around her, and he felt her lean into him.

"After this, I don't want to deceive anyone else ever again," Damaris said. "I had promised to put that behind me, then this happened."

Stefan pulled away to face her. "When else have you deceived someone? I have a hard time believing that. What, do you have another secret identity?" He laughed.

"No, no. It's nothing like that. When my brother, Dominic, met the woman who is now his wife, Adriana, she wasn't Amish. She was in a car accident near our community, and we took care of her in our house for a while until she was better. It's a long story, but she didn't want to go to the hospital. Anyway, I was set on my brother marrying my friend so that he would stay Amish. A few years ago, he left the Amish for a while, and after he came home, I never wanted him to leave us again, especially after my father died."

"Your father died? I'm so sorry, Damaris," Stefan said.

"Yes. I wanted to tell you about that before, but when you told me about your mother passing away, you thought I was Arabella. So, I wasn't able to tell you about my father," Damaris said.

"What happened to him?"

"He died of an undetected heart condition. Basically, from when he was born, his heart continued getting weaker and weaker until it just gave out. He died so suddenly. He and my mother were true soul mates, so she was devastated when he died," Damaris explained, still remembering it vividly.

"I'm so sorry, Damaris," Stefan murmured, rubbing his thumb over her arm.

"I've been trying to take care of my family the best I can ever since. My older brother Dominic, has been too. Anyway, about what I was saying before... I made up rumors about Adriana, and I was rude to her, hoping it would make her leave so that Dominic wouldn't fall in love with her, marry her, and leave my family again. I never should have done that. I was afraid if he fell in love with her, he'd leave the Amish like he did before," Damaris explained with a sigh. The memories and shame flooded back to her.

"You thought you were protecting your family."

"I was so wrong. They got married anyway after Adriana joined the Amish church. Most of all, she forgave me after I told her what I did. I have come a long way since then, and I'm not that person anymore. I just wanted you to know in case you heard about it from someone else. In a

220

small community, things like that become widely known. It was embarrassing, but now Adriana and I are close friends."

"We all make mistakes. It's good that she forgave you. I thought you were going to tell me that you are an ex-con artist or something." Stefan chuckled.

"No, no, nothing like that. Anyway, after lying to you about me being Arabella, I just want you to know that I don't want to lie anymore. That's not who I am. Let's promise to always tell each other the truth." Damaris looked up at him, and he smiled at her, warming her heart.

"I promise," Stefan said, kissing her cheek.

"It was so hard on my mother when he passed away. She's been trying her best ever since, but I can see the toll it has taken on her."

"Your mother sounds like a wonderful woman."

"She truly is. I feel terrible for deceiving her like this. I hope she won't be too upset with me for lying and leaving like I did, but I'm so glad everything worked out with your father and Arabella's parents," she murmured.

He took her left hand in his, which no longer wore the engagement ring since she'd given it back to him.

"You were wrong about one thing," he said.

She looked up at him with her dark brown eyes. "What?"

"When you told me the truth here, you told me the ring wasn't meant for you."

"But it wasn't. When you proposed to me, you thought I was Arabella." Her face was lined with confusion.

"It doesn't matter." He shook his head. "It is you I have fallen in love with, and it was you I proposed to. The ring was meant for you, Damaris. It always was." His heart slammed against his ribs as he withdrew the small black box from his pocket, and a slow smile spread on her face. She sat up, and he knelt on one knee before her.

Stefan took in a deep breath and let out the words he'd been practicing in his head over and over. "Damaris Kauffman, you've captured my heart from the first moment we met. It doesn't matter that I didn't know your name at the time. It was you all along—it was always you. Your kindness, your boldness, your beautiful mind. I want to spend the rest of my life learning everything about you, every day. Will you marry me?"

Damaris beamed, joy radiating from her face. She threw her arms around him, laughing. "Yes! Yes!"

Sudden tears of joy sprang up in his eyes as an overwhelming elation filled him. He removed the ring from the box and slipped it onto her finger once again. For several long moments, he held her in his arms.

"When you go back home to say goodbye to your family, I want to come with you, if that's what you want," Stefan said.

Damaris pulled away and wiped away a tear that had fallen onto his cheek. "Of course, I want my family to meet my future husband. Nothing would make me happier."

***

After flying to Maine, Damaris, Arabella, and Stefan stepped out of the taxi at Damaris' house. As they walked toward the house, Damaris' siblings and her mother came out of the house. The children called her name, crowding around her to greet her.

When they saw Arabella, they looked back and forth between the two women, clearly confused. Damaris was wearing her Amish clothing out of respect, though she no longer felt at ease wearing the attire she'd grown up wearing.

"You look like twins," Daisy said, her eyes wide. "Are you twins?"

"Of course, they're not. We'd know if we had another sister," Danny said gruffly.

Desmond tugged on Damaris' skirt and hugged her legs. Smiling, Damaris bent down to hug him.

"I missed you all so much," she said.

"But… You weren't gone that long," Delphine said.

"We have a lot of explaining to do," Arabella added.

"Who's he?" Danny asked, looking Stefan up and down with a scowl. Stefan gave him an awkward smile.

"You go on inside," Constance said, shepherding the children back into the house.

As the children went inside with Arabella, peppering her with questions, Constance hugged Damaris as they remained standing in the driveway. "I'm so glad you're back. The children will be confused, so it's best we explain everything right away." Her gaze fell on Stefan. "Is this Stefan?"

"Yes," Damaris said, beaming. "*Maam*, we are engaged." Pride and excitement bubbled up within her in anticipation for her mother's reaction.

Constance's hands covered her mouth. "Truly? Oh, how wonderful!"

Damaris held out her left hand, showing her mother the sparkling diamond ring.

"Damaris! You know it is not the Amish way to wear jewelry." Constance wagged her finger.

"I know, *Maam*," Damaris said softly, tears stinging her eyes at the implication of her words.

Constance's smile quickly faded as realization set in. She placed her hand over her heart. "Does this mean… Will you be leaving us, Damaris? For good?"

"So much has changed so quickly," Damaris explained. "Stefan and I will be married, then run the Blackwood-Castle Bakery company together. I haven't officially joined the church yet, so I will come back and visit often, I promise."

"But... But..." Constance's eyes quickly filled with tears and her chin trembled. She whispered in a shaky voice, "Damaris, I don't want to lose you."

Damaris' heart ached at the thought of even causing her mother pain. "You're not losing me, *Maam*. I love Germany. That is where I want to live. I know you can't come to see me, but I promise, I will come to see you as often as I can."

"I will make sure she does visit," Stefan put in, who had been standing there quietly the entire time. "Family is the most important thing. I will make sure she sees you often. Also, Damaris told me how hard it has been on your family financially since your husband died. We will provide for you so you don't have to work anymore, and we will cover your living expenses—anything you need."

"I can't accept that." Constance shook her head adamantly. "It's too much."

Stefan took both of Constance's hands. "I believe it is our duty to take care of our parents and in-laws. Please let us do this for you. I promise, it will be no burden to us. The company is a multi-million-dollar company."

"We want to do this for you, *Maam*," Damaris pleaded. "You've done so much for me. Now let me take care of you. Now you can retire. You shouldn't have to work so hard."

Constance let out a sob, then covered her mouth again. She smiled. "Oh, thank you. Thank you so much. I can't tell you how grateful I am. I am so happy for you both." She pulled them both into a hug. When she finally let go, she wiped her eyes. "I always knew Damaris was meant for something more," she told Stefan. "Her mind is too vast for this place. I hope you will be happy together."

"We are," Damaris said.

Stefan put his arm around her. "I promise I will do everything I can to make your daughter happy, and I will treat her like the princess she is." He squeezed Damaris' shoulder.

"I wish Damaris' father could have met you, Stefan. He would be so happy," Constance said, her smile tainted with sadness.

Damaris nodded, knowing if she spoke, that she would start crying.

"Let's go inside, shall we?" Constance beckoned for them to follow her, then she turned and walked toward the house.

Inside, the children were asking several questions at once, except for little Desmond, who watched quietly while sucking his thumb.

Damaris put her hand up. "I know you're confused about what's going on. If everyone quiets down and listens, I'll explain."

The children all sat down and looked at her expectantly. She told them everything, how she went to Germany and how Arabella was here in her place.

"Is that why her cooking was so terrible?" Danny asked, his arms crossed.

"Shh," Daisy scolded. "Her baking was so much better than Damaris'."

"Anyway." Damaris put her hands on her hips. "There's more. This is Stefan, and we are engaged to be married."

The children started talking all at once again.

"Will you live here?" Daisy asked.

Damaris took a deep breath. "We will be living in Germany. You know I love you all, but I want to live in Germany with Stefan. I promise I will come back to visit often. It's a dream come true for me."

"We know," Daisy said, rolling her eyes. "You've always wanted to go to Germany."

"How did you know that?" Damaris had not spoken about her dream much, in fear of being scolded for wanting to fly on an airplane.

"I've heard you talking about it to Ella Ruth a few times." Daisy smiled and shrugged.

Or, maybe her sister had been reading Damaris' diary, but that was another discussion. Damaris eyed her suspiciously.

"Anyway, I promise I will come back and visit as much as I can. Very often," she promised.

"Does that mean you won't be Amish anymore?" Danny asked.

"Yes, Danny. I won't be joining the church. I will still hold on to many of our beliefs, but I will be an *Englisher*." She gave them a sad smile. "This is what I want."

The children looked at each other, silent for once.

"We will miss you," Daisy said in a soft voice.

All the children stood and hugged her, even Danny. Tears sprang up in Damaris' eyes as she hugged them. When she saw her mother crying on the couch, Damaris lost her composure and broke down crying.

Still, in her heart, she knew she was making the right decision without a doubt. It would be hard to leave Unity, but Germany was her home now.

Chapter Twenty-two

Arabella watched with tears in her eyes as Damaris' siblings hugged her, saying they'd miss her. All her life, Arabella had longed for siblings. She'd give anything for a brother or sister. Damaris and Gilbert were blessed to have so many siblings.

Gilbert. She needed to see him.

She turned to Stefan. "I need to go find Gilbert. Let Damaris know I'll be back later."

He nodded to her, and she slipped out the door.

She walked the short distance to Gilbert's house, not knowing if he would be home. She knocked on the door, then waited on the porch, tapping her foot. Exhilaration filled her at the thought of seeing him again. Even though she'd been gone only a short time, she'd missed him.

The door suddenly opened, and Gilbert stood in the doorway. He was wearing a wrinkled white shirt and his hair was tousled, as though he'd been running his hands through it. When he saw her, his eyes lit up. He stepped onto the porch, closed the door behind him, and took her hands.

"You're back! What are you doing here?" A shadow crossed his face. "So… What happened? Do you still have to marry that other man?"

Arabella grinned. "No. We figured out another way."

He drew his eyebrows together in confusion. "What? So, that means you can marry whomever you choose?"

"Yes. I'm free, Gilbert." She gazed up at him, running her hands up his arms, longing for him to wrap her in them again.

He granted her silent wish, pulling her close in a warm embrace. He bent down and captured her lips with his, kissing her softly at first, then deepening the kiss with longing. She felt the same way and had been afraid to show too much affection for him, just in case she'd never be able to see him again.

But now she was free to be with him.

"I love you, Arabella," he said once he finally pulled away. "But I'm Amish. The only way I could marry you is if—"

"If I also became Amish?" Arabella smiled up at him. "That's what I want, Gilbert. I want to stay here and join the Amish church."

"Really?" His eyes widened in amazement. When she nodded, he kissed her again, and she wished he'd never let her go.

She touched his cheek. "I'm so sorry I lied to you about who I was, Gilbert. I lied to everyone."

"I forgive you, and the community will too. So what about your parents and the bakery company?"

Arabella explained everything. "Damaris and Stefan make a great team. I know they'll do great things for the company."

Gilbert chuckled. "I'm happy for them. Everyone got what they wanted."

"I never thought I'd want to live here, and I never expected to meet someone like you. I guess I didn't know what I wanted until I found you."

"Well, I'm so glad God brought you to me," Gilbert said with a smile, running his hand through her hair. "I guess I didn't know what I wanted either, but we both ended up with more than we ever dreamed of. God knows better than we do."

***

As Stefan watched Damaris with her family, guilt ate at him for taking her away from this. Was leaving here to live with him in Germany really what she wanted?

This place was fascinating. He looked around the simple yet cozy home, warmed by the woodstove and the love of family. The scent of apple pie and donuts lingered in the air, and the sun shining on the fields outside and the Amish homes in the distance were breathtaking.

How could Damaris leave all of this behind?

He was so deep in thought, he didn't notice Damaris walking up to him. "Are you okay?" she asked.

He took her hand. "Are you really sure you want to leave your family to come to Germany with me?"

"Yes," she said adamantly. "Of course. It's been my dream to go to Germany for so long, and now I get to live there with the love of my life."

His face heated at her words. "I'm so afraid you'll get homesick and want to come back. If you do, that's okay. We can come back. I will leave everything behind in Germany and come live here if that's what you want."

Damaris shook her head. "Stefan, what I want is to marry you and live with you in Germany while running the company. That is what I want, and I won't change my mind. I promise. I always felt I was meant for something beyond Amish life. I never fit in because I wanted to do something more. Not just a small shop or bakery—something bigger. Around here, that's not normal." She smiled. "Because of you, I get to do everything I ever wanted to do and more."

"I'm so glad, Damaris. But..." He stared at his shoes. "I'm afraid you'll come to resent me for taking you away from your home."

"Impossible," she spat out. "Besides, you're not taking me away from here. I want to go with you. Now, please stop worrying. We're going to make dinner. If you want, you can play some games with my brothers and sisters and get to know them a bit."

He grinned. "I'd love that."

Arabella and Gilbert went for a walk down the lane, and she told him more about everything that had happened, especially about when she and Damaris had told her parents the truth.

"I'm so glad they came around and realized the arranged marriage was wrong," Gilbert said. "And now Damaris and Stefan get to be together."

"Yes. I'm so grateful everything worked out. I was afraid Stefan's father was going to back out and we'd lose everything, and it would be my fault," Arabella admitted.

"No. It wouldn't have been your fault. Your parents shouldn't have put that pressure on you in the first place."

"Hi!"

They looked to see Ella Ruth scampering down the lane toward them.

"Arabella?" she asked.

"Yes, it's me."

Ella Ruth threw her arms around her. "You're back? What on earth happened?"

Arabella quickly explained everything. "I want to join the Amish church."

"That's wonderful! But first, you'll need to go before the congregation and explain why you lied and ask for forgiveness."

"Yes, of course. I was planning on it."

"I'm so glad you'll be staying, but I'll miss Damaris."

"Thank you, Ella Ruth, for helping me while I was here. I couldn't have done it without you," Arabella said. "I want to keep working at the store in Damaris' place, if your father will allow me."

"I will talk to him about it," Ella Ruth said. "And you will also want to keep working for the Millers, too?"

"Yes. They have the most wonderful baking recipes. I want to keep working with them and develop new recipes for the bakery company."

"That's amazing!" Ella Ruth cried. "I'll keep on helping you learn our ways, Arabella. I'll help you through your confession at church, too, if you want."

"I'd appreciate that." Arabella smiled.

"Well, I better get home. I'm so happy for you both." Ella Ruth waved and hurried down the lane.

Arabella let out a long breath. "I deceived a lot of people here. I'll be glad to get this over with."

"They will forgive you, Arabella. We always forgive," Gilbert reassured her. "Don't worry."

***

"They're here!" Arabella cried, standing by the Kaufmann's living room window. "My parents are here."

She rushed outside to help them with their bags, her long purple skirt flying behind her as she ran. She was followed by Stefan, Damaris, and the rest of the Kaufmanns.

As Helene stepped out of the taxi in her black high-heeled boots, Arabella stifled a giggle, remembering when she'd first shown up here dressed the same way. Now, she wore sturdy black shoes, an apron, and a prayer *kapp*.

"Mother, when I said to bring boots, I meant to bring boots that you don't mind getting dirty," Arabella said with a chuckle. "Not high-heeled boots."

"I'm not going to traipse around in rain boots," Helene said, waving her hand. She looked up and saw Arabella's attire, not bothering to hide the shock on her face. "Oh, my. I know you said you'd be wearing this, but..." Helene waved her hand again, then smiled. "Well, you look lovely, Arabella. It might take me a bit to get used to it."

But Arabella didn't miss a flash of emotion in her mother's eyes. Was it disgust?

"Hello, dear," Henry said, kissing the top of Arabella's hair. "You could wear a sack and still look beautiful."

Arabella laughed. "Thanks, Father."

"Anyway, I reminded her about what you said about wearing practical shoes, but your mother doesn't own sturdy boots," Henry added, taking their luggage from the driver. Helene had clearly over packed with two large suitcases just for herself.

"You'll only be here a few days, right?" Arabella asked.

"I told her not to over pack, but you know how she is." Henry rolled his eyes.

"Yes, but I wanted to be prepared." Helene raised her cell phone into the air. "I have no signal here."

"There's hardly any reception here," Arabella explained. "You probably won't be able to charge your phone, anyway. The Kaufmanns have one outlet in the basement to charge their battery-operated appliances, but I don't know if any of the other Amish homes do, or if the bed and breakfast does."

Coco, the Kaufmann's German shepherd, pranced over and barked happily at the newcomers.

"Oh!" Helene shrieked, backing away. "I didn't know you had a dog."

"She's very friendly. A terrible watchdog," Damaris said with a laugh. "Coco, hush. Sit."

The dog immediately quieted and sat, tail wagging and tongue lolling out of the side of her mouth as she panted.

Henry's eyebrows shot up. "Wow. She's well-trained."

"I trained her myself," Damaris said, scratching the dog's ear.

Helene looked around and sniffed. "What's that horrid smell?"

"Manure," Damaris said, hands on her hips. She and Stefan each took one of the bags and hauled them to the house.

"Lovely." Helene raised her eyebrows and put a finger under her nose.

"Come on inside!" Damaris called over her shoulder. Helene and Henry followed them into the house as the taxi drove away.

Constance opened the door. "Welcome! I'm Damaris' mother, Constance." She ushered them inside. "Please, have a seat and make yourselves at home."

"So nice to meet you," Helene said.

"Yes. It's nice to put a face to the name," Henry added.

"I've heard so much about you. We're so happy to have you here," Constance said.

Helene eyed the rustic style of the home and the woodstove. Though she was acting polite and pleasant, Arabella could see disapproval in her eyes. "You have a lovely home," she said cheerfully.

"Thank you," Constance said with a smile, clearly not seeing through Helene.

"May I use your bathroom? You do have an indoor bathroom, correct?" Helene said, glancing around with one eyebrow raised. Helene was excellent at hiding her disgust. The only reason Arabella could see through it was because she knew her so well.

"Mother," Arabella whispered, her cheeks flaming. "I told you they do." Had she already forgotten or was she trying to embarrass her on purpose?

"Yes, of course. It's this way," Constance said, unfazed, as she led Helene down the hall.

Soon Constance returned, and they sat in the living room as Damaris set out homemade banana bread and tea. Some of the children were already playing with games and puzzles in the living room, but the rest came scampering down the hall.

When Helene returned a few minutes later, Damaris introduced her and Henry to the children. "This is Daisy, Delphine, Desmond, Dean, and Danny. My oldest brother Dominic lives down the lane. Children, this is Arabella's mother and father, Mr. and Mrs. Blackwood."

The children each greeted them, waving and saying hello.

"Wow, there are so many of you!" Helene cried. "There are seven of you in total? I could barely handle just Arabella as a child."

Arabella rolled her eyes. She hadn't been that difficult.

Constance gave an awkward laugh. "Well, I always knew I wanted many children. Some of the families here have twelve children or more."

"Twelve? Oh my!" Helene exclaimed, her hand flying to her heart.

"I would have had more, but I lost my husband before we could." Constance stared at her hands in her lap.

A look of surprise or distaste—Arabella couldn't tell which—flashed across her mother's face but was quickly replaced by a sympathetic look. "I'm so sorry to hear that. It must have been hard, being left with seven children to raise on your own."

Henry said, "Damaris mentioned it before. We are very sorry."

"Thank you. Well, the people here take care of each other. The community has helped cover our expenses, and the families supported me so much by bringing meals and helping me with childcare. If someone's house or barn burns down, the community will build a new one. I was not alone. Even Damaris has helped support the family financially by working two jobs to help us get by." Constance smiled at Damaris proudly.

"Arabella tells us that is one of the things she loves about this place—how much people take care of one another," Helene said.

"It is very true," Damaris said. "That is probably one of the things I will miss the most."

A look of sadness crossed Constance's face.

To change the subject, Arabella stood up. "Would you like a tour of the outside?"

"We can show you the inside too," Constance said. "What time will you be going to the Millers' Bed and Breakfast?"

"We can go whenever you'd like," Henry said.

Constance waved her hand. "Please, stay for dinner, won't you? Then you could go in the evening."

"That would be lovely, as long as we aren't imposing," Helene said. "We will be going to meet Gilbert later this evening."

"We already have dinner cooking, and we planned on having you here. Please stay. Maybe you could tell us some funny stories about Arabella as a child." Damaris smiled mischievously.

Henry guffawed. "Oh, yes, we have plenty of stories to tell."

Arabella laughed. "That is true."

"Come on," Damaris said. "Let's show you the barn."

***

That evening after dinner, Gilbert rushed around his cabin, checking over everything for the umpteenth time. He wanted the place to look its best for when Arabella's parents arrived and met him for the first time. He just wanted to make a good first impression.

235

What would they think of him, the man who was the reason why their daughter was moving here, far from home? They probably already disliked him.

He shook his head. *Lord, please help me to stay positive and not be so nervous.*

Gilbert wiped his sweaty palms on his pants again, then busied himself with sweeping the floor again, even though it was already pristine. He adjusted the vase of flowers on his small table, wiped down the counter again, checked on the kettle of hot water, then paced back and forth.

Moments later, he heard voices outside and rushed to the window. His heart leapt when he saw Arabella walking down the lane toward his house with her mother and father. His pulse spiked.

What would they think of him? Would they like him at all?

Before they saw him gawking, he bolted from the window and went to the door, waiting a moment before opening it.

"Hello," he said, wondering if his voice was audibly wavering. "I'm so glad you made it. Please, come in and make yourselves at home."

"Thank you," said the man, Arabella's father, as they walked inside.

Arabella gave him a reassuring smile, and it warmed his heart.

As they removed their coats, he said, "I'm Gilbert Schwartz."

Arabella's father now had his jacket off and extended his hand toward Gilbert, looking him squarely in the eye, sizing him up. "I'm Henry Blackwood. It's nice to meet you, Gilbert."

"I'm Helene Blackwood, Arabella's mother. We're glad to finally meet you. Arabella has told us about you." Helene smiled at him, but Gilbert could see that she was also looking him over, and then her eyes flitted around his cabin. She took in the rustic, handmade table and cabinets, the wood floors, and lack of any sort of décor. "Your home is so…quaint."

"Thank you. The community helped me build it. It's small now, but in the future, after I get married, I plan to add on to it," he explained, then his cheeks burned at the implication of his words. "Here, let me take your jackets." He took their jackets and hung them on a hook on the wall.

Helene's eyes widened just a bit at his words, but she said nothing.

"Would you like to have a seat at the table?" he asked. "I have hot water on the stove if you would like some tea."

"Thank you. That would be lovely," Helene said, sitting down in one of the handmade chairs. Arabella and Henry followed suit.

Gilbert dashed into the kitchen to make the tea and returned with the tray of teacups, milk, and sugar, then sat down.

"Thank you," Helene said, taking a teacup from him. He didn't miss her pulling a small handkerchief from her pocket and wiping the rim of the cup before taking a dainty sip.

"So, what are your intentions with my daughter, Gilbert?" Henry asked boldly, almost knocking Gilbert right off his chair.

His eyes widened. For a moment, his brain froze, at a complete loss for words.

Should he tell them the honest truth or a watered-down version of it? Should he make his feelings plain with complete honesty and possibly scare them off?

Arabella's face paled, and she gave him an apologetic look. Helene eyed him suspiciously, and Henry was staring at him with blazing intensity.

Gilbert cleared his throat. "I love your daughter," he began cautiously. "And to be honest, I want to ask her to marry me one day soon."

Arabella grinned, placing a hand on her heart, which swelled in her chest.

"Here, we only date someone with the intention of marriage. I do intend to marry you one day, Arabella, if you'll have me. I'm not officially asking now, but I will," he said, barely noticing her parents as he watched Arabella smiling at him.

He could watch her forever.

"Also, I would like to ask your permission to marry her and for your blessing," Gilbert said, looking at Henry, then Helene. "I've always believed it's the right thing to do."

Henry cleared his throat, glancing at his wife, who was now as pale as the white teacup she was holding.

"And if you two did marry, how would you support her?" Henry asked.

"I'm a carpenter. I have very steady work. My father is soon handing down his business to me. Don't worry, she will be provided for." Gilbert nodded.

"I hope you can understand our perspective, Gilbert," Helene said. "But we don't know you, and if Arabella marries you, she'd be moving here, to a different country."

Arabella interrupted. "You both said you were fine with this."

"No. That's not true. We never said we were fine with it. We said we'd come here and meet Gilbert and see Unity. I'm not so sure about this, Arabella," Helene said. "I'm sorry. We won't give you our blessing."

Chapter Twenty-three

Arabella's blood boiled. Why wouldn't they give Gilbert a chance? "This is what I want. I told you even if things didn't work out with Gilbert and me that I wanted to live here and become Amish," Arabella reminded them.

"If things don't work out between us? What do you mean, Arabella?" Gilbert asked, his heart sinking to his toes. Did she think they weren't right for each other?

Arabella lifted her hand defensively. "That's not what I meant, Gilbert. I was only saying that I wanted to move here for me first and foremost. For the right reasons."

"You'd be taking our daughter away from us," Henry blurted out to Gilbert, his face reddening.

"He is not. Why are you doing this? Why are you changing your minds?" Arabella asked her parents.

"I'm sorry, Arabella. I thought I could get used to the idea of you marrying him, but I can't let you do this. I can't just stand by and watch you make the biggest mistake of your life," Helene said, raising her hands.

"This is my choice! It's not a mistake. Gilbert is not making me do anything," Arabella retorted, slamming the table with her palm. "I want to live here because I want to be Amish and I want to serve God."

"She's right," Gilbert said, his voice cracking. "I'm not taking her away from you. This is her choice. She wanted to move here even before I mentioned marriage."

"But if it weren't for you, she never would have wanted to stay here," Helene said, her eyes welling with tears. Henry nodded in agreement.

Gilbert's ears rang, his heart slamming his rib cage.

"It's not Gilbert's fault!" Arabella cried, standing up.

"I can't bless a marriage that is the cause for my daughter leaving home to move to another country and become Amish, giving up her inheritance to become a farmer's wife in the middle of nowhere with no electricity," Helene said through clenched teeth, setting down her cup with a thud. She pushed her chair back and also stood up.

"I concur." Henry abruptly stood up and marched to the door, grabbing his coat off the wall.

"He's a carpenter, not a farmer," Arabella put in, but her parents ignored her.

Gilbert was so stunned by what had just happened, he didn't even move. It had happened so fast, and his mind was still reeling.

"Gilbert, I'm so sorry." Tears were now coursing down Arabella's cheeks. She let her face fall into her hands for a moment, then looked up.

"How could you do this?" she demanded, looking at each of her parents.

Helene was now standing next to her husband, grabbing her jacket off the hook. "Arabella, I'm sorry. One day you'll understand."

"You're not thinking clearly because of this man," Henry said. "Your feelings are clouding your judgment."

"That is not true," Arabella said. "I'd move here even if I had never met Gilbert."

"But you have no way of knowing that for sure." Helene turned to Gilbert. "Look, we've heard you're a nice, hard-working young man. But we can't grant your request. We can't give you our permission to marry our daughter."

"Arabella, let's go," Henry said sternly.

"Let me stay and talk to Gilbert," she said, swiping a tear away.

"No. I meant let's go home, back to Germany. This is over," Henry said, and Helene nodded.

"Go home? What? No!" Arabella shouted. "I'm not leaving. This is my home now. I'm joining the Amish church. I was going to apologize to the community in church."

"You've had your adventure, and now it's time to get back to reality," Helene said, walking over to Arabella and tugging on her arm. "Let's go."

"I'm a grown woman now, Mother," Arabella protested, jerking away. "I appreciate everything you and Father have done for me, but I'm an adult now and I can make my own decisions."

"Not when you're not thinking clearly," Helene snapped. "Trust me. You will regret this decision. Let's go home before things get any worse."

"No!" Arabella cried, but her parents took hold of her arms and steered her out of the cabin into the dark of the evening. Gilbert watched helplessly, frozen. What should he do? Stop her parents and bring her back to the cabin, or let her go? If he tried to stop them, would they think even worse of him?

"Gilbert!" Arabella screamed as they went out the door, wrenching around to look at him. His heart clenched at the sight of her being taken away from him, but he didn't want to disrespect her parents by demanding that they stop.

They were her parents, and they thought they were doing what was best for their daughter. No matter how much it hurt, he felt as though he should honor that. Maybe once they had a chance to think, talk things over, and calm down, maybe they'd realize Arabella truly did want to stay here and that was the right decision for her.

Gilbert dashed to the door, watching as Arabella's parents pulled her away, taking her farther away from him.

Would he ever see her again?

Tears leaked from his eyes as a physical pain crushed his chest, watching her fight and protest, trying to break free from their hold. Since it was already dark out, no one else was on the lane; otherwise, people would have been concerned.

He found himself following them, at least so he could make sure she was all right. Where were they going?

Arabella and her parents hurried down the lane and approached the street. Maybe they were heading back to the Millers' Bed and Breakfast to pack up before leaving for the airport. Gilbert ran to catch up with them as they crossed the street.

Now on the other side of the street, they walked in the direction of the Millers. Gilbert sprinted toward them, not even sure what he was going to say to them.

But now he knew he had to do something, say something to try to change their minds. Was this his last chance?

In the dark, Gilbert could barely make out Arabella turning her head as she walked. She noticed Gilbert standing on the other side of the street.

"Gilbert!" she shouted.

The sound of the distress in Arabella's voice ripped apart Gilbert's heart, and he looked both ways, about to cross the street.

Arabella suddenly thrashed and fought her way out of her parents' grip, breaking free and sprinting toward him. During her hurried escape, she didn't look before running into the street toward him.

He felt as though the blood was draining from his head.

A car barreled around the corner, speeding right toward Arabella. Time seemed to freeze as the car grew closer at an alarming rate. With her eyes trained on Gilbert, Arabella didn't even notice the oncoming danger.

"Arabella! Stop!" Gilbert screamed, but she kept on running.

Before he could think or comprehend what was about to happen, he dashed into the street and pushed her out of the way as hard as he could.

In a fleeting moment, he barely registered the blinding headlights rushing toward him in the dark of the night.

Pain jolted through him, and the world went black.

Chapter Twenty-four

"Gilbert!"

The scream was deep and guttural, a sound Arabella barely recognized coming from her own throat.

Gilbert lay on the pavement, motionless. The car that had hit him was stopped, the driver frozen as if his hands were glued to the steering wheel, eyes wide. Before Arabella could register what was happening, the driver backed up, drove around Gilbert, then sped away as the tires squealed on the pavement.

Arabella didn't care about the driver. All she cared about was Gilbert, the love of her life who was now bleeding, who'd taken the hit for her.

Was he...?

"Oh, no!" Helene cried, rushing toward Arabella and Gilbert. "Henry, call an ambulance!"

"I already am," Henry said, phone to his ear. Thankfully he was able to get cell service.

"Gilbert!" Arabella cried again, emotion cracking her voice. She felt his pulse on his neck, her own pulse racing. "He's still alive, thank God. What do we do? I don't know what to do!"

"I don't know. Just don't move him," Helene said. "But we have to make sure cars go around us."

"He saved my life." Arabella let out a sob as she knelt beside him, grabbing his hand. "He put himself in danger to push me out of the way of that car."

"I saw everything," Helene said as Henry was still on the phone. Her eyes reddened with tears. "It was so...selfless."

"I told you he loves me." Arabella wiped away the tears, fighting the urge to not rest her head against his chest and throw her arms around him, in fear of hurting him more. She looked up at her mother, who stood beside her. "He could have been killed, but he got me out of the way, anyway. It should have been me who was hit, not him."

"Arabella—" Helene began.

"They'll be here in a few minutes," Henry cut in, stepping closer.

"This is your fault. Both of you. If you hadn't forced me to leave like that, I wouldn't have tried to run back to him," Arabella spat out. Even as she said the words, she knew how cruel and unjust they were, but she didn't care.

"You're the one who ran into the street without even looking!" Helene shot back.

Henry raised a hand palm up. "Please. This doesn't help anyone."

Another car drove around the corner, actually going the speed limit, and Henry waved his hands, getting it to slow down even more. The car parked in the street sideways, blocking off any oncoming traffic.

"What happened?" The elderly man jumped out of his car and ran over to them. "Is that Gilbert Schwartz?"

"Yes. He was hit by a car. He pushed me out of the way and saved my life," Arabella choked out.

"Where is the car now?"

"They drove off."

The man grunted. "A hit and run. Terrible. I'm Bob. I sometimes act as a driver for the Amish here, and I know everyone. I'm sure his family won't try to find out who hit him."

Arabella couldn't understand why they wouldn't report the hit and run, but it was the Amish way here. A few minutes later, the police arrived and questioned Arabella and her parents.

"He pushed me out of the way," Arabella told them. "He saved my life."

"And the driver drove away?" the police officer asked her. "What did the vehicle look like?"

As Arabella described the driver and vehicle, the ambulance arrived. Arabella watched, feeling helpless, as the medical workers loaded Gilbert onto a stretcher and wheeled him into the ambulance.

"Are you all right, miss?" one of the EMTs asked. "You have scrapes on your arms and face."

"I do?" Arabella reached up to her forehead and pulled her hand away. Blood and bits of gravel stuck to her fingers. "I didn't even realize it. Everything happened so fast. But I'm fine. It's nothing. Just get Gilbert to the hospital."

"That young man pushed her out of the way," the police officer told the EMT. "She fell on the pavement."

"You should ride in the ambulance with us. We can treat the cuts and scrapes on the way. It may be nothing serious, but a doctor may want to take X-rays or other tests to make sure. You could have fallen harder than you think."

"Okay." She turned to her parents. "I'm going to ride in the ambulance."

Her mother stared at her, gaping. How could she argue with that? "Arabella," Helene said, touching her daughter's arm. "Of course. We will go to the hospital with you. Right, Henry?"

"Yes. He just saved our daughter's life. It's the least we can do." Henry bent his head.

"We're taking them to the Unity Hospital," the EMT said. "You can meet us there."

"Do you need a ride?" Bob asked Arabella's parents.

"Yes, please. We'd appreciate it," Henry said.

"Please, Bob, can you go tell Gilbert's parents what happened first? They need to know right away," Arabella asked.

"Of course, miss. I'll go right now." Bob was already getting into his car, followed by Henry and Helene.

Arabella thanked him and climbed inside the ambulance and watched as the medical workers took care of Gilbert. Though she stayed out of the way, she wished she could sit near him and hold his hand.

They drove away, red lights flashing and sirens blaring.

***

After Arabella was treated, she was allowed to leave, but returned to the waiting room.

Arabella's parents were waiting there, but Arabella ignored them and approached Hannah and Ernie Schwartz. As Arabella slowly approached them, her cheeks reddened with embarrassment. This was the first time she was speaking to them as Arabella, not Damaris.

When they saw her, they stood up. "Gilbert told us about how you traded places with Damaris," Hannah said, still with a warm smile on her face. "Don't worry, we aren't upset with you. I'm glad my son met you. We are grateful you and Gilbert are safe now."

"It's nice to meet you officially, Arabella," Ernie said, nodding to her.

"Thank you. It's nice to meet you too," Arabella said as they all sat down in the waiting room chairs. "I'm glad that you know the truth. I'm sure Gilbert told you why I asked Damaris to switch places with me."

She couldn't help but glance at her parents, who were shifting uncomfortably in their seats.

Hannah also glanced at Henry and Helene, as if not sure how much she should say. "I'm sorry, Arabella. I hope everything will work out,"

247

Hannah said with a sympathetic look. She patted Arabella's hand in a motherly way.

Awkwardness was thick in the air, but Arabella just smiled at Hannah. "Thank you." Under different circumstances, maybe they would have discussed it more, especially if Arabella's parents were not in the room. However, Arabella could only think about Gilbert anyway, and she was sure his parents felt the same.

Time seemed to crawl by as slowly as honey dripping from a spoon as none of them spoke.

Finally, a doctor entered the room. Arabella shot up out of her seat along with Ernie and Hannah.

"Are you Gilbert Schwartzs' parents?" the doctor asked Hannah and Ernie.

"Yes," Ernie replied. "How is he?"

"He sustained a concussion and a broken arm," the doctor explained, but his eyes were hopeful. "He's doing well. He will make a full recovery, but he will have to not use his arm for a while so the bones can heal properly."

"Oh, thank the Lord." Arabella let out the air she'd been holding in.

"May we see him now?" Hannah asked, twisting the ribbon of her prayer *kapp* in her hand.

"Yes, but keep your voices low," the doctor said and led them to Gilbert.

Out of respect, Henry and Helene remained in the waiting room.

At the sight of the man she loved with a cast on his arm and a bandage on his head, Arabella's heart physically ached. It should have been her on that hospital bed, not him.

"Oh, my son!" Hannah cried, rushing toward him. "I'm so glad you're going to be all right."

"I'm fine, *Maam*," Gilbert said. His eyes sought Arabella out as he looked past his mother. "Arabella, are you okay?"

"Me? Don't worry about me. You got me out of the way and saved my life. You could have been killed!" Arabella cried, joining Hannah at his bedside. Gilbert's good hand reached for hers.

"I love you, Arabella. I'd die for you," he said in a low voice.

"Please don't plan on it," Arabella choked out. "It was foolish of me to run out into the street like that. I'm so sorry."

"You were upset," Gilbert said. "Don't be sorry. What's done is done."

"All that matters is you're both safe now," Ernie said.

A few minutes later, Henry shuffled his feet awkwardly and Helene cleared her throat as they approached the doorway, but Arabella ignored them. This was their fault for dragging her away like they had.

"Arabella, we should go," Henry said.

"I don't want to leave Gilbert," Arabella said, looking her father right in the eye with determination. "Not now, not ever."

"You're welcome to stay here with us," Hannah offered to Arabella.

"You can all go home and get some sleep," Gilbert said. "Really, I'm fine."

"No." Ernie shook his head. "We will stay. A neighbor is staying with our children. Arabella, whatever you decide is fine with us."

"I want to stay," Arabella said.

"I see," Henry said, shifting his weight uncomfortably. "Well, then, I guess we'll call Bob and go back to the bed and breakfast."

Helene gave one last look of regret to Arabella. "Are you sure you won't come with us, dear?"

"I need to stay here," Arabella said, seeing that they were trying. It seemed as though they had so many things to say to her, but now was not the time or place. They'd have to talk later.

Her parents backed out of the room, and Arabella found herself sighing in relief as the awkwardness in the room evaporated.

***

"You didn't have to stay at the hospital all night, you know," Gilbert said again after he'd returned home. He was staying at his parents' house for a while until his arm was healed, so Arabella visited him there.

Together, they sat on the couch in the living room. Gilbert's younger siblings played with wooden toys and puzzles at their feet.

"I wanted to," Arabella said. "Trust me."

"I know you won't do anything you don't want to do," Gilbert said with a laugh.

Arabella sighed, staring off into the distance as she remembered the way her parents had forcefully removed her from Gilbert's cabin.

"Have you spoken to your parents yet?" Gilbert asked, reading her expression. "Have you seen them since?"

"No. I guess they extended their stay, and they've stopped by Constance's house to talk to me, but I've been avoiding them," Arabella admitted. "To be honest, I have been feeling like this was their fault. I know that's wrong. But when you were unconscious in the road, I blamed them." She bent her head. "Even as I said the words, I knew I'd regret it, but I said it anyway."

"You should talk to them, Arabella. It wasn't their fault. Things just happen," Gilbert said in a gentle voice. "Yes, maybe they went about things the wrong way, but we all make mistakes. I think they truly want what's best for you and they thought they were doing the right thing at the time. Maybe since then they've changed their minds."

Arabella shook her head. "They made their opinions clear. I doubt it."

"Look, Arabella! I did the puzzle!" six-year-old Jacob shouted, jumping up and down. He pointed to the puzzle on the floor he'd just completed, which was advanced for his age.

"That is wonderful, Jacob. You're so good at those," Arabella said, ruffling his hair. The boy giggled and then proceeded to wreck the puzzle he'd just finished, only to do it all over again.

Gilbert chuckled. "He does the same ones over and over."

"I was the same way as a kid." Arabella smiled. "I had this book about a squirrel that I used to ask my governess to read to me every night." Her smile faded. "I remember I used to ask my mom, and she was always too busy to read it to me."

Gilbert touched Arabella's arm. "It's not too late to change things, Arabella. You need to give them a chance."

There was a knock on the door, and Hannah came out of the kitchen and opened the door.

Henry and Helene stood on the porch. Arabella sucked in a breath. Of course, they knew she was here.

"Hello, Hannah," Helene said. "We came to speak with Arabella."

"Come in," Hannah said, opening the door wider. "Please, make yourselves at home."

"Thank you," Henry said.

"Sorry, I have something on the stove. I'll be back. Children, come with me, please." Hannah rushed out of the room with Gilbert's siblings. The room was suddenly quiet.

"We went to Constance's house, and she told us you were here," Helene explained, approaching Arabella. "We've gone there a few times to talk to you. You've been avoiding us, haven't you?"

251

Arabella just stared at her hands in her lap. Yes, she had. Guilt tore through her veins, and she refused to look up.

"I don't blame you for not wanting to talk to us after what we did," Henry said as they stood before her. "Maybe the accident was our fault."

"No, please. Don't blame yourselves," Gilbert interjected.

"If we hadn't been dragging Arabella away from you, she wouldn't have run toward you," Helene added.

"Either way, we are sorry," Henry blurted.

Arabella's head shot up as she met her parents' eyes. "You're...sorry?" she asked, stunned. It was rare for them to admit when they were wrong, so she knew this wasn't easy for them.

"Not only for how we behaved and made you leave the cabin but also for how we treated you, Gilbert," Helene said, turning to him. "We were incessantly rude to you and harsh. Of course, none of this is your fault. Arabella has fallen in love with you because you are a kind, selfless young man. Now we see why she loves you and why she wants to stay here."

"Thank you," Gilbert murmured, eyes wide.

"Really?" Arabella asked, hope rising within her.

"When we saw how you put yourself in front of that car to get her out of the way, we realized how you truly do love Arabella. That was an act of true, selfless love," Helene said, her hand over her heart. "Never in my life have I ever seen anyone do anything more noble."

"Not only that, but we would be proud to call you our son-in-law," Henry told Gilbert, walking over to him to shake Gilbert's good hand. "We give you our blessing and permission to marry Arabella, Gilbert."

Arabella let out a sob, covering her mouth with her hands. Was this truly happening? Had they truly had a change of heart? Recently, she'd seen her parents change for the better, especially when they'd admitted they'd been wrong to ask her to marry Stefan, and when her mother had stood up for her in front of Philip Castle. So...maybe this was truly happening. Maybe it wasn't too good to be true.

"Are you sure? You won't change your mind?" Arabella asked, looking at her mother. "You are giving me your blessing to move here, far from home?"

"Yes," Helene said. "And we will visit you often, just like Damaris will come here to visit her family and friends."

"We were wrong, and we couldn't be sorrier. Your entire life, we've been insensitive to what you want, Arabella. We just wish we would have realized it sooner," Henry added, patting her knee where she sat.

"And I wish I had been a more present mother to you instead of working all the time," Helene said, sniffling as her voice wavered and a tear slipped from her eye. "I can't go back and change things, but from now on I want to be a better mother to you, and I think this is the best way to do that."

Arabella stood up and hugged both of her parents, throwing her arms around their necks. "Thank you both so much."

Arabella heard sniffling and looked to see Hannah standing there, wiping her eyes. "How lovely," she said. Ernie stood by her side, smiling, and Gilbert's siblings had gathered around to see what all the commotion was about.

"Well, I think now is the perfect time to ask Arabella a question," Gilbert said, and Arabella whirled toward him, her heart leaping in her chest.

He took her hand and gently tugged, and she sat back down next to him.

"Arabella Blackwood, I love you more than my own life. I want to hear you laugh every day until I die, and I want to spend the rest of my life making you happy. I know you haven't officially joined the church yet, but I don't want to wait to ask this until then. Will you marry me?" Gilbert asked, his brown eyes searching hers.

"Yes!" Arabella cried, not even hesitating for a moment. Joy and elation surged through every molecule of her being as he kissed her hand softly while his siblings cheered.

"Congratulations!" Helene shouted over the noise as she hugged Arabella.

"We're so proud of you," Henry said as he pulled her into his arms.

She'd never heard her father say that before, so tears welled in her eyes as she squeezed him back. "I love you both so much. Thank you."

Helene pulled away just enough to touch Arabella's face. "We should have told you that for your entire life. We've always been proud of you, dear."

Arabella smiled, just grateful they were saying it now and making things right.

Hannah was now sobbing tears of joy as she came over to hug Gilbert, then Arabella. "I am so glad you are going to be my daughter-in-law," she said. "Welcome to the family."

As the children cheered, hugging her and Gilbert, tears of joy continued to drip from Arabella's cheeks. She looked at Gilbert, who smiled back at her. At the sight of his handsome face, her heart soared.

Finally, her heart was home.

Chapter Twenty-five

Arabella knew she wasn't supposed to worry about Sunday morning, when she would stand before the entire community and ask for forgiveness, but she did worry. She'd already received permission from the elders, and she'd been dreading it all week. At the same time, she was ready to get it over with, hoping she'd be accepted into the community after.

She'd also spoken with the elders and the bishop about joining the church. She was surprised that even though she'd lied about who she was, they had granted her request, forgiving her. She would begin taking classes and would be baptized into the church soon after.

"Even after I lied to you all, you still are willing to welcome me into the church?" Arabella had asked, stunned.

"God says to always forgive," the bishop had said with a smile.

But what about the community? What if they didn't want anything to do with her after this? And she didn't blame them.

Not to mention, this would be the first time the community saw both Damaris and Arabella together at the same time.

As Arabella rode to church with Stefan, Damaris, and the Kaufmanns in the back of their buggy, she wrapped her arms around herself. Constance was up front driving, and Stefan sat in the front seat with her, chatting happily about the scenery. He was clearly enjoying his time here.

"Are you cold?" Daisy asked.

"She's just nervous about standing before the church today," Danny said.

"Are you?" Dean asked.

Damaris gave the children a warning look. "Please. Give her a moment."

"It's okay." Arabella nodded. "Yes. I'm very nervous."

Delphine, who sat next to her, quickly patted Arabella's knee and gave her a shy smile, but said nothing.

"Don't be nervous," Daisy said.

"I lied to everyone and pretended to be Damaris. I wouldn't blame them if they never trust me again."

"We all make mistakes," Danny added.

Damaris nodded. "He's right. God calls us to forgive."

She hoped they were right as they drove into the parking lot of the church and Constance parked the buggy. Arabella helped the younger children out and grabbed the box of cherry tarts she'd made for the church potluck lunch. Now it seemed like a feeble peace offering.

Everyone else turned and walked to the church, but when Arabella heard someone walking up behind her, she stopped.

"Arabella," Gilbert said in a quiet voice as she turned around. He stood before her, giving her an encouraging smile, his arm still in a cast. When he saw her face, his smile faded. "Are you okay?"

She nodded, not trusting herself to speak. How would she confess her sins to an entire church when she couldn't even speak to Gilbert, who was so easy to talk to?

"We're here for you," he reminded her. "Soon, you will look back on this and wonder why you were so worried."

She nodded again. "I'm really nervous. This is so important to me, and my future depends on it. But I do hope you're right, Gilbert. I hope they can forgive me and maybe, one day, they'll trust me again."

"Well, I trust you and I forgive you. I'd offer to take that box for you, but I don't think I can hold it with one hand. Come on. Let's get inside."

The Millers' buggy drove into the parking lot, and Helene and Henry quickly got out.

"Well, that was terrifying!" Helene cried, stepping around a pile of manure. "I thought for sure those narrow, rickety wheels were going to break or a car was going to crash into us."

"Oh, Helene. Please," Henry said, waving his hand.

"There aren't even seatbelts. How are these things legal on the road?" Helene persisted.

Mortified, Arabella glanced around, wondering who'd heard her. One family was hurrying into the church, eyeing the newcomers curiously before going inside.

"Mother, please," Arabella said in a warning voice. "People can hear you. Please be respectful."

Helene looked up to see her daughter. "Oh. I'm sorry," she said, putting her hands up. "You're right. I didn't mean it that way. I was only saying—"

"I know things here are very different from what you are used to, but please," Arabella pleaded.

"I'm sorry, dear. I guess I say things without thinking sometimes. I need to work on that." Helene sighed.

Henry rolled his eyes. "Well, that's the understatement of the year."

"Hold on," Laura said, who had been watching the exchange. "Damaris? Why did you call her Mother?"

Had her mother told the Millers? Arabella touched a hand to her forehead, hoping her mother hadn't told them a more dramatic version of the story.

"Look, I have a lot to explain, and when the service begins, I'm going to tell the whole church what's going on," Arabella said. "But right now, there isn't time."

Laura gawked at her. "What is going on? Do you have two mothers?"

"Laura, come on," Lydia said, grabbing her sister's arm. "Let's take in the pastries or we'll be late."

Mae and Ed looked like they also wanted to ask several questions, but they walked inside the church with their daughters instead.

Arabella sighed and turned to her mother. "Did you tell them?"

Helene threw up her hands innocently. "What? All I said was I was here with my daughter, Arabella. I didn't tell them the rest. That's your place, not mine."

For once, her mother had not overstepped. "Good. Thank you, Mother. Come on, let's go in."

They made their way into the church. Damaris was already inside, talking with several of the other women. So, when Arabella stepped into the church, they turned to stare at her.

"Wait, what?" Adriana, Dominic's wife, asked in confusion.

"Damaris, do you have a secret twin?" Charlotte asked in a joking voice.

Damaris hurried over to Arabella. "Look, I know this is shocking, how much we look alike. In a few minutes, you'll understand."

"Yes, I'm going to explain everything," Arabella added.

Liz's eyebrows shot up, and several of the other women had similar expressions of shock and confusion.

The service was about to begin, so Arabella took the tarts downstairs, then went upstairs and sat next to Damaris. Her heart raced, and she wiped her sweaty palms on her skirt despite the chill outside. Several more people were staring at them as they sat down. Even some of the men glanced over in confusion.

Damaris squeezed her hand. "It'll be over soon."

The service started, and before they began singing hymns, the bishop stood at the front of the church while the congregation was still seated.

"This morning will be a little different. Well, I will let her do the explaining, but Damaris and a young woman asked for permission to speak to you all this morning. I ask that you listen with open hearts." The bishop nodded to her and stepped back as Arabella stood up on shaky legs and walked to the front of the church. Damaris walked with her.

Dozens of pairs of eyes watched them, and Arabella felt her stomach turn queasy, but she persisted.

When Arabella hesitated, Damaris began. "Good morning. I know it must be confusing, because we look so alike. No, we are not twins. We are not even related. I'm Damaris."

Arabella took in a deep breath and let it out. "And my name is Arabella Blackwood."

No one spoke out loud, but several people gasped and glanced at each other in shock.

"It's a bit of a long story, but Damaris and I switched places temporarily." Arabella explained how she'd come here and convinced Damaris to go to Germany in her place. "We never meant to hurt anyone. I just wanted to live in someone else's shoes and get some time away before my wedding. But now that the wedding is not going to happen, I would like to stay here. Being here has changed me, and I see life differently now. I want to live more mindfully and savor each day, serving God and putting Him first in my life. You've shown me what true friendships look like and what strong families look like. I want to give up modern conveniences and devote my life to God. I hope to be baptized into the Amish church here, but if I've lost your trust and you want me to leave, I understand. However, I do ask for your forgiveness."

"I also ask your forgiveness," Damaris added.

Arabella bowed her head, expecting someone to speak up and ask her to leave and never return. But when she looked up, everyone was smiling at them.

"I forgive you," Constance said, standing up.

"So do I," Gilbert added, nodding to her.

"Me too," Ella Ruth said.

Damaris smiled through reddened eyes and grabbed Arabella's hand.

Arabella's eyes flooded with tears, and her vision blurred as several more people spoke in agreement and no one objected. She covered her face with her hands, overwhelmed at the mercy of these people she'd outright deceived.

"Thank you," she managed to choke out as she turned to face the congregation. "Thank you all."

The bishop nodded to Arabella, who then took her seat. He addressed the congregation. "The elders and I have already spoken with Arabella about the process of becoming baptized into the church, so we will soon begin the process. That is what she believes God wants her to do. We are glad to have her join us."

Murmurs of surprise and delight filled the room.

"Having said that, now that Arabella will soon be baptized into the church, I'm also happy to announce that Arabella and Gilbert Schwartz are engaged," the bishop said. "Their wedding, of course, will take place after she is baptized."

Even more of a joyous response came from the congregation. Everyone smiled, exchanging excited whispers. Arabella was grateful they approved of the engagement here even though she hadn't officially joined the church yet, which may not have been allowed in other communities, or at least frowned upon. But here in Unity, everyone seemed overjoyed.

Her heart full, Arabella glanced over at Gilbert, who was grinning even bigger than she was.

Chapter Twenty-six

Damaris nodded to Arabella, who smiled back at her with tearful eyes. Damaris was happy for her friend who'd found where she belonged.

"And now we have some very happy news from Damaris Kauffman," the bishop said, nodding to Damaris.

Damaris still stood at the front of the church. Stefan stood up and joined Damaris.

Damaris said, "I'm happy to announce I am engaged to Stefan Castle." She gestured to Stefan. "He's from Germany, and I will be moving there to live with him after the wedding."

Constance looked at Damaris with tears in her eyes.

Several more gasps sounded throughout the room, but everyone smiled at Damaris and Stefan. Here, there was no judgment, as one might expect, even though she'd be leaving them. They were still happy for her. She felt her face burn with so many eyes on her.

"I think I speak for everyone when I say we will be sad to see you leave," said the bishop as Damaris and Stefan returned to their seats, glad the announcement was over. She didn't like being the center of attention.

"Now, let's begin our service." The bishop directed everyone to open their copies of the *Ausbund,* and the congregation began singing one of the old songs from the book.

Damaris couldn't help but glance over at Stefan, who sat on the men's side of the room, wondering what he thought of the church service. He seemed to be enjoying it, singing along. And throughout the sermons, he seemed to be intently focused, taking notes, even though the speaker spoke in Pennsylvania Dutch. Since Stefan grew up in Germany and also knew German, Damaris figured he would probably have no trouble understanding most of what the speaker was saying.

After the service, everyone went downstairs for the potluck lunch. The women flocked to Damaris and Arabella, asking them questions.

"We are so happy for you!" Adriana cried, pulling Damaris into a hug. "It's about time you get your happily ever after."

"Congratulations, Arabella. We're all so happy for you and Gilbert," Ella Ruth gushed.

"Wait… So, in the restaurant, that was you who knocked over the waiter?" Laura asked Damaris.

Damaris laughed. "Yes, it was me. We were trying on each other's clothes, and then you walked in."

"And that was your cell phone ringing at my house?" Laura asked Arabella.

"Guilty. That was me," Arabella said.

Laura laughed. "Wow. Now it makes sense. And that's why you knew so much about social media and had that idea at the farmers market."

The other women looked at each other in confusion.

"After we sit down, we will tell the whole story," Damaris told them, and they made their way to get in line for lunch.

"So, you're moving to Germany, Damaris?" Charlotte asked.

Maria's eyes widened. "What's it like there? Arabella, you're so fortunate to have grown up there. Is it wonderful?"

"Oh, it is wonderful!" Damaris cried. After they got their food and sat down at a table to eat lunch, she told the group of women about her stay there.

Laura clasped her hands together and sighed, smiling at Damaris and Arabella. "Your lives are like fairy tales."

Damaris laughed out loud. "It sure didn't feel like a fairy tale at times, especially when I had to confess to Stefan that I'd been lying to him. I was afraid Arabella's family's business agreement would fall apart, and it would have been my fault."

"And I didn't feel like I was living a fairy tale when I was betrothed to a man I didn't know," Arabella said.

"But everything worked out," Liz said.

"I'm sure your families will miss you both," Ella Ruth said. "We will miss you, Damaris."

"I'll come back to visit often," Damaris told them. "I promise."

"Arabella, I'm so excited for your wedding. If you need help from any of us, please ask," Maria said.

"Amish weddings are wonderful," Damaris said. "I'm sure you'll have plenty of help."

"Thanks," Arabella said with a smile. "I'm sure I'll need it. This is still new to me."

"I can't wait to hear about your fairy-tale wedding, Damaris," Adriana gushed. "Will you get married in Germany?"

"I don't know yet. Maybe. It is where I met Stefan, but I grew up here. If I get married in Germany, none of you could come. We might have the wedding here."

"But where will you be living after the wedding? Does Stefan have a mansion too?" Charlotte asked.

"Well, yes, but I am not sure if we will be living there. This has happened so fast." Damaris chuckled. "It's so wonderful, sometimes it doesn't even seem real."

Stefan took in a deep breath as he sat with the other men on the men's side of the room, feeling slightly overwhelmed with everyone talking to him at once. Yes, he knew they meant well and were just trying to get to know him, but he could barely keep up with all the questions.

"We've known Damaris since we were kids," Gilbert said with a playful twinkle in his eye. "So, I hope you're going to take good care of her."

"Of course!" Stefan said, a little too enthusiastically. His heart raced at the way they were looking at him. What did they think of him? Did they think he was good enough for Damaris? "I promise, I will treat her like a queen."

"My sister can be a handful sometimes," Dominic said, elbowing him. "You think you're up for the challenge?"

"Oh, don't listen to him," Gilbert said. "We hope you and Damaris will be very happy together. You two seem like you belong together."

Stefan just smiled. "Thank you. I do hate to have Damaris leave her home, but this is what she wants."

"She's always wanted to go to Germany," Dominic said. "Now she gets to live there. I know my sister. She wouldn't leave here unless she really wanted to. Don't worry. You're not making her do anything she doesn't want to do."

Stefan breathed a sigh of relief. So they didn't think he was whisking her away. "She will come to visit often, I promise."

"Good. Because none of us will be able to get on a plane and go see her," Dominic said.

"I know. She told me about that. That's why I'll make sure she comes here to see all of you as much as possible," Stefan said.

"You can afford the travel? The plane tickets?" Dominic asked.

"I've heard flights from Germany are expensive," Gilbert added.

"Well, yes. It won't be a problem," Stefan assured them, his face burning at the way they were staring at him.

"Damaris mentioned your family runs a huge bakery company," Dominic said. "And you will be inheriting it soon?"

"Yes," Stefan stammered. "My father is retiring after our wedding, so Damaris and I will be inheriting it and running it together. Arabella's parents are also retiring and the two companies will be merging together. We will be running it."

"Wow," Gilbert said. "Sounds like a lot of work."

"Damaris is so good at it, and she told me she's always wanted to run a business," Stefan said. "With her helping me, I know we can grow the company even more."

"My sister always wanted to do more than what she could here," Dominic said and clapped Stefan on the shoulder in a friendly way. "You're making all her dreams come true."

Stefan smiled, glad her brother and the other men approved of him.

"So, will you be getting married in Germany? Or here?" Dominic asked.

Stefan's eyebrows shot up. "Well, we haven't decided where or when yet. I was thinking Germany, but here would be wonderful. I'll have to ask Damaris what she wants. I don't care where we get married."

"Well, why not get married here, in the community?" Dominic suggested. "All her family is here."

"An *Englisher* wedding in an Amish community?" Stefan asked. "Would that be allowed?"

"Allowed?" Dominic touched his chin thoughtfully, then smiled. "Of course! I don't think there would be a problem with that. Check with the bishop, of course, but maybe the elders would let you use this church if you wanted to." He paused. "Well, maybe not. I don't know. You'd have to ask them. Or, you could get married outside or somewhere else in town. The bishop only marries Amish couples, so you'd have to have a pastor come and marry you."

"And the Amish would come to an *Englisher* wedding?" Stefan asked.

"Of course!" Dominic cried jovially. "We've been to *Englishers'* weddings. We've never had a non-Amish wedding here before, though. It would be great."

"Wow," Stefan said slowly. "I never even thought of it. Thank you, Dominic. I'll definitely see if she wants to do that and if we could use the church."

***

After the potluck lunch, Damaris' family returned home to have a restful afternoon and evening.

While Constance drove the children home in the buggy, Damaris walked home through the woods with Stefan.

"Dominic had a great idea for our wedding," Stefan said. "He suggested that we have the wedding here, outside the church."

"Really?" Damaris asked. "But it wouldn't be an Amish wedding. Would they allow it?"

"Actually, I talked to the bishop after church. He said he would be fine with us having the wedding here, as long as it is not inside the church, and he will speak to the other elders. He only marries Amish couples, so we will need to have a pastor come here to marry us. What do you think, Damaris? We could get married here and have a reception in Germany as well, if you want to."

"Wow," Damaris said as they walked through the trees. "I always imagined getting married in that church, but now that I'm not Amish anymore, I'm fine with not having the wedding there. If we get married here in town, my family and community can attend. If we got married in Germany, they wouldn't be able to come." She glanced up at him.

"I am happy with whatever you want to do, Damaris." He gave her a crooked grin and her insides melted. "How about if we have a simple outdoor wedding and reception here, then another reception in Germany?"

"That's the best of both worlds. I can still get married here, even though it will be an *Englisher* wedding. I never imagined it, but I know it will be perfect," Damaris said, and kissed Stefan's cheek.

"Your brother said that, too. I wouldn't care if we got married in the Arctic, as long as I get to marry you." He touched her nose, and she laughed.

Just then, Arabella and Gilbert ran up to them.

"Hi!" Arabella called. "We were walking home and saw you."

"I've been meaning to ask you—do you have a place to stay until you're married?" Damaris asked. "I am sure my mother would be happy to have you stay with her."

"Well, Constance already told me I can live with her until the wedding, actually. I get to stay in your old room. Is that okay?" Arabella asked.

"Of course! I'm glad you can use it and keep my family company." Damaris grinned. "So, we were just talking about our wedding. We decided to get married here so all of you can come."

"That's wonderful! I can't wait," Arabella said.

"Why don't we just have a double wedding next November?" Gilbert said, laughing, obviously joking. He turned to Stefan. "November is traditionally when Amish couples get married."

Damaris and Arabella looked at each other, then smiled.

"What do you think, Arabella?" Damaris asked.

"I think it's a great idea," Arabella cried, throwing her hands up.

"What? Are you serious? I can't tell if you're kidding," Stefan said, looking at each of them.

"We're serious," they both said.

Gilbert and Stefan looked at each other and chuckled.

"I'm fine with it if you are," Stefan said.

Gilbert nodded. "I'm fine with it too. So, how would that work?"

"Well, we could have our wedding in the church, and Damaris and Stefan can get married somewhere nearby outside, then we can all have one large reception, as long as you're not planning on having drinking or dancing," Arabella said.

Damaris laughed. "Definitely no drinking. As for the dancing..." She laughed. "I had enough dancing at our engagement party to know I'm terrible at it. I'd rather not."

"I would be fine with skipping the dancing, too," Stefan added.

"Well, it would be nice since Stefan and Arabella's families will be traveling from Germany. They can attend both weddings in the same trip," Gilbert added.

They all nodded in agreement.

"It will be cold for an outdoor wedding in November, but we can keep the ceremony short, and the rest will be inside," Stefan said.

"The fall foliage will be beautiful." Damaris chuckled. "A double Amish-Englisher wedding. I've never heard of such a thing."

***

Chapter Twenty-seven

One Year Later

On a cool November morning, the day of her wedding, Arabella woke up before the sun. Well, she hadn't slept much that night, so instead of waiting in bed, she got up and dressed in a blue dress which was similar to the ones she now wore every day.

Her heart thumped wildly in her chest. Today she was going to marry the man of her dreams, Gilbert Schwartz. She knew the day would go by quickly, and she hoped she could remember every moment. Her wedding was one of several that would occur in the community this month.

In the glow of the battery-operated light, she smoothed her hands over the white apron covering her skirt. Now, instead of designer dresses, high heels, and handbags, she wore plain dresses with aprons and white prayer *kapps*.

And she wouldn't have it any other way.

For now, before the wedding, she would wear this dress because she had baking and cleaning to do that might dirty it. After, she would change into a dress very similar to this one for her wedding.

Arabella made her way to the kitchen to see that Constance was already awake, baking pastries.

"You're up already?" Arabella asked.

"Of course. There's so much to do," Constance said, smiling. "Let me guess. Couldn't sleep?"

"Nope," Arabella said, beginning to wash the dishes that had piled up in the sink.

"Me neither. Good morning, early birds," Damaris said, joining them in the kitchen.

"Happy wedding day to both of you," Constance said with a grin, hugging Damaris and kissing her on the forehead. "Ah, my oldest daughter is getting married."

"Oh stop it, *Maam*," Damaris sniffed. "You'll make me cry."

"So, you couldn't sleep either?" Arabella asked Damaris, who began drying the dishes Arabella washed.

"Barely at all," Damaris said.

"I remember I was the same way the night before my wedding. I was much too excited to sleep. But I knew I was marrying the love of my life, my soul mate. So I had no doubts at all," Constance said with a wistful sigh.

"I feel the same way," Arabella said with a grin.

"Me too," Damaris added. Though she was not technically Amish anymore, she still wore a long, gray dress. It wasn't an Amish dress, but it was very modest. Damaris wore it out of respect for her upbringing. But at home in Germany, she wore *Englisher* clothing. And later on that day, she would wear her white wedding gown.

They worked together harmoniously until everyone else woke up. The children each wandered into the kitchen, ready for breakfast.

A few minutes later, Arabella's parents Henry and Helene arrived.

"Arabella!" Helene cried, hugging her daughter as soon as they walked through the door.

"You look beautiful, my dear," Henry said, hugging her once Helene finally let her go.

"It's not the white gown I always imagined for you," Helene said, looking over her blue dress. "But it suits you."

"Thanks. This isn't the exact dress I'll be wearing for the wedding, but it looks almost the same as this one. How is your stay at the Millers' Bed and Breakfast?" Arabella asked.

"Oh, it's lovely there. A quaint little place," Henry said.

Arabella chuckled. "I know it's not one of the five-star resorts you're used to. I'm just glad you're here."

"We wouldn't miss it for anything," Henry said.

"Come on. Let's go eat." Arabella led them to the kitchen.

Soon a breakfast feast was ready, and they set out sausage, gravy, and biscuits on the table. They bowed their heads for silent prayer, then everyone began chatting at once.

As Arabella looked around the table at each person she loved, she knew in her heart this was what she wanted.

After eating, Arabella changed into her blue wedding dress. As she was pulling it up over her shoulders, a knock sounded on the door.

"It's me," she heard her mother say. Arabella opened the door.

"I want to help you get ready," Helene said. "I know there isn't a veil for me to put on your head or buttons for me to fasten for you, but I'd like to be here with you while you get ready."

"I'd love that." Arabella opened the door wider and let her in.

After securing her hair in a low bun, Arabella held out the white prayer *kapp* to her mother. "You're right. There is no veil, but you can put this on me if you want."

Tears glimmering in her eyes, Helene nodded and took the head covering from her. She lifted it up and placed it gently on Arabella's head, tugging on the ribbon ties. "Perfect."

Arabella smiled. She always thought she'd have a team of makeup artists and hairstylists helping her get ready for her wedding day, but today, she wouldn't even wear makeup or curl her hair. She turned to the mirror.

Satisfied with her reflection, Arabella knew this was exactly what she wanted.

Helene rested her hands on Arabella's shoulders. "My dear, I have to ask you one last time. Are you completely sure this is what you want? This way of life, this man?"

Arabella took her mother's hands in her own. "Yes, Mother. I promise. I have never been more sure of anything in my life. Besides, I've already taken the classes and have been baptized into the Amish church."

"We just had to make sure. You're giving up so much," Helene said, her eyes pleading with her.

"No. I'm gaining so much more than what I'm giving up. Besides, we will visit each other often. My life is here now. I hope one day you'll understand that this is what makes me happy. Gilbert makes me happy."

Helene swiped away the tears that had suddenly flowed. She nodded. "If you say so, my dear." Helene smiled at her, adjusting Arabella's prayer *kapp*. "Again, it's not the elaborate wedding gown I always imagined you'd wear. But you are the most beautiful bride I've ever seen, Arabella. I'm proud of you, and I support you."

Arabella's breath caught in her throat as she blinked rapidly, tears falling down her cheeks. "I love you, Mother. Thank you. That means the world to me."

"I love you too, my daughter." Helene hugged her tightly.

"Let's go," Arabella said, smiling at her.

Everyone went to the church. The schoolroom divider had been moved aside, so there was one large room where the wedding would be held. The desks had been moved to the corner, but the shelves of books remained along with the educational charts and students' artwork on the walls.

The chairs for the wedding guests were set up in a circular shape, so they all faced the middle of the large room where the rooms met—this was where the speakers would stand and where the ceremony would take place.

"It's beautiful," Arabella said, gazing around the church. "I always thought I'd have a huge wedding with flowers, a beautiful gown and decorations, and a huge cake. But honestly, this is all I want."

Damaris looped her arm through her friend's. "None of those things matter. What matters is who you're marrying and the people you love who come to support you."

It was still early, so few guests had arrived except for those helping with the wedding.

Ella Ruth approached them, grinning. "Happy wedding day, Arabella. How are you feeling so far? Did you sleep at all?"

"I barely slept, but I actually feel great. I'm just so excited and so happy. I can't believe I get to marry Gilbert today."

As more people began to arrive, several women went up to Arabella to congratulate her. Soon, the bishop signaled Arabella that the wedding was about to start.

Gilbert walked into the room, and at the sight of him, Arabella's breath was stolen. He wore the same type of dark pants and white shirt with suspenders that he normally wore, and his hair was a bit mussed, probably from tossing and turning all night like she had. But he was the most handsome man she'd ever seen, and she felt so blessed to call him hers.

Her heart beat faster with each step he took as he walked toward her.

"You're beautiful," he whispered into her ear.

Her face burned in response to the unexpected compliment. "You know you're not supposed to comment on outward appearance."

"You said that the day we met, but I can't help it," he said with a mischievous grin. "And I want to tell you that every day for the rest of our lives, so get used to it."

She wanted to kiss him right there, but it would have to wait until they were alone. They took their seats near the center of the room where the chairs faced, near the bishop.

The wedding started a few minutes before nine o'clock. Arabella didn't walk down the aisle with her father escorting her as she'd imagined. She held no bouquet, and there were no instruments playing. Only the sound of voices singing hymns in harmony filled the church and filled her heart.

She was truly content, even as they continued to sing the slow German hymns for the first hour.

Arabella noticed her parents getting a bit antsy, fidgeting in their chairs. At least they got to sit in chairs while many of the teens sat on long, backless, wooden benches. A year ago, Arabella wouldn't have thought she could sit on one of those benches for that long without getting up and stretching her legs. Now, she was used to it and it no longer bothered her.

After the hymns and three sermons, the service carried into the third hour. The sermons focused on how a husband and wife should love and respect each other, and how God should be the center of the marriage. Arabella listened intently, soaking it in.

Now, it was almost noon. To Arabella's relief and delight, it was time for the vows.

The actual marriage ceremony took about five minutes out of the entire three-hour service. Arabella and Gilbert stood up and said their simple vows. At the end, the bishop joined their hands together. Sparks shot up her arm at Gilbert's touch, filling her entire being with warmth. She smiled up at him, wondering what adventures were in store for them.

There was no kiss, and there were no rings. Instead, they only promised to love each other for the rest of their days.

Instead of a large home near a castle, they'd live in the sturdy home that Gilbert had built with his own hands along with the help of his community. Instead of elegant balls, she would attend barn raisings, work frolics, and church services with these people who she now called family.

For Arabella, that was more than enough. It was what she never knew she always wanted.

***

Damaris watched with pure joy as Arabella and Gilbert were married. As soon as the wedding was over, she quickly hurried into the downstairs bathroom where she put on her modest yet beautiful long-sleeved white wedding gown with a white shawl. She didn't want to take any attention away from Arabella during her wedding, so she'd waited until it was time for her own wedding to change.

It was the wedding gown she'd secretly dreamed of all her life, complete with a full skirt and intricate beadwork which she had done herself.

As Constance helped Damaris button the back, her hands shook. "I am so happy for you, my dear. I just can't believe my oldest daughter is getting married."

"I know," Damaris said, smiling at her over her shoulder. "Remember, *Maam.* You are not losing me. I promise, I will come visit you often. Stefan is looking for a house for us to buy nearby so we can stay there during our visits."

"Oh, that's wonderful," Constance said, wiping away a tear.

Upstairs, they could barely hear the bishop making an announcement, inviting everyone to go to the nearby field for Damaris and Stefan's wedding.

"It's time, my dear," Constance said, finishing with the buttons. She hugged Damaris, who also felt a tear running down her own cheek.

She pulled away and smiled. "Let's go."

They walked outside together, through the path in the trees, to a nearby field in front of the woods. The fall foliage was breathtaking, something people traveled for hours to see in Maine. The leaves were fiery orange, red, and yellow, as though they'd been ignited.

Long wooden benches were set up, simply decorated with white flowers. There was a white wooden arch draped with sheer white fabric where she and Stefan would be married. The morning was chilly, but the scent of autumn in the air and the fiery colors of the leaves were breathtaking.

Unlike Amish weddings, there was music. An *Englisher* violinist played a sweet melody as the guests arrived from the church and sat down.

"I've never seen anything like this," Constance said. "It's our two worlds colliding."

Though the Amish of Unity did not play instruments themselves, they were still allowed to listen to *Englishers* play instruments.

"It's why I didn't want to get married in the church building," Damaris said. "I love that church, but I wanted to do it my own way while still honoring God. I believe music with instruments is a way to worship the Lord."

Constance squeezed her hand. "I always knew your mind was too much for this place."

They watched behind the trees as the rest of the guests arrived. Once everyone was seated, Stefan took his place with the pastor. The violinist changed the song to the one Damaris had chosen for when she would walk down the aisle, which was Pachelbel's Canon.

She looked at her mother and nodded. "I wish *Daed* was here."

"He's here with us in our hearts," Constance said, tears glimmering in her eyes.

Damaris walked with her mother down the aisle toward Stefan. She was overcome with a wave of gratitude when she saw the smiling faces of every person she loved beaming at her. They were all here for her and Stefan on the most important day of their lives. With that realization, she began to cry tears of joy, especially when she set eyes on Stefan. He wore a dark suit with a red tie. He gazed at her, a wide grin on his face, and her heart soared.

Ella Ruth, Emily, Arabella, and Damaris' old friend Belle were her bridesmaids, and Gilbert and Dominic were Stefan's groomsmen. Gilbert, Ella Ruth, Arabella, and Dominic wore their usual Amish attire that they'd worn to Arabella's wedding. Yes, there were more bridesmaids than groomsmen, but this was a very non-traditional wedding.

After their short and simple ceremony, they decided not to kiss out of respect for the Amish customs, who did not show physical affection publicly. She didn't want to make anyone feel uncomfortable.

As they made their way to the double wedding reception back in the church building, Stefan leaned close to Damaris' ear.

"You look beautiful, Mrs. Castle."

She giggled. "Thank you, Mr. Castle. And you look very handsome."

"No one is looking right now." They walked behind everyone else. He took her hands, turned her toward him, and kissed her on the lips.

Damaris laughed. "I love you."

"I love you, too."

At the double reception, the tables were covered in dishes of food that the guests had brought, ranging from desserts to casseroles and salads. Damaris chose to not have a cake, since she knew her Amish friends would be bringing so many sweet treats.

They spent the afternoon in fellowship, and Damaris' face hurt from smiling so much, but she savored every moment. Arabella came over and hugged Damaris.

"I knew this was a good idea," Arabella said.

"It surely was," Damaris agreed.

"Your grandmother is loving this." Damaris laughed at the sight of Elizabeth, who was having an animated conversation with several Amish women, who were laughing.

"I even saw Ms. Libby shedding a tear at your wedding," Damaris said.

"No way. Did she really?" Arabella laughed.

"She did. And so did I. It was beautiful."

"Thank you. Your wedding was also so beautiful. I'm so glad we did them together."

Emily hurried over to them, putting her arms around both of their shoulders. "I am so happy for both of you!" She looked around the room, then whispered, "So, which of these Amish men are single? I didn't expect them to be so handsome."

"Emily!" Arabella chided, then laughed.

"I can't tell because they aren't wearing wedding rings. Help me out here," Emily said with a wink.

Arabella rolled her eyes.

"Thinking of joining the Amish too, Emily?" Damaris asked.

Emily touched her chin thoughtfully. "If I met the right man, maybe."

Stefan joined Damaris, taking her hand in his.

Belle and her husband Cole Henderson, otherwise known as the well-known sci-fi author Tony Graham, walked over to them. Stefan stared, star-struck, as his favorite author shook his hand. It wasn't because half of Cole's face was covered in burn scars—Stefan was wide-eyed because he was a huge fan of Cole's novels.

"Congratulations," Cole said, letting go of Stefan's hand. "I'm Cole. It's nice to meet you."

"Thank you," Stefan stammered. "I'm Stefan. I'm a huge fan."

As the two men were talking, Belle leaned in and whispered in Damaris' ear, "Cole got Stefan an entire autographed collection of all the Tony Graham books as a wedding gift after I told him what a big fan he was of his work."

Damaris laughed out loud. "Oh, trust me. He will absolutely love that."

Philip Castle walked over, clapping Stefan on the back, then hugged him as Belle and Cole excused themselves. "I'm proud of you, and I love you."

Damaris noticed tears shining in Stefan's eyes as he pulled away from his father. "Thank you," he said. "I love you, too."

"I have to admit I never thought you'd get married, and I'm so sorry now for that. I am so glad you have found your other half. Congratulations to both of you." Philip gave Damaris a rare smile. "I look forward to seeing you run the company together."

"Thank you, Mr. Castle," Damaris said.

"Please, call me Dad."

Damaris smiled. "Thanks, Dad."

Philip moved away, and Damaris turned to Stefan. "Are you okay?"

"He's never told me he's proud of me before. I can't believe he apologized. And he hasn't told me he loves me since Mom…" Stefan sniffed, wiping his eye. "That meant a lot."

Damaris squeezed his hand, silently communicating with him as several more people came up to them to congratulate them. Damaris thanked them as Stefan continued to hold her hand.

She looked up at him and grinned. Her happily ever after was about to begin.

***

"Are you ready to go home, my love?" Stefan asked.

Damaris turned to him and smiled. "I think so."

They stood outside Damaris' house, taking in the sights as they waited for Bob to pick them up and to drive them to the airport.

"What a wonderful wedding we had," Damaris said with a wistful sigh.

"It really was. And I can't believe Tony Graham came to my wedding!" Stefan said, laughing. Damaris smiled at the memory. She looked around and sighed again.

"I know it must be hard leaving home," Stefan said.

"This is all I've ever known." Damaris looked out across the fields, admiring the way the golden fingers of the setting sun brushed over the swaying grass. She bent down and scooped up a handful of dirt, letting it sift through her hands. "I love this place. I wish I could bring a piece of it back to Germany with me."

"Don't forget, Damaris. I'm going to make sure you're back here to visit several times a year," Stefan said, reaching for her hand to help her up.

She nodded, feeling her eyes sting as tears threatened. If she spoke, she knew she'd crumble.

The sound of a motor caused them to look down the lane where Bob's car was approaching.

281

"He's here to take us to the airport," Stefan said. He took Damaris' bag. "I'll give you a minute."

Behind them, Damaris' younger siblings talked and laughed in the yard as they waited, and the younger ones ran around, carefree. Constance approached them, pressing something into Damaris' hand.

Damaris looked down to see her old white prayer *kapp* in her hand, the first one she'd ever made that her mother had helped her sew. Damaris had never been very good at sewing.

"No matter where you go, never forget where you came from and who I raised you to be. Whether you're running a multi-million-dollar bakery company or traveling the world, you will always be Amish at heart. And that means putting the most important things in life first—loving God, loving family, and loving people." Constance closed Damaris' hands around the *kapp*, a symbol of their steadfast faith. "Even though you have chosen not to be Amish anymore, and I support your decision, I hope you will still hold these values."

"I will, *Maam*," Damaris choked out, a sob wracking her chest. She threw her arms around her mother. "You are the best mother in the world. I love you."

Her mother squeezed her tightly. "I love you, too. I am so proud of you, my daughter, and I know your father would be too."

Stefan finished putting the bags in Bob's trunk and approached them. Damaris' siblings gathered around, joining the group hug. Constance grabbed Stefan's sleeve and also pulled him into the circle.

"We will miss you," Daisy cried.

"I'll be back to visit soon and often. I promise," Damaris said, the hug finally breaking up. "I love you all."

They each told her they loved her, and Damaris treasured it in her heart. "It's time for me to go now." She looked at them, smiling through her tears, then forced herself to turn away and get in the car before she completely broke down. Stefan reached for her hand and gently squeezed, silently supporting her.

As they got in the car, she quickly shut the door, waving to them. They waved back to her, Constance's eyes still red with tears.

"Are you ready for the new adventures that lie ahead?" Stefan asked, rubbing his thumb over her knuckles as he scooted closer to her. "This is just the beginning, Damaris."

The car drove down the lane, and Damaris turned around in her seat to see her family waving in front of the house she grew up in. No matter where she went, this place would always be a part of her.

"Yes," Damaris said, swallowing her sorrow and embracing the joy of the days to come. "I'm ready."

Epilogue

Arabella, Laura, Lydia, and Mae busily worked in the kitchen at the new Blackwood-Castle Bakery location in downtown Unity, Maine. The sun had barely risen, but Arabella and the Millers had been up baking for hours already.

Arabella was continuing to learn Pennsylvania Dutch, which was coming easily to her since she could already speak German.

"Think we will sell out of cherry tarts again today?" Mae asked.

"I wouldn't be surprised," Lydia said.

Arabella smiled. Having this bakery here was like having a piece of home here with her in Unity. And since Damaris was running it, she was here often to oversee how the business was doing—and to also visit friends and family.

Arabella worked in the bakery, trying to keep up with the orders. The location had stayed busy so far, since it was the only true bakery around. Yes, the Community Store also sold their goods, but it sold so many other types of things as well.

Several hours later, Arabella rested her hands on the bakery counter as her gaze swept over the several tables which were full with customers enjoying their purchases. Yes, this was the type of job she enjoyed doing. She created her own recipes, then baked and sold the products directly to her customers. Best of all, she had the privilege of seeing them enjoy her creations.

The bell on the door rang, and Arabella turned to face the customer.

"Damaris!" Arabella cried as her friend came behind the counter to hug her.

"I wanted to surprise you this time," Damaris said.

"How are things going in Germany?" Arabella asked.

"Honestly, things couldn't be better. Now that we have a house here, I get to visit as often as I like." Damaris' cheeks turned pink. "I have big news."

"What is it?" Arabella asked.

"I'm pregnant!" Damaris blurted out.

Arabella gasped. "Me too!"

They both laughed and hugged each other again.

"I just told my family, and they're thrilled," Damaris said. "Stefan is still there with them. Have you told your parents yet?"

"Yes. They were so much more excited than I expected. My mother is learning to sew so she can make Amish clothing for the baby, and she's learning to knit baby blankets. Can you imagine that? She can't wait to be a grandmother. She said she will be visiting every month when the baby is born," Arabella said with a laugh.

Damaris chuckled. "Of course, she will! I didn't expect anything less from her. That's going to be one spoiled baby."

"How long are you staying?"

"We will be staying a few days. You should come by and see the new house. It's right down the road."

"I will! I'm so happy for you, Damaris," Arabella said.

"I'm happy for you too. You know, none of this would have happened if you hadn't talked me into switching places with you," Damaris said. "Thank you, Arabella."

Arabella's eyes stung with tears as she grabbed her friend's hand. "This was God's plan, Damaris. We each got our own happily ever after, even if it wasn't what we expected at all."

About the Author

Ashley Emma knew she wanted to be a novelist for as long as she can remember. She was home-schooled and was blessed with the opportunity to spend her time focusing on reading and writing. She began writing books for fun at a young age, completing her first novella at age 12 and writing her first novel at age 14, then publishing it at age 16.

She went on to write 8 more manuscripts before age 25 when she also became a multi-bestselling author.

She owns Fearless Publishing House where she helps other aspiring authors achieve their dreams of publishing their own books.

Ashley lives in Maine with her husband and children and plans on releasing several more books in the near future.

Visit her at ashleyemmaauthor.com or email her at:

ashley@ashleyemmaauthor.com. She loves to hear from her readers!

If you enjoyed this book, would you consider leaving a review? Reviews tremendously help authors because they help other customers decide whether or not they want to buy the book or not.

Here is the link:

https://www.amazon.com/gp/product/B089PR9ML1

Thank you!!

Download free printable checklists at
www.AshleyEmmaAuthor.com!

Looking for something new to read? Check out my other books!

Click here to check out other books by Ashley Emma

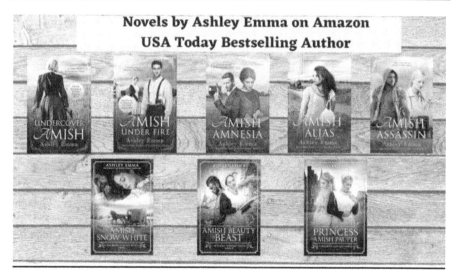

GET 4 OF ASHLEY EMMA'S AMISH EBOOKS FOR FREE

www.AshleyEmmaAuthor.com

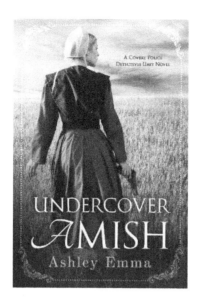

(This series can be read out of order or as standalone novels.)

Detective Olivia Mast would rather run through gunfire than return to her former Amish community in Unity, Maine, where she killed her abusive husband in self-defense.

Olivia covertly investigates a murder there while protecting the man she dated as a teen: Isaac Troyer, a potential target.

When Olivia tells Isaac she is a detective, will he be willing to break Amish rules to help her arrest the killer?

Undercover Amish was a finalist in Maine Romance Writers Strut Your Stuff Competition 2015 where it received 26 out of 27 points and has 455+ Amazon reviews!

Buy here: https://www.amazon.com/Undercover-Amish-Covert-Police- Detectives-ebook/dp/B01L6JE49G

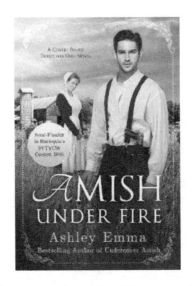

After Maria Mast's abusive ex-boyfriend is arrested for being involved in sex trafficking and modern-day slavery, she thinks that she and her son Carter can safely return to her Amish community.

But the danger has only just begun.

Someone begins stalking her, and they want blood and revenge.

Agent Derek Turner of Covert Police Detectives Unit is assigned as her bodyguard and goes with her to her Amish community in Unity, Maine.

Maria's secretive eyes, painful past, and cautious demeanor intrigue him.

As the human trafficking ring begins to target the Amish community, Derek wonders if the distraction of her will cost him his career...and Maria's life.

Buy on Amazon: http://a.co/fT6D7sM

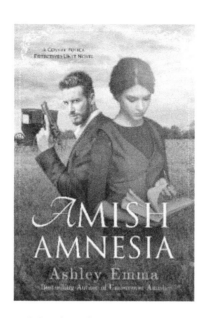

When Officer Jefferson Martin witnesses a young woman being hit by a car near his campsite, all thoughts of vacation vanish as the car speeds off.

When the malnourished, battered woman wakes up, she can't remember anything before the accident. They don't know her name, so they call her Jane.

When someone breaks into her hospital room and tries to kill her before getting away, Jefferson volunteers to protect Jane around the clock. He takes her back to their Kennebunkport beach house along with his upbeat sister Estella and his friend who served with him overseas in the Marine Corps, Ben Banks.

At first, Jane's stalker leaves strange notes, but then his attacks become bolder and more dangerous.

Buy on Amazon:
https://www.amazon.com/gp/product/B07SDSFV3J

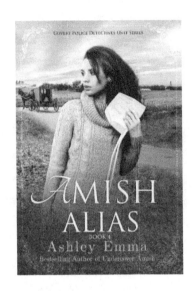

Threatened. Orphaned. On the run.

With no one else to turn to, these two terrified sisters can only hope their Amish aunt will take them in. But the quaint Amish community of Unity, Maine, is not as safe as it seems.

After Charlotte Cooper's parents die and her abusive ex-fiancé threatens her, the only way to protect her younger sister Zoe is by faking their deaths and leaving town.

The sisters' only hope of a safe haven lies with their estranged Amish aunt in Unity, Maine, where their mother grew up before she left the Amish.

Elijah Hochstettler, the family's handsome farmhand, grows closer to Charlotte as she digs up dark family secrets that her mother kept from her.

Buy on Amazon here: https://www.amazon.com/Amish-Alias-Romantic-Suspense-Detectives/dp/1734610808

When nurse Anna Hershberger finds a man with a bullet wound who begs her to help him without taking him to the hospital, she has a choice to make.

Going against his wishes, she takes him to the hospital to help him after he passes out. She thinks she made the right decision...until an assassin storms in with a gun. Anna has no choice but to go on the run with her patient.

This handsome stranger, who says his name is Connor, insists that they can't contact the police for help because there are moles leaking information. His mission is to shut down a local sex trafficking ring targeting Anna's former Amish community in Unity, Maine, and he needs her help most of all.

Since Anna was kidnapped by sex traffickers in her Amish community, she would love nothing more than to get justice and help put the criminals behind bars.

But can she trust Connor to not get her killed? And is he really who he says he is?

Buy on Amazon:
https://www.amazon.com/gp/product/B084R9V4CN

Ever wondered what it would be like to live in an Amish community? Now you can find out in this true story with photos.

Buy on Amazon: https://www.amazon.com/Ashleys-Amish-Adventures-Outsider-community-ebook/dp/B01N5714WE

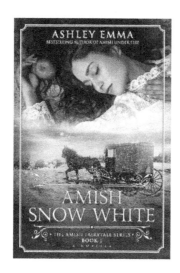

An heiress on the run.

A heartbroken Amish man, sleep-walking through life.

Can true love's kiss break the spell?

After his wife dies and he returns to his Amish community, Dominic feels numb and frozen, like he's under a spell.

When he rescues a woman from a car wreck in a snowstorm, he brings her home to his mother and six younger siblings. They care for her while she sleeps for several days, and when she wakes up in a panic, she pretends to have amnesia.

But waking up is only the beginning of Snow's story.

Buy on Amazon:
https://www.amazon.com/Amish-Snow-White-Standalone-Fairytale-ebook/dp/B089NHH7D4

She's an Amish beauty with a love of reading, hiding a painful secret. He's a reclusive, scarred military hero who won't let anyone in. Can true love really be enough?

On her way home from the bookstore, Belle's buggy crashes in front of the old mansion that everyone else avoids, of all places.

What she finds inside the mansion is not a monster, but a man. Scarred both physiologically and physically by the horrors of military combat, Cole's burned and disfigured face tells the story of all he lost to the war in a devastating explosion.

He's been hiding from the world ever since.

After Cole ends up hiring her as his housekeeper and caretaker for his firecracker of a grandmother, Belle can't help her curiosity as she wonders what exactly Cole does in his office all day.

Why is Cole's office so off-limits to Belle? What is he hiding in there?

https://www.amazon.com/gp/product/B089PR9ML

Sample of Amish Beauty and the Beast
Chapter One

"Belle? Where are you?" Aunt Greta called outside the barn.

Belle reluctantly closed the pages of her sci-fi novel and propped herself up on the hay. "In here." It was a cold, snowy morning in Unity, Maine, but that didn't stop Belle from curling up on a pile of hay to read a novel by her favorite author as she took a break from her chores.

Aunt Greta entered the barn, then scowled when she saw the book Belle was reading. "What is that?"

"It's the latest book in the sci-fi series I love," Belle said. "It's about time travel and secret identities and—"

"Books like that will just fill your head with nonsense." Her aunt shook her head and put her hands on her hips. "They'll distract you from your work, and some of them have inappropriate content that will corrupt your mind. It's better to avoid them completely, so you aren't tempted. You should be focusing on other things, like being baptized into the church. Have you decided yet?"

Taken aback, Belle frowned. "No, not yet. It's such a big decision. Once I'm baptized into the church, if I leave the Amish, I would be shunned, so I really want to make sure before I commit. And about my reading, in my old community in Ohio, no one ever minded that I read so many different kinds of fiction."

"Well, as you know, each Amish community has different rules."

"Is it against the rules here to read fiction?" Belle countered.

"Well…" Aunt Greta hesitated. "No. Not exactly. But it might be frowned upon, and I certainly don't approve. I'm sure your uncle won't, either. I think you should only read Bible study guides, devotionals, or books of that sort."

"My friends here read all kinds of novels. Ella Ruth, Damaris, and Adriana read clean Christian romance novels, mysteries, and other types of fiction as long as they are clean and have no swearing, sexual content, violence, or anything like that. I like wholesome, clean reads, anyway. I don't read anything inappropriate. I promise."

"They don't live with me, so I don't have any say in what they read. I don't know what your parents allowed you to read while they were alive, but while you're living in my house, I expect you to follow my rules. If I see you reading them again, I might have to confiscate them. Now go do your chores and help me with breakfast." With a stomp of her foot, Aunt Greta pivoted and walked out of the barn.

Belle's heart sank to her toes as she let the book slip from her fingers and onto the hay.

There was no way she could give up reading. It was her one escape from her life, her one way to shut out the memories that haunted her, even in her dreams.

Could she keep it a secret? It would be wrong, but without her books, she knew she'd slip into a dark void.

Lifting herself from the pile of hay she'd been sitting on, she mucked out Phillip's stall and gave him fresh water and hay. After she finished, Belle hurried to the house to help her aunt with breakfast.

When she heard the voices of her aunt and uncle in the house, she paused at the door.

"I found her in the barn reading some time travel novel," Belle heard her aunt tell Uncle Josiah in the kitchen.

"Belle has good judgment," Uncle Josiah said. "I don't think she'd read anything immoral."

"Still, I don't want her filling her head with such nonsense. She should be reading only books that are biblical."

"If you think that is best," Uncle Josiah said. "She has been through so much, maybe reading fictional stories is her way of coping."

"Perhaps. I wonder what my sister let her read when she was alive. I guess we never really talked about it. Anyway, she's too old for such fictional novels. She should be more concerned with joining the Amish church and finding a husband."

"She just moved here a few months ago, Greta. Don't be in such a rush to make her join the church and then marry her off."

"She's twenty-six years old. That's far beyond old enough to get married and be baptized into the church. All our children are married and moved out, and I thought we'd finally have some time to ourselves." Aunt Greta let out a sigh, then regret tinged her voice. "It's horrible of me to say that. I miss my poor sister dearly. I miss all of them. Poor Belle. I can't even imagine what she's going through, being the only survivor."

"As I said, maybe her novels help her get her mind off of missing her parents and siblings. Yes, I know you were looking forward to us being empty-nesters, but we promised Belle's parents that if anything ever happened to them, we'd take care of their children," Uncle Josiah reminded Aunt Greta. "She's no burden. It's a joy to have her here, and she's such a help to you."

"Yes, of course. You're absolutely right. I just never imagined that all of them would be killed, leaving behind Belle as the lone survivor. The poor thing."

Belle shuddered, willing herself to not run back into the barn and hide under the pile of hay, burying her nose in her book.

They say I'm not, but maybe I really am a burden to them, Belle thought. *And they pity me, which is worst of all.*

As the firstborn in her family, she'd always had the responsibility of helping her mother care for her younger siblings. It was a duty she had loved and respected…until it had ended. Belle's heart ached. What she wouldn't give to change one more cloth diaper, to help her younger siblings with one more homework assignment, or to help her mother make soup one last time.

What is my life worth now? I'm useless. Maybe I should have been murdered along with the rest of them.

Her heart twisted as a tear trailed down her cheek. She knew she should walk in before she started sniffling, and then they'd know she'd been eavesdropping. Forcing herself to open the door, she wiped her eyes and pasted on a fake smile.

"Sorry I'm late. What are we making for breakfast?" she asked.

Belle helped Aunt Greta make scrambled eggs, sausage, and toast with freshly squeezed orange juice.

"I'm sorry if I was too harsh in the barn," Aunt Greta said as she grilled toast in a pan on the woodstove. "I just think it's not appropriate for Amish women to read fiction. It's my personal opinion. I'm very traditional, as you might have noticed." She gave a small chuckle. "I shouldn't have reacted like that."

"I understand. It's all right. You're just looking out for me."

"Well, I won't take your books away, but I would appreciate it if you didn't read them. Maybe that's too much to ask. Does it help you? You know, with the grief?"

"Well, yes, it does. When I'm reading, I get lost in the story, and I feel like I'm one of the characters. For a little while, it helps me forget about what happened," Belle explained, flipping local sausage in a crackling pan on the woodstove next to her aunt.

"I never read fiction much, so it's hard for me to understand."

"Oh, I can't even imagine. It's my favorite thing to do," Belle gushed.

"Well, I don't want to take it away from you, if it helps you that much, but I do ask that you read only material that is moral. No swearing or sexual content or violence."

"Of course. I only read clean books, as I mentioned."

"Well, then. I think that will be all right."

"Thank you," Belle said, but guilt marred her words as she remembered what her aunt had said about Belle being a burden to them. Maybe if she helped Aunt Greta enough around the house and the farm, they'd realize how much of an asset she was. She'd do her best to earn her keep.

Most of all, maybe they'd stop pitying her so much.

Belle went about the kitchen as she placed the food onto serving dishes. Aunt Greta set the table, then Belle, Aunt Greta, and Uncle Josiah sat down, ready for the first meal of the day.

"Let us pray," Uncle Josiah said. He bent his head to reveal his receding hairline. His long beard bobbed as they prayed silently.

Once they had prayed, they began to talk and pass around dishes of food as they munched on their breakfast. Belle ate quietly, mentally reviewing her routine for the day.

After breakfast, Belle had a moment to herself. Because she had recently moved here after the tragedy, she hadn't yet found a job, but she hoped to find one soon. Maybe it would help take her mind off the memories.

She went to her room and pulled a cardboard box from under her bed. Resting it on her bed, she stared fondly at it.

Belle had begun reading when she was four years old. At least that was what her mother had told her.

Thoughts of her mother brought up bittersweet memories. Belle remembered the beautiful and caring blonde woman who always had a smile and had been filled with concern for everyone who came her way. How she missed her mother!

A shudder ran through her body as she tried to push away the horrible memories. She opened the cardboard box and stared at several books in piles. This was her solace—a world away from the turmoil she really felt. Belle had read countless books of different genres. She loved adventure stories and clean Christian romances. Her favorite genres, however, were sci-fi and fantasy—her new interest and one she believed would never fade. She loved how captivating it was, from the first page to the last, leaving one wanting more.

Hallowed Ground was the book she was currently reading. It was by her favorite author, Tony Graham. She thought she'd read captivating works in the past, but Tony Graham's works blew her mind. She wanted to have just five minutes with him, during which she would find out where he got his ideas for the stories he wrote. They were incredible. It was no surprise that all his works were bestsellers and had won many awards, even if the man refused to make an appearance so that he could receive any of them in person.

"Belle? Someone is here to see you!" Aunt Greta called up the stairs.

Who could that be? Maybe one of her friends, probably Damaris or Ella Ruth. She got up and hurried down the stairs, but her stomach sank when she saw Gilbert Schwartz standing in the entryway.

Her aunt gave her a knowing smile and left the room.

At twenty-six, Gilbert was well-built with sandy brown hair and freckles scattered all over his face. Belle had spoken with him many times at social gatherings. In her opinion, he was rather boring but very persistent in getting to know her.

It was no secret in the community that he was already smitten with her.

"Hello, Belle. I'm on my way to the wood shop for work and I was wondering…Would you like to go to the Singing with me tonight? It's at the Holts' house. It would be really fun, and you'd get the chance to get to know more people."

"Oh, I don't know, Gilbert," she began, trying to think of a valid excuse. "My aunt may need my help with chores."

"No, I don't!" Aunt Greta called from the kitchen. "I don't need your help tonight, Belle."

Belle tried not to roll her eyes at her aunt's meddling.

"Come on. You'll have a good time, I promise. Did you like going to Singings in Ohio?" Gilbert asked with hopeful eyes.

"Well, yes—"

"Then come with me. Please?"

She couldn't think of a good reason not to go. Besides, she'd see her friends there. "Oh, all right then."

"I'll pick you up in my buggy just before six," Gilbert said with what he must have thought was a charming smile. "Really, it'll be fun."

She raised her eyebrows. "Sure. See you then."

***

That night, after the Singing ended, she walked out of the Holts' house with her two best friends, Ella Ruth and Damaris. They'd eaten popcorn and sung several hymns. Belle had enjoyed the night. Because of the singing, she hadn't had much of a chance to talk to Gilbert, but she knew she would when he brought her home in his buggy.

"I can't believe you're here with Gilbert Schwartz," Ella Ruth gushed. "You know every single woman in the community is after him, right?"

"*Ja,* I bet they're all so jealous of you. Why wouldn't they be?" Damaris gazed at Gilbert, who was laughing with a group of his friends. "He's so handsome and kind."

"And kind of boring." Belle laughed out loud.

Damaris scrunched up her nose, looking offended. "He is not. He's sweet, though a bit awkward sometimes, but that's only because he gets nervous."

"I'm sorry," Belle said when she realized she'd insulted Damaris, who had been friends with Gilbert since they were children. "I've gotten to talk to him enough that I know we don't have much in common. All he talks about is fishing and carpentry, and on the way here, he was so quiet."

"He's probably just nervous, as Damaris said, being out with such a beauty," Ella Ruth said with a wry smile, playfully swatting at Belle's arm.

"Oh, stop it." Belle swatted Ella Ruth back, laughing.

"So, you aren't interested in him, then?" Damaris asked, twirling a stray piece of hair that had escaped her *kapp.*

Belle kept her voice low. "No, I'm not. I see him only as a friend."

"Well, I've heard rumors that he thinks you're the one. So, you better make that clear to him before you string him along and break his heart," Damaris whispered.

Gilbert was now staring at Belle with a lopsided grin.

Ella Ruth chuckled. "I think it's too late for that."

A group of the younger teenagers was huddled together beside them, talking loudly enough to overhear.

"I've heard he's disfigured, with burn scars all over him," one of the boys said, motioning with his hands. "And he never leaves his mansion."

"Have you ever seen the manor? It's huge!" said one of the other boys.

"I've heard he only comes out at night," one of the girls added.

"And what else? That he eats children for dinner?" A boy laughed. "Come on. Really?"

"Well, he really never does leave his house. He's probably afraid of people seeing him."

"What happened to him? Was he in a fire?" one of the teenage girls asked.

"I heard he's a spy, and he was in an explosion."

"I dare you to ring his doorbell."

"No way!" shrieked one of the girls.

"What are they talking about?" Belle asked Ella Ruth and Damaris.

"There's a man who lives all alone in the manor on the hill," Ella Ruth said, a mischievous look on her face.

"Oh, yes. I can see it through my window. It's on a hill down the street, through the woods," Belle said. "And I've seen his light on late at night."

"Maybe he's nocturnal," Ella Ruth added.

"Nocturnal? Don't be ridiculous." Damaris waved her hand. "He probably just works late."

"Well, it is true that he never leaves his home. He is wealthy and has a housekeeper run all his errands and do everything for him. He doesn't even go to the grocery store."

"Sometimes kids will ring his doorbell on a dare," Ella Ruth added. "Hardly any of them actually get close enough to do it. Most of them are too afraid."

Gilbert walked over to them, smiling at Belle. "Ready to go, Belle?"

"Sure," Belle said, then turned to her friends. "I'll see you both later."

Ella Ruth and Damaris grinned, waving.

Gilbert helped Belle into his buggy, letting his hand hold hers for a moment longer than necessary. She couldn't help but pull away from his grasp.

He got in the driver's seat and clicked his tongue to get the horse moving.

"So, what did you think? Did you have fun?" he asked.

"Yes, it was fun."

"What were you and your friends talking about?"

"We heard the younger teens talking about the man who lives in the manor on the hill. Do you know anything about him? Sometimes I see his light on from my window late at night. Is it true he never goes outside?" she asked.

"I think so. That's what I've heard. You should probably stay away from there. He doesn't like visitors," Gilbert said. "He's not a nice man."

"I'll remember that," she said.

They talked about their favorite hymns that had been sung, and then the conversation lulled. The awkwardness was thick in the air, like the clay-like mud that the horse plodded through.

"What are your hopes for the future, Belle?"

She glanced at him, stunned by his surprisingly deep question. "Well, I'd like to get married and have a family, of course, but I'd also like to work."

"Work? Where?"

"There's an anti-sex slavery organization that I follow. I get updates in letters from them monthly. They rescue children from slavery all over the world, even here in Maine. I'd like to somehow work for them, even if I do it for free," she said, unable to hide the passion in her voice. Just talking about it fired her up. "Did you know that so many people aren't aware that sex slavery is happening right here in the United States, even in Maine?"

"Well, yes. We know about it well because of the girls who were abducted by traffickers here in the community. Two of them were Ella Ruth's sisters, as I'm sure you know," Gilbert said. "It was a scary time. Perhaps that line of work is too..." He paused. "I worry that type of work might be too hard on you."

Ella Ruth had indeed told Belle about how her sisters had been abducted by traffickers. Ella Ruth had actually played a huge role in their rescue by going on fake dates with a man who worked for the traffickers. This helped the police locate where the girls were being kept. Ella Ruth and her sisters had inspired Belle's desire to work for the organization. "I know it might be intense, but I want to help," Belle persisted.

"Don't you think you'll be too busy raising children and running a household to work?" he asked, giving her a sidelong glance.

She couldn't help but scoot a few inches farther away from him. "I can do both. I want to do both. There's no rule against Amish women here having a job after they get married. Why, even Aunt Greta was a schoolteacher for a few years after she got married and had children."

"Then it became too much for her, so she quit, handing the job over to a younger, single woman."

"True. But that doesn't mean I'll do that."

"When I marry, I'd want my wife to be concerned only with raising our children and running our house, not to be spending time working somewhere else," he told her.

Belle scrunched up her nose. "What if your wife wants to make extra money outside the home? Even the Millers have a bakery, and Mrs. Miller and her daughters sell their baked goods at the market. I heard that even Damaris and her mother are thinking of working for them, baking goods to sell."

Gilbert said nothing. He just stared at the road ahead.

Yes, Mrs. Miller's daughters were teenagers and Damaris' father had passed away, so they needed the income, but still.

Belle crossed her arms, annoyance welling up in her like a flame. "Even the Proverbs 31 woman worked outside the home, selling her goods in the market, trading, and buying land."

Gilbert flicked the reins, his eyebrows knit together. The silence weighed heavily upon them.

We clearly have nothing in common.

As they approached her uncle's house, Belle stepped down from the buggy before Gilbert could get around to her side. Disappointment lined his face.

"Well, I had a good time, Belle. Did you?"

"Yes, I did. Thank you for taking me," she said, trying to hide her irritation, but she knew she was failing.

"I hope I didn't offend you."

"You didn't. We can just agree to disagree."

"Right. Well, goodnight." He took her hand and kissed it in the moonlight. What was meant to be a secret yet romantic gesture just aggravated Belle, making her pull away.

"Goodnight," she said, rushing into the house, leaving Gilbert standing in the driveway. She quietly went inside, where Aunt Greta was knitting by the light of a battery-operated lantern.

"Did you have a nice time with Gilbert?"

Ugh. "Well enough. We don't have much in common, so we don't have much to talk about." She took off her jacket, scarf, and boots.

"Give him a chance. You just met him. Maybe a few more dates and you'll change your mind."

"I don't think I'll be going on another date with him."

Aunt Greta set down her knitting. "Why not?"

"I'm not interested in him. I see him only as a friend. I don't have feelings for him, and as I said, we don't have much in common."

"That could change, Belle."

"I don't think so." She shook her head vehemently.

"Well, have you given more thought to being baptized into the church?" Aunt Greta asked.

Belle heaved a sigh. This was the last thing she wanted to talk about right now, let alone think about. "Yes, but I haven't decided yet. Well, I'm really tired. I'm going to bed." Belle trudged up the stairs.

Why was her aunt pushing her so much to join the church? Yes, Belle knew she was well beyond the average age most youths joined, but in her heart, she was afraid to make such a huge commitment.

Her new home was nice, but she missed her old Amish community in Ohio. She missed her old friends. She missed her family, but she had faith in God that everything would work out for good. This was what she prayed for every night.

Lying comfortably in bed, she opened her new book. Usually, books by this author enraptured her, making her stay up well past midnight. She had to find out what happened next. However, this one was different from the others.

Using her battery-powered bedside light, she finished the last pages of the book she'd been reading, *Hallowed Ground*. She should have felt satisfied, yet she wasn't. While the other books in the series had been complex, page-turning, and full of adventure, this book had been a disappointment. She'd struggled to finish it, but had been determined to do so, as she'd read all the other books in the series.

Had the author run out of good ideas?

Maybe the next book would be better. Was it in the local bookshop yet? Maybe she'd go tomorrow.

Belle looked out her window toward the hill with the manor that the teens had talked about.

Now the manor was shrouded in darkness, showing no signs of life.

Suddenly, she saw a light flicker in one of the windows. Her eyes widened. As quickly as it appeared, it disappeared, the hill once again dark.

A draft of cold hit her and she shuddered, her heart racing with sudden fear. She quickly closed the window and pulled down the curtain, shutting out her thoughts of the reclusive and strange man who lived up the hill.

***

"I have to quit. I'm so sorry."

Cole set down his fork and looked up at his housekeeper of three years, stunned, completely forgetting about his omelet. He and his grandmother, Claire, sat at a long table in the ornate dining room filled with fine art, complete with a chandelier above them.

"Abigail, why?" Cole demanded.

"I'm sorry, Cole. Claire, I apologize to you most of all. You've become like family to me, and I've enjoyed our time together as your companion," Abigail said.

"Me too," Claire said. "This is a shock. We thought you liked working here."

"I do," Abigail said. "My mother fell and broke her hip, and I need to move back home to be with her and take care of her. Her health has been deteriorating lately, and recently it's gotten much worse. I'll miss you both, but I'm not sure how much time she has left, and I need to be with her. Family is the most important thing."

"Absolutely. I'm so sorry to hear about your mother, Abigail. We'll miss having you here," Claire said.

"You've been good to me. But to be honest, working here has been making me depressed," Abigail explained. "Cole, you're a young man who should be out in the world, meeting people and doing the things you used to do, exploring nature and rock climbing. Instead, you never leave this manor."

"You know why I can't go out," Cole said, gesturing to his face. "People would take one look at me and reject me. They don't call me 'the monster on the hill' for nothing."

"I think you're wrong," Abigail said. "I think most people would be kind, and you might meet some people who treat you differently. It would be a small price to pay for you to have the life you used to live."

"I've been trying to tell him that," Claire said, shaking her head. "He's too afraid."

"I am not afraid," Cole retorted, then stared down at his plate, knowing it was a lie.

"Either way, I need to go back home and take care of my mother. It all happened so suddenly," Abigail said. "So, this is my last day. I'm sorry I can't give you a week or two notice."

Cole set down his fork with a thud. Where on earth would he find a new housekeeper and companion for his grandmother? How could he find someone who wouldn't run away at the sight of him? The interview process would be a nightmare.

He stood and backed away from the table. "I've lost my appetite. I'm going to get some work done." Cole walked up to his office and shut the door, then sat at his desk and ran his hands through his hair.

What was he going to do now? Who would be a companion to his grandmother?

Humming happily, Belle led her uncle's horse, Phillip, out of the barn to hitch up to the family buggy. She was off to the bookstore in town and could hardly contain her excitement, hoping the next book in the series would be just as good as the other ones before *Hallowed Ground*.

"Belle?"

Consumed with her thoughts of what might happen next in the *Hallowed* series, Belle hadn't noticed Gilbert walking down the lane until he wasn't far behind her.

She groaned inwardly, resisting the urge to turn around and walk away.

How would she tell him that, after the Singing, she didn't want to go on any more dates with him?

"Where are you off to?" Gilbert asked as he approached.

"Just running some errands in town," she said, busying herself with hitching up the horse to the buggy.

"You mean…going to the bookstore?"

Belle whirled around. "How did you know that?"

"Come on." Gilbert laughed. "You think it's a big secret? I know you read a lot. In a tree, in the barn, by the pond…"

Belle felt her face heat and her temper flare. "Have you been watching me?"

Gilbert laughed. "No, of course not. Damaris told me. You're not the only one. It's okay, you know. It's not forbidden here. Many people here like to read books besides the Bible."

"I know that," Belle said, keeping her voice low. "My aunt doesn't like it. She says it fills the mind with nonsense. Although, she's not forbidding it."

Gilbert chuckled, and Belle couldn't tell if he agreed or disagreed.

"Do you read?" she asked.

"Me? No. I don't like reading. Never have." Gilbert shrugged, looking at the sky.

"Really? Why not? It's my favorite thing to do. There's a whole new world inside each and every book, just waiting to be discovered."

Gilbert laughed again. "Maybe your aunt is right. That sounds like a bunch of nonsense to me."

"Excuse me?" Belle asked and crossed her arms, not bothering to hide her offense.

"I'm sorry," Gilbert said, waving his hands. "I'm kidding. I just don't find reading interesting, that's all."

That confirmed it. She and Gilbert had nothing in common, besides the fact that they both lived here in Unity and were Amish.

"Well, I better get going," Belle said, climbing into the buggy and keeping her eyes ahead. "See you around."

"Belle, I'm sorry. I didn't mean to offend you...again," Gilbert said, coming to the side of the buggy.

"You didn't," Belle said. He'd just made it even more obvious that they shared no common interests.

Not waiting for a reply, Belle clicked her tongue. Phillip clip-clopped down the lane.

As Belle drove through town, she paid close attention to where she was going. Although she'd arrived in the community a few months ago, it still seemed strange to her. She headed to the market, where she purchased everything on her aunt's list. Then she ventured farther into town toward the bookshop and lost her way.

"Excuse me," Belle addressed two women who were walking by on the sidewalk. She leaned toward them in her seat at the front of the buggy. "Do you know which way the bookshop is?"

"Not far. It's just down there, the next block over." One of the women pointed.

"Thank you." Belle clicked her tongue and Phillip started walking.

The woman turned to her friend and muttered, "I'm surprised she even knows how to read. Did you know they go to school only until eighth grade?"

Belle felt her face grow hot, annoyance bubbling up inside her. Growing up Amish, she had heard many rude comments and had seen the stares from people on the street. While she tried to shrug it off, sometimes she just couldn't help herself. Her mother had always taught her to turn the other cheek, but Belle just couldn't suppress a retort sometimes.

Before she could think twice, Belle told them, "Yes, we go to school only until the eighth grade, but I read over a hundred books a year. Thanks again."

The women's eyes widened as they glanced at each other, but Belle turned her eyes back to the road and drove the buggy away.

O'Malley's Books was a small, quaint bookshop that didn't seem like much from the outside, but inside it was a haven of books from great writers. Belle had discovered the little bookshop a few weeks after her arrival. This was probably her third visit there, and she had to get as many books as she could, as she had no idea when her next trip would be.

The bell rang as she walked into the shop and headed for the counter. Mr. O'Malley, the shopkeeper, flashed her a kind smile. The bald old man weakly stood up as he pushed his glasses from his nose up to his eyes.

"Hello, dear. I haven't seen you in a while," he said.

Belle beamed at him. He remembered her. "Yes, I've been busy."

"How were the last reads you got?" he asked.

Belle's eyes shone with excitement. "They were all good, except the fifth book in the *Hallowed* series, *Hallowed Ground*. It just wasn't as good as the rest, but I'm hoping the next one will be better. Please tell me you have the next book in the series."

"Sadly, I don't have the next book. It probably won't be out for a long time, maybe a year or two at least."

Belle sighed with disappointment. She had been looking forward to spending the night under the covers reading the next book. "Do you have any other similar books?" she asked.

"Hmmm. I do have one of his older works, but it's in the back in the discounted section. It might take a while to find," the old man said regretfully. "It's a mess back there."

"I can find it," Belle persisted. "And if I don't find it, I'm sure I'll find something else just as intriguing."

As the old man opened his mouth to reply, the door opened and a group of school kids walked in. Belle took the opportunity to slip into the back room, which held the discounted book section.

Mr. O'Malley had been right—it was indeed a mess. Bins were overflowing with books. Some of the books were in horrible shape, with their pages ripped out. Belle shuddered at their battered state, wondering where to begin. How long would this take? She took a deep breath and began her search.

About a half-hour later, just as she was about to give up, her eyes caught a name. A wide, satisfied smile spread on her lips as she stared at an early work of Tony Graham. It was certainly worth the search.

She dusted herself off and returned to the front room, where Mr. O'Malley was still attending to the kids, who were now creating quite a ruckus.

"I found it," Belle said, waving the book.

The old man nodded with a smile. Her eyes caught another work of one of her other favorite authors on the shelf, and she grabbed it, along with a few others. Seeing that he was busy with the children, Belle placed them in a bag in front of him. He quickly looked through her books and rang up her order.

"Looks like you still found some good ones in that pile of donated books. I'll have something better for you the next time you come around!" Mr. O'Malley called as she walked out the door.

"Thanks."

She hoped so. Belle climbed into the buggy and began the trip back home, eager to find a nice spot and start reading.

However, minutes later, Belle pulled over to the side of the road. Even if it was just a page, she had to read it, to have an idea of what to expect. Her heart was racing in anticipation of what Tony Graham had in store for her. She went straight for the early publication and started reading.

As she continued turning pages in the book, she saw something else. A white envelope was tucked between the pages. Her eyebrows shot up in surprise.

What was this? Perhaps it was something that Mr. O'Malley had forgotten. She would have to return it to him the next time she went to the store.

Looking at the handwriting on the envelope, she realized it was a letter. Written in pencil, the letter was addressed to a Sergeant Hender—, but the end of the last name had been smudged off. The names and addresses on the envelope were all smudged, and she couldn't make sense of them.

The seal was still intact, so the letter hadn't been opened, but it belonged to someone. Perhaps the person had forgotten it in the book, and one way or another, it had been donated to the bookstore with the letter still inside.

Reading the letter was invading someone's privacy, which wasn't right. The best thing to do was to keep the letter safe and give it to Mr. O'Malley when she next went to the bookstore. Maybe he'd know whose it was if he remembered who had donated the book. But she had no idea when she'd get another chance to go back to the bookstore.

Belle was intrigued by this letter from a stranger that had been found in her favorite author's book.

Maybe the name of the letter's owner would be on the letter itself. Because she couldn't see the names clearly on the outside of the envelope, opening it up could be the only way to find out how to return the letter to its owner.

She struggled internally over the right thing to do. To read or not read the letter? As her curiosity took over, Belle opened the envelope and unfolded the letter, ignoring her guilt.

Dear Son,

I don't even know where to begin. I am so sorry for those hurtful things I said to you. I was so wrong. I also forgive you for everything. I do realize now that selling the logging company was the right choice.

You have the right to choose your career, and now that I've read your first book, I can see that you are remarkably talented, Son. Once I read your book, especially the part about the father and son who have a terrible argument but finally make amends, it all became clear to me.

I can see now you wrote that about us, and now I understand all the things you probably wanted to say but maybe you were afraid of how I'd react. I understand what you wanted to say now because of the story. The story pays tribute to our family history.

I understand you, and I am proud of you for serving your country, following your dream, and being a wonderful son.

I will always love you,

Dad

Tears had filled Belle's eyes by the time she finished reading the letter. Although short, it was emotional. She had no idea what the son had done, but his father's forgiveness showed his love for his son.

It reminded her of how, even after all the sins she'd committed, God continued to love and care for her. She patted her eyes dry, willing herself to not cry more. Reading the letter had thrown her into a private world of this father and son.

Perhaps she shouldn't have read the letter. But the deed had already been done. She shoved it back into the book. Next time she went to the bookstore, she would give it to Mr. O'Malley.

Belle looked around. She had been so consumed in her thoughts that not only had time flown by, ushering in the evening, but she had also lost track of where she was.

She looked around for another buggy, but the road was empty. She had taken this road before…or had she?

Belle urged the horse to walk, determined to find her way home. She soon found herself at a crossroads. She looked left and right, trying to remember which direction she had taken earlier on. Yet, she couldn't remember. Right or left?

"I think it was right," Belle mumbled to herself. "I hope this is the right way."

However, the right path seemed to take her uphill, or was it just her imagination? The earth seemed to rise. There was no doubt that this was not the direction she had taken earlier in the day. She was on the wrong path. Phillip neighed as she tried to grasp the reins to turn him around, but the road was getting narrow, and the day was getting dark, not to mention colder. Just like her, the horse was clearly alien to these parts.

"Shhh. It's okay, Phillip. We can just turn around," Belle said gently, now getting worried. The horse calmed down for a bit, yet it trudged on, refusing to listen to her instructions to turn around. The once-smooth road had given way to gravel. That fact, combined with the steep hill, meant that Phillip's hooves became unsteady. He was not used to such terrain under his hooves.

Belle tried again to get Phillip to turn, but she wasn't familiar with him yet, and maybe she was using the wrong cues. When a car flew by out of nowhere, beeping its horn, the horse suddenly took off running.

Leaves hit Belle's face as she tried to dodge them. She closed her eyes, holding on tightly to the seat of the buggy as Phillip careened into a bush. Her mouth opened into a scream as the ground seemed to give way.

Everything went dark.

If you enjoyed this sample, check out Amish Beauty and the Beast here on Amazon: https://www.amazon.com/gp/product/B089PR9ML

Made in the USA
Coppell, TX
12 October 2021